THE MASTERMIND

BRIAN O'SULLIVAN

This novel is dedicated to my new friends in Walnut Creek. They are masterminds in their own right; convincing me to go out on the town when I should be at home writing novels for you, my fans.

PART ONE: THE CRIMINALS

CHAPTER 1

SHANE

"Please help me!"

I'd been woken up at eleven p.m. by an unexpected knock on my door.

A young woman stood before me. She was in obvious distress, her face littered with fear.

She was wearing a white nightie, a big tear on its right side. There was no visible blood, but it looked like a bruise was forming under her right eye.

I gazed beyond her to make sure no madman was running in our direction, a knife or gun in hand. Nothing.

"Come inside," I said.

She quickly darted in. You know a woman is in trouble if she'll gladly walk into a stranger's house. Especially a male stranger.

I locked the door behind me.

I had a million questions.

"Do you want me to call 9-1-1?" was the first that came to mind.

"Maybe in a bit," she said. "I'd like to decompress first."

"Are you in any immediate danger?" I asked.

By extension, I was asking if I was as well.

"I don't think so."

That was hardly reassuring.

"Just give me the word and I'll call the police."

"Do you have somewhere I could sit?" she asked.

"Of course. Follow me," I said.

I led her into my kitchen, which was a mere fifteen feet from the front door. I lived alone in an extremely small house. It was a two-bedroom place that I'd turned into a one-bedroom, using the second one as my study.

An upcoming divorce from Christie, my soon-to-be ex-wife, made the second bedroom superfluous. The baby we'd planned to inhabit the other room was no longer in our future.

"Would you like some coffee or tea?" I asked.

"Coffee sounds good," she said sheepishly.

I pressed the power button on my Keurig. I could have spent five more minutes making it with my French Press, but I doubted this woman was going to be too picky.

She had a lot more on her mind than the type of coffee I brewed.

"You let me know if you want to talk. No pressure," I said.

I was leaving it open-ended. I was afraid of pushing her too hard, but I certainly wanted to know why a random young woman had knocked on my door at eleven at night.

She looked up at me, making eye contact for the first time. The swelling was worse than I'd first thought.

"Can we talk after this coffee?" she asked.

"Of course."

It took the Keurig a minute to heat up and then about twenty seconds to spit out the coffee.

I set the mug in front of her as I put a second K-cup in for myself. It was going to be next to impossible to fall back asleep after this, so why not introduce some caffeine into the mix?

We sat in silence for the next few minutes. And then, to my surprise, she managed the slightest of smiles and extended her cup in my direction.

We clinked mugs, undoubtedly the weirdest "Cheers" of my life.

"Thank you," she said. "You're a lifesaver."

I only nodded, feeling it would be weird to take credit for merely opening my house to a woman in distress. Anyone would have done the same thing in my situation. And I knew I was no saint. I didn't deserve her adulation.

Neither of us said a word for another minute.

Maybe I should have been scared.

An ex-boyfriend or a jealous husband could have seen her walk into my house, ready to snag her back and hurt me in the process. Shit, maybe he'd think she was cheating with me and I'd be killed in the process.

But instead of being scared, I was fascinated.

I wanted to know everything about the woman in front of me. She was clearly attractive, despite her long, light-brown hair being clumped together and her doe eyes being puffy from having recently cried. And obviously, the bruise that would be making an appearance sometime soon.

None of that took away from her attractiveness. She was alluring, without question. A mid-twenties bombshell. Would she fall for an average-looking guy ten years her senior?

Stop being an asshole!

I berated myself for not concentrating on the issue at hand. Her well-being.

I really wanted to know what thug had led her to my place today. Honestly, I'd like to kick his fucking ass. Not that I was the toughest guy, but at least I'd have tried. That would put me in a good light with her. Right?

She took the last sip of her coffee and looked up at me.

"I guess I should explain," she said.

"Take your time. You don't have to tell me anything you don't want."

"Thank you for everything. What's your name?"

"I'm Shane Doyle," I said.

"Irish much?" she said, barely above a whisper.

I smiled.

"Just a bit."

"I'm Lexi."

I didn't bother asking for a last name. Lexi may have been made up for all I knew and it's not like I could blame her.

Before she began her story, we made eye contact once again. I knew I was out of line considering the circumstances, but I couldn't help but think those eyes would be easy to fall in love with.

She was beautiful in the worst of circumstances.

I couldn't imagine what she looked like when dressed up.

Or, not dressed at all.

Fuck, I'm going to hell.

"His name is John," she said. "He's my ex-boyfriend."

CHAPTER 2

LEXI

S hane Doyle was such an easy mark.

The first few minutes had gone better than I ever could have imagined. He was eating out of my hand. I just batted my little doe eyes two or three times and knew he was mine. Men are so easy. Like molding Playdough into any form you wanted.

But now it was time to tell my bullshit story and I couldn't fuck this up. I'd been perfect thus far.

"His name is John," I said. "He's my ex-boyfriend."

"I'm sorry."

The truth was we'd invented the name out of thin air. We decided to go with one of the most common names out there, just in case Shane eventually tried to go and find him. Which would be fruitless, considering he didn't exist.

We'd even picked the last name in case Shane asked. Miller. John Miller.

My real partner-in-crime was named Ben, but no one in Los Angeles called him that. He'd been telling people his name was Knox since arriving in the City of Angels. He wanted to be known by a name that wasn't on his driver's license, lease agreement, or anything else binding.

It's safe to say that Knox knew he'd be up to no good. He was tall, skinny, tattooed, and had a fuck everyone attitude that I found sexy.

We had no choice but to keep Lexi as my name. The goal was to start dating Shane, bringing him to my bar, and generally being out and about.

That wouldn't work with any other name than my own.

I was taking all the risks. In Knox's defense, he'd brought this opportunity to me. I wouldn't even be in the ballgame if it weren't for him.

I realized my mind was wandering at the most inopportune time.

"Don't be sorry," I finally said to Shane.

I could tell he took my late reaction as a sign I was in mental distress. Perfect.

"What did he do to you?" he asked, his eyes just a little too razor-focused on me.

Shane had greenish blue eyes and a full head of brown hair that he parted a little close to the middle. He was neither handsome, nor bad-looking. He was neither tall, nor short. He was neither in-shape, nor out-of-shape.

In most regards, Shane was quite average. He didn't stand out - for better or worse - like Knox did.

I'd been able to gather a lot of information on him over the last few weeks. Knox and I followed him, learning as much as we could. Overall, he was a decent man - despite some character flaws we could exploit - but he was still a man, and he was falling for my sad-eyed, damsel-in-distress look. He was far from a lady killer so I knew he'd go all googly-eyed for me.

Might have been imagining me naked for all I knew. Good. That would make all of this easier.

"He physically assaulted me tonight," I said.

"That's so terrible, Lexi. And you ran?"

"Yes. I live a few blocks down the street and when he hit me, I just took off. My door could still be ajar for all I know."

Shane looked me over and I deftly, slowly swiveled my head in his direction so he could see the bruise on my cheek more closely. If it was even bruising yet. Knox had hit me about thirty minutes before I arrived at Shane's house. Intentionally, of course. This was all a charade. That doesn't mean it didn't hurt, but it had to be done. Even though he hit me harder than I thought necessary, I didn't speak up. It wasn't advisable to piss off a guy like Knox.

"That's going to get worse over the coming days," Shane said.

"At least I'm safe, " I said.

"Yes, that's the most important thing. Did he chase after you?"

"I don't think so. When I turned around after a few hundred yards, he wasn't behind me. I was still genuinely scared so I knocked on the first door I saw, which happened to be you."

"I'm so sorry."

"Thanks, Shane."

I used his first name on purpose, hoping to build a quick camaraderie.

"You could have gone straight to the police and reported him for domestic violence."

"And then what? Go to court for the next several months? Get a temporary restraining order and just piss him off even more? Be looking over my shoulder for months to come?"

"I get where you are coming from, Lexi, but he did hit you. I guess that decision has to be up to you."

"Thanks, Shane. You're a good guy."

And then I made my saddest possible expression.

I thought he was going to melt like the witch from *The Wizard of Oz*.

I've been with a lot of men in my life, but never did I have one under my thumb this quickly. He'd known me for all of ten minutes and he was already at my beck and call.

As I said, men are easy.

In Shane's defense, this situation was extreme. What man wouldn't want to help/save me in this scenario?

I'm a twenty-five-year-old knockout with a perfect body and big, brown eyes that men would kill for.

"I'll ask one last time, Lexi," Shane said. "Do you want me to call the cops?"

"No, for all the reasons I already mentioned. What I would like is to look out your front window and make sure he's not standing out there," I said, knowing full well no one would be there.

"Of course."

We got up from the coffee table and I put Shane through the farce of slowly, deliberately opening the blinds and peeking out. I spent a good forty-five seconds peering from one side of the window to the other and then back again. It was an Oscar-caliber performance.

"Did you see him?" Shane asked.

"No, he's not out there."

We walked back to the kitchen table.

"Do you want another coffee?"

"Sure, I'll take one more, thanks. And then I'll go."

"Go where? You can't go home to an abusive boyfriend."

"John doesn't live with me. He is an ex-boyfriend. He arrived at my door and said he wanted to talk. I made the grave mistake of letting him in. It started going downhill shortly after that."

I almost mistakenly called him Knox. I had to watch myself.

"What if you go home and he's still there waiting?"

"That is possible."

I wanted Shane to ask me to stay, but I couldn't be Captain Obvious about it. I had to let him bring it up.

"You can stay here if you'd like," Shane said.

Bingo.

"I can't stay here," I said, playing my part to perfection.

"Of course, you can, Lexi," he said. "You can sleep on the couch. Or, if you want, you can sleep on my bed and I'll sleep on the couch."

I should have asked for a suite at the Ritz. He would have booked one.

"You're too nice," I said, glancing upward.

As you might have guessed, eye contact is a big one for me. The easiest way to seduce a guy.

"Would you prefer the couch or the bed?"

As much as I'd have preferred a bed, I had to keep playing the innocent, battered, bereaved ex-girlfriend.

"The couch is just fine," I said.

"Alright. I'll go put a sheet and a comforter on it after we finish this coffee."

Shane walked back to his Keurig machine and started making me a second cup of coffee.

Everything was working to perfection.

Knox would be proud.

CHAPTER 3

KNOX

L exi was a tough, street-wise girl.

She was also extremely gorgeous and could play the sad, dejected girl when needed. The kind any guy would want to help out, which is exactly what was necessary.

I had no doubt Shane would fall for her.

And it was a necessity. If you set a plan in motion, part one has to be successful for all the other parts to follow.

And when Shane did inevitably fall for Lexi, our plan would work like a well-oiled machine. Maybe he wouldn't fall for her the first night, but at that point, Lexi had her in. She could invite Shane to coffee in a few days or tell him she'd like to repay him by buying him dinner.

Once coffee or dinner happened, Shane would have no chance. I'd seen the guy walking around Santa Monica while we vetted him. We knew his wife had just dumped him. And let me tell you, she wasn't exactly a play-mate. Then again, Shane didn't appear to be a Lothario.

A guy down on his luck would be easy pickings.

Especially with a woman like Lexi. The fact that she was also playing the battered woman would only make him feel closer to her. My guess is they'd have sex within the next week. Maybe sooner.

And then he was all ours and we could start with phase two of my outlandish scheme.

∽

I'd been very meticulous and planned everything to perfection.

Including the time of night that we had Lexi knock on Shane's door. We'd staked out his apartment for a few weeks and the lights would go out right around 11:30 every night. We had to make sure Shane was still awake and he'd hear the knock at the door.

So we decided on eleven.

It was these small details that could make all the difference.

I continued to let Lexi think we were in this together.

I told her everything on our end would be split 50/50. I made it out like we were equal partners.

That wasn't the case. I was in charge. Completely and totally.

She could play the vixen all she wanted, but she was no match for a bastard like me. I could - and would - resort to worse tactics than her. Much, much worse.

Shit, I even hit her harder than necessary.

I'll concede that Lexi was tough, but after all, she was still just a woman.

She would prove useful, but I'd have to dispose of her at some point.

Too bad, because she is one beautiful, sexy woman. I mean, like an all-timer. Those dimples. Those breasts. Those legs. That ass.

None of those would save her though.

At some point, allowing her to stay alive wouldn't be worth the risk.

But that would have to wait.

For now, I needed her hooks firmly implanted into Shane.

CHAPTER 4

SHANE

I put a sheet over my couch and tucked it under the cushions to make it as bed-like as possible. I replaced the uncomfortable couch pillows with a few from my bed and grabbed a comforter from the closet.

"You're going above the call," Lexi said.

"No, I'm just trying to show you that not all men are pigs," I said.

"I'm glad I knocked on your door," she said and slightly smiled.

For obvious reasons, I'd only seen the miniature version of her smile. I'm sure it would light up a room in all its glory.

"There's a bathroom at the end of this tiny hallway," I said, pointing in that direction. "I put an extra towel in there if you want to shower in the morning. I wake up early so I can get you up if you'd like."

"Please do. I'm a guest, I don't want to sleep in."

"Is six a.m. alright?"

"That's fine."

"If you need anything, just knock on my door," I said. "I've deadbolted the lock on the front door. You're going to be okay tonight."

"You said no compliments, but you're getting one last one. Thanks for everything you have done, Shane."

"You're welcome, Lexi. I'll see you in the morning."

∾

I was actually up by five a.m., but I stayed in my room and gave Lexi an extra hour of beauty sleep. She certainly could use it.

At six, I opened my door and made my way to the couch. She was cuddled in the most minute ball imaginable. It was as if she made herself as small as possible so the big, bad world couldn't get to her.

I tapped her on the shoulder.

"Lexi," I said.

She bolted up really quickly, terror-stricken.

It's like she'd woken up from a nightmare, only in this case the nightmare was real. She'd been attacked by her ex-boyfriend.

"It's me, Lexi. It's Shane."

It took her a second and the recognition finally came.

"My good samaritan."

I'm pretty sure I blushed.

"That's me."

"What time is it?"

"Six. I would have let you sleep, but I didn't know if you have a job you need to get ready for."

"I'm a bartender and I work nights. What do you do?"

"I'm a lawyer."

"You must be a really bright guy."

"Ah, I'm middle of the road."

"I doubt that. A good guy and a bright guy. Not so easy to find."

Was she flirting with me?

She must have sensed what I was feeling.

"I'm sorry," Lexi said. "For all I know you're married with six kids."

I looked around my modest home.

"I think we both know that's not the case. Actually, I am newly single."

"Her loss."

I enjoyed where this conversation was heading but decided to steer clear of it. At least for now. It was debatable whether I was a good guy or not. For the moment, I was going to play one.

"How is your cheek feeling today?"

Lexi felt it.

"Has the bruise gotten worse?"

It had.

"Yes. Do you want an ice pack?"

I realized it was something I should have offered her last night, but there was a lot going on. It slipped my mind.

"Sure, thanks. I think I'll leave after that. I've already taken up enough of your time."

"I don't leave for work until around eight, so you're free to stay here until then."

I quickly reconsidered.

"And if you're too scared to go home, I guess you could stay here while I work."

No, I didn't know Lexi well, but I'd rather have her at my place than walk back to her place where her ex could potentially be waiting for her.

"I'll leave when you are going to work, but could you do me one more favor?"

"Anything," I said, a bit too quickly for my own liking.

"Can you walk with me to my place, just to make sure John isn't there?"

"Of course."

"Thank you, Shane."

CHAPTER 5

LEXI

Shane walked me to my place and I had to act relieved that "John" wasn't there.

I really did live three blocks away from Shane. Of course, like everything else, that was part of the plan. I'd only moved in last month.

Once we "realized" my apartment was unoccupied, I asked Shane for his phone number. He happily gave it to me.

"Can I call you in a few days and maybe we can hang out?" I asked.

"That would be great, but take care of yourself first," Shane said.

"I will. You'll see a different Lexi next time we hang out."

"Looking forward to it."

Shane hugged me goodbye and started walking down 10th Street towards Wilshire and back to his place. In Santa Monica, the streets went in descending order as they neared the beach which meant I was a mere ten blocks from the Pacific Ocean. A nice perk of living in west Los Angeles.

Once Shane was out of sight, I picked up the phone and called Knox.

"How did it go?" he asked.

"To perfection."

"That's my girl."

Knox was a mean-spirited guy who didn't care about anyone but himself. Unlike Shane, he never would have let a random woman stay the night unless he planned on banging her.

Shane wasn't perfect, but he was a far better human than Knox.

Not that I was one to be judging morality.

I was seducing a man for all the wrong reasons.

And the sad fact is that most women would choose Knox over Shane. Or, maybe that's just cold-hearted women like myself.

"I told Shane I'd call him in a few days," I said.

"Good. Let's try to make this happen quickly. We don't want too much time to pass. He might consider how you two met as being a bit fortuitous. We want him to get into you soon. And I mean that literally."

"Don't be crass, Knox."

He laughed.

"You love it. You're probably already tired of that little pushover. You're ready for a real man like me."

"Can I come see you?" I asked.

"You can come over later tonight, but as I told you, we can't be seen in public for a while. Not until we finish our business with Shane. It's just too risky."

"I understand. So what time tonight?"

"Swing by around eleven."

"See you then."

I hung up the phone.

I'd now played two guys in the last five minutes.

To Shane, I'd played my role of the broken girl.

To Knox, I'd played my role as the subservient girlfriend who did anything and everything he told me to.

The truth was I was only looking out for myself. I knew this Shane situation could go in a thousand different directions and I had my eyes on Knox. Not for the reason he was thinking, though. I was suspicious of him.

I was in this for myself and no one else.

If I even had an inkling that Knox might try to cut me out, he'd have another thing coming.

CHAPTER 6

KNOX

Lexi may have had Shane wrapped around her little finger, but I had Lexi wrapped around mine.

She came over at eleven that night and we had sex twice before falling asleep in each other's arms. It would be considered romantic if I believed in fictional notions like love.

We were two peas in a pod that way. We both loved sex - especially the carnal, animalistic aspect of it - but felt the romantic side of it was for the birds.

Leave that to schlubs like Shane Doyle.

Speaking of him, it was time to start planning for phase two. I was considering it inevitable that Lexi would have sex with him soon.

And then it would be all over for Mr. Doyle.

Lexi was damn good at sex.

And I should know.

CHAPTER 7

SHANE

I spent the next few days at work, preparing for the mundane case I was about to begin. A DUI. How freaking boring! Now, my trial coming up after that? It was the polar opposite and completely fascinating.

While my body was at my office at the Santa Monica Courthouse, my brain would often drift to Lexi. Or maybe it was the other way around. My brain was at work and a certain body part was thinking about Lexi.

She'd called me the night after I walked her home and we set up a date for Friday night.

Well, maybe get-together was more accurate. It was hard to be sure.

Sure felt like a date, though.

It was only three days away, which still felt like a damn eternity.

Yes, I think it's safe to say I was slowly falling for Lexi.

And by slowly, I mean quickly.

Friday rolled around and I drove the three blocks to pick up Lexi. I hated thinking about her being abused in that apartment.

Would she ever be able to stop thinking about it?

Maybe once she moved.

Into my place?

Slow down, Shane!

I walked to the door and she opened it, wearing a beautiful red dress. It was understated and not a gown or something you'd wear out in Beverly Hills. She was wearing a small silver necklace and looked approximately fifteen times more attractive than when she showed up at my house.

And I'd already thought she was gorgeous then.

"Hey, Shane."

"You look stunning, Lexi."

"Thanks. You look pretty good yourself."

I was wearing some light green dress pants with a crisp, blue shirt. It was a little wild for me stylistically, but what can I say, I wanted to stand out.

"Are you ready?" I asked.

"Sure am. Let's do this."

I led her to my car where I opened the passenger side door for her.

I was being the consummate gentleman.

My car was nothing to write home about. A five-year-old Kia Optima. I may have been a Los Angeles District Attorney, but I was far from rich. I'd had a few financial issues in the past. An aversion to betting the NFL would have benefitted me. It was one of my fatal flaws.

Add my divorce to that and things weren't exactly ideal financially. But hey, I had a beautiful girl on my arm now. Things could be worse.

The car didn't seem to matter to Lexi - I'd hoped not - as she smiled seductively. It was the full smile that I didn't get that first night.

We set off for Sugarfish, the best sushi in Santa Monica, and possibly all of Los Angeles. I drove down Wilshire Boulevard in the direction of the beach.

I looked sharp, had a gorgeous girl with me, and was about to eat some delicious sushi. Life was good. Financial issues or not.

I parked at a neighboring parking garage and we walked one block to Sugarfish. I gave the host my name and she seated us at a little booth. It gave us a little more privacy than the tables in the middle of everyone else.

They handed us two menus and we quickly smiled at each other.

"This is a nice place," Lexi said.

"Wait till you try the sushi."

"Looking forward to it."

"I hate to do this, but let's get the awkward shit out of the way first. Anything you want to tell me?"

She knew what I was referring to.

"John texted me and apologized. I told him not to contact me again and if he did, I'd go to the police. He texted back that he'd give me my space."

"Do you believe him?" I asked.

"He seemed genuine, but who knows?"

"I can't imagine he's the most trustworthy person."

"No, admittedly not."

"Anything else?"

"No, really that's it. As long as he keeps his distance, I'm happy."

I waved my hands like I was calling an NFL play dead. The same NFL I never should have bet on.

"Alright, now that we have that out of the way, tell me about yourself, Lexi."

"What do you want to know?"

"For starters, your last name."

"Grant."

"Lexi Grant. A very pretty name. And where is Lexi Grant from?"

"I grew up in San Antonio. My father was a construction foreman and my mother was a stay-at-home Mom. I had a brother, but he died in a car accident when I was in high school."

"I'm so sorry."

"Thanks, but it's been a long time now. It doesn't hurt like it used to. I moved to LA a few years back. I had dreams of being an actress, but I've led a mostly normal life since I've been here. I bartend four times a week and I work as a freelancing web designer."

"You didn't tell me the web designing part."

She looked down.

"I'm still in the early phases."

She didn't appear too keen on talking about her web designing. I'm sure it was a tough business to break into with everyone and their cousin knowing how to do it.

"Did you ever go on any auditions?"

"A few when I first got to LA. I'd look around and there were fifty women and forty of them were hotter than me."

"I find that hard to believe," I said.

She blushed.

"Thanks."

"I'm quite serious. You're striking. I don't care if it's the Miss America pageant, there's no way forty out of fifty women would ever be prettier than you."

Was I laying it on too thick? Probably, but I believed it.

"Stop," Lexi said playfully.

"So you didn't book a gig?"

"No. And maybe it's for the best. I see these women who get an acting role right away and they think it's going to be all roses and red carpets. Five years later, they are addicted to coke or something worse, and looking like shit."

"That's somber."

"I don't think I'm wrong."

"There are certainly a lot of examples of that. So are you done auditioning?"

"Never say never, but I'm happy with where I'm at."

"Where do you bartend?"

"It's a place called The Belly Flop."

"I've heard of it. Didn't the owner get killed in some crazy case a few years back?"

"Sure did. His name was Barry Gant, but I started working there after he was killed. It's under new ownership now."

"Wait, he's not running it from six feet under?"

Lexi laughed quite loudly.

"You're funny," she said.

I decided to run with it.

"Uh, Barry, we're thinking about hiring a new girl named Lexi," I said. "Knock once on the dirt for yes, knock twice for no."

We both busted out in laughter.

I was definitely guilty of laughing at my own joke.

The waiter came and checked on us. We hadn't even looked at the menu. I asked him for a few minutes.

"I'm not that well versed in sushi," Lexi said. "Why don't you order for us?"

"Sure. Anything you don't want?"

"Anything that's still alive."

I smiled.

"I think you're safe."

When the waiter came back a few minutes later, I ordered something called the *Don't Think. Just Eat. Trust Me.* which included a variety of sashimi, nigiri, and rolls.

It was "only" $59, which considering the price of sushi in Los Angeles, was pretty damn cheap.

I felt like the date was going well. We'd gotten the uncomfortable part out of the way and since then had flirted and laughed.

"You said you were a lawyer, right?" Lexi asked.

"I am."

"What kind of law?"

"I'm a district attorney."

"For Los Angeles or Santa Monica?"

"I'm based out of Santa Monica, but it's all of Los Angeles county."

"That must be a pretty big job. The DA of LA County."

I realized my mistake.

"I should clarify. I'm an Assistant District Attorney. There's only one official DA in LA, but there's tons of ADA's which is what they call us."

"Do you still prosecute the cases?"

"Oh, yeah. It's not like the DA could prosecute every single case in LA county."

My comment came off as snider than I'd intended.

"You're a little more sarcastic than I remember. What happened to that quiet, caring man from a few days ago?"

I laughed.

"He's still in here somewhere. Just wanted to make sure you don't think I'm a pushover."

She smiled ever so slyly. I took it as a good sign.

"Any fun cases you're working on?"

"I've got a wild one starting in a few weeks."

Lexi moved her arms forward.

"Tell me more."

"A guy who owns a few apartment complexes killed a man over some sort of drug deal gone wrong."

"I think I saw it on the news."

"Yeah, it got some airplay. The trial is going to bring a lot of attention as well."

"On you?"

"Yeah, since I'm the ADA trying it, but the murderer will receive the lion's share of the media attention."

"Don't you say alleged murderer?"

"Certainly, if you're a defense attorney. Since I'm a prosecutor, I can kind of get away with it."

Lexi laughed.

"Yeah, that makes sense."

Our sushi arrived several minutes later. They put the whole order in the middle of us, leaving us to decide who got what.

"I'm going to let you be the guinea pig," Lexi said.

I grabbed my chopsticks and picked up a roll with blue and Dungeness crab, dipping it into a small soy sauce/wasabi/ginger concoction that I'd quickly put together.

"It's delicious!" I exclaimed, possibly a bit too loudly.

There were two rolls, so I pointed to Lexi and told her the next was hers.

She fumbled with her chopsticks, dropping the roll on her first and second attempts. On the third try, the roll made it to her mouth. For a few seconds, she didn't respond.

She then looked up at me.

"Holy you know what. That is fan-freaking-tastic."

"Told you."

Before I had a chance to reach for a piece of nigiri, Lexi had taken down a piece of Albacore sashimi.

"This was great too. I've been missing out."

"Don't tell me you've never tried sushi?"

"I haven't."

"Why didn't you say something?"

"I didn't want to rock the boat once you brought up sushi. I just wanted to go out with you."

I just wanted to go out with you.

Bingo.

"I'm glad you're enjoying it."

"I was always a little scared of raw fish. To be honest, if it weren't for you and this date, I might never have tried it. So thanks."

I had been wondering if this was a date. I guess it was.

"You're welcome. Glad I converted you."

I could tell that Lexi was waiting to choose her next piece, so I grabbed some salmon sashimi.

She quickly followed with a piece of nigiri.

"Each one gets progressively better," she said and reached out and touched my arm, holding on for a few seconds longer than necessary.

The date was moving in the right direction.

Did I want to sleep with a woman who'd been hit by her boyfriend several days earlier?

I mean, I wanted to, but should I?

I decided Lexi would have to instigate it. I wasn't going to be the one.

A few minutes later, we'd demolished the *Don't Think. Just Eat. Trust Me.*

"We could order some more," I said.

"As good as it was, I don't want to get too full. I have some plans for later tonight."

She looked at me flirtatiously and that's when I knew I was going to sleep with Lexi that night.

Fuck it!

I was tired of playing Mr. Nice Guy with her.

Time to show her I had an edge to me.

CHAPTER 8
LEXI

Shane and I ended the night with a bang.

And yes, I mean that in the carnal sense.

He wasn't great, but I managed to enjoy myself despite this all just being a means to an end. And honestly, most men weren't great with me the first time. They'd finish a bit too early for my liking. And I knew I was to blame. I was just too damn sexy. Sorry, modesty is not my specialty.

Knox had set out two early goals for me. Getting Shane to fall for me and soon thereafter, having us sleep together.

Mission accomplished on both fronts.

Dinner was excellent, and yes, I'd eaten sushi before. I just thought Shane would appreciate thinking he'd turned me on to it.

The only potential mistake I'd made was being a bit upfront about his next case as Assistant District Attorney. I hadn't blown my cover, but I needed to be careful.

Hopefully, he just wrote it off as me being interested in his work. During subsequent meetings, I'd make sure that he broached the subject.

There was no reason to mention that little tidbit to Knox. More than anything, I didn't want Knox mad at me. He would just be happy I'd slept with Shane and that he was now smitten with me. Which he was.

CHAPTER 9

KNOX

It wasn't going to continue being this easy.

It couldn't.

Everything had transpired in the exact manner I'd hoped.

Sure, my meticulous planning deserved some of the credit. The fact that I decided to go after an ADA and not some lone juror looked like the right call.

Of course, I did have a little help with that one. Some slick-looking guy in an expensive suit approached me outside of my complex one day.

"Shane Doyle should be your mark. He'll be confirmed soon as the ADA assigned to prosecuting Roger Theus. He's going through a divorce and likes to gamble a bit too much. Go after him. That comes from our mutual friend."

With that, the man walked away.

～

Inviting Lexi on as the femme fatale now seemed like a no-brainer, but there was a time when I was looking to do this all myself. Hoping to not have to share the money with one or two co-conspirators.

Which brought me to my latest conundrum.

If it came to the point where I had to, how would I do away with both Lexi and Shane?

I still had some time, but my wheels were churning.

Did I seem like the type of guy who wanted to split the money three ways?

I'll bet you can answer that question.

CHAPTER 10

SHANE

I woke up the next morning with a smile on my face and a yearning for Lexi.

You'd think after a night of passionate sex, I might want some time off, but it was the opposite. I'd had a good thing the night before and was up for round two. Unfortunately, Lexi had left early that morning, and there would be no encore.

I was willing to wait. Not that I had a choice.

She was so much sexier than Christie. I hated to badmouth my soon-to-be ex-wife, but comparing the two of them in bed was an epic mismatch. Lexi won in a landslide.

Plus, Christie had left me. I shouldn't be worried about pulling punches with her. Screw her! In the "Fuck off" sense. As far as actually screwing, give me Lexi any day.

How great would it be if I was out with Lexi and we ran into Christie?!

That would be perfection. Christie would immediately know that I'd taken a step up. I'd have won my little one-on-one battle with her.

Maybe that was petty, but it's how my mind was working.

As for what I'd say when people asked how Lexi and I met, that would be a little tricky. I certainly couldn't tell the truth. Maybe I'd say I met her online. No one likes hearing that, but it was better than the alternative.

I hated admitting it, but I wish this John guy would vanish from the planet. If it took a bolt of lightning to strike him down, I'd be okay with that.

The thought of him still out there worried me. How was he going to react when he found out Lexi had a new man? Probably not very well.

Maybe John would run onto Santa Monica Boulevard and a fully-loaded Hummer would take him out.

Shut the fuck up, Shane! Don't be that guy.

Maybe I wasn't that guy, but I still felt ill-will towards him.

I wanted to find out more about the guy and pulled out my laptop.

It was Saturday so no court for me. I should have been preparing for my upcoming trial. Not the vapid DUI case, but the big one that followed.

But I couldn't let a sleeping dog lie. I had to know more about this mysterious John.

I googled, "Lexi Grant John." I didn't know his last name, so this was likely a wild goose chase. Maybe he'd been arrested for assaulting Lexi in the past. The google search produced nothing productive. There were a few articles that popped up by a reporter named Lexi Grant where the name John had been used in the article. Out of curiosity, I clicked on the picture of the reporter. The two Lexi Grants looked nothing alike.

Without John's last name, I didn't have much hope. I googled "Lexi Grant", but I couldn't find my Lexi Grant. I wasn't too surprised. While Lexi wasn't exactly an everyday name, it wasn't unheard of either. And Grant was very common.

I tried "Lexi Grant Santa Monica" to no avail.

I set aside my laptop and asked myself a question.

Why so suspicious?

I told myself I wasn't, but there was something eating at me.

Was it odd the way Lexi and I met? Yes, a little bit.

But I believed every word she said.

Plus, who would go after me? I was hardly rolling in the dough. In fact, Christie had been the breadwinner, working in pharmaceutical sales. Assistant District Attorney sounds like a big job, but it only pays 7k a month. Our rent was 3,500 a month and now that I was paying it alone, there wasn't much left over. And like I'd mentioned, gambling had taken a few chunks over the years.

So no, no one was using me as a mark.

There was no money to squeeze out of yours truly.

STOP!

I actually yelled aloud.

I was pissed at myself. I'd just slept with the sexiest girl of my life and my mind wouldn't let me enjoy it.

Was Lexi out of my league? Probably. Was I great with women? No, probably not.

But I'd helped her in her time of need and that could go a long way. I'm sure the last thing Lexi wanted was to be around some asshole like John.

For once, being the nice guy had been advantageous to my sex life.

Smile, you asshole!

And so I did.

～

The next time I saw Lexi was on Monday at The Belly Flop, the bar she worked at. By then, I'd forgotten about my ridiculous speculation. I was just happy to see her.

Her bar was on Wilshire Boulevard, halfway between the 405 freeway and the ocean. And yes, as a native Angelo, I do put "the" in front of my freeway names. I'd been born in Temecula and slowly made my way further north and further inland. That included a stint at UCLA for undergrad and I ran it back there for law school.

The guise for meeting with Lexi was for an after-work drink, but really I just wanted to see her. I got out of court around 4:45 and arrived at The Belly Flop a few minutes after five.

I was currently prosecuting that tedious DUI case, surely the lowest case an ADA can land. The guy was going to be convicted, but insisted on going to trial and tried saying the cops had it in for him. Not just that, he alleged the lab had screwed up his BAC, which was an astronomical .26.

For my money, he's lucky he didn't kill anyone and should have just accepted his punishment. But no, he had to take a trial, and sure enough, yours truly got assigned to this shitty case.

What I'm saying is, I was looking forward to that drink.

Only one, though. I didn't want to be on trial for my own DUI.

I parked on the street and walked into The Belly Flop. It was bigger than I expected. There were lots of TVs and a huge "island bar" in the middle of the room. I saw Lexi, along with a male bartender, patrolling the bar.

I took a seat on one of the barstools.

Lexi looked over and immediately walked in my direction.

I doubted she was going to kiss me. This was her workplace. These were her regulars. You didn't want them to know more than they had to.

"How are you, Shane?" she asked and then leaned in for a quick little peck on the mouth. I felt vindicated. She didn't mind kissing me in public.

"Long day at work," I said.

"Oh, yeah?"

"Yeah, working that boring DUI case I told you about."

"That's a bummer. Can I get you a drink?"

"Sure. I'll take a Shirley Temple."

She looked at me, not sure how to react.

"You're joking, right?" she said.

"Yes, Lexi, I'm joking."

She laughed.

"I'll take a Tito's and Tonic."

"Coming right up," she said and started pouring it directly in front of me.

I saw the male bartender look in my direction. He probably realized I was not just a random customer. Especially if he'd seen the quick kiss.

Was he jealous? Probably. If you worked with Lexi, being attracted to her was basically inevitable. I can't imagine many heterosexual men who wouldn't see Lexi as sexy.

Did that bother me? That Lexi's co-workers and regulars likely imagined her naked?

Maybe a little bit, but I decided to wear it as a badge of honor. I had seen her naked. I had slept with her. Let the other ones gawk at her. It was me they wanted to be.

Lexi brought me out of my daydream.

"That will be $9," she said.

I looked at her, surprised she'd charged me so suddenly. Don't you let someone run a tab, especially someone you just slept with?

And then I realized she was joking.

"That's for your Shirley Temple comment," she said.

"You got me."

"And I got you. This drink."

"Thanks, Lexi."

There were no two ways around it. I was smitten. Bordering on falling in love.

I took a long sip of my Tito's and Tonic and told myself to slow down a bit.

I was behaving like a teenaged girl.

CHAPTER 11

LEXI

I f I cared what other people thought, I might have been annoyed by all the questions once Shane left.

Are you dating him?

Have you screwed him yet?

And that was just from Buddy, my co-worker.

The regulars were much more to the point.

He definitely out-kicked his coverage.

He's fighting out of his weight class.

"He's just a close friend," was my response.

Their expressions told me they weren't buying that.

"Do you give all your close friends a kiss on the lips?"

I had no answer to that and ignored it.

It hadn't been my idea to invite Shane to The Belly Flop. Knox had suggested it. He said we had to make this believable. We had to make Shane feel like he was dating me. That's why I decided to give him a kiss.

"Plus, you've already been out to dinner with him and I can assure you he's told a few friends about you. Sorry, there's going to be no hiding this," Knox had said.

"It sounds like I'm taking all the risks," I said.

"I came up with the plan. That means I make the rules. And it's not like I can be the one seducing Shane."

That made me laugh, which wasn't a very common occurrence with Knox. Comedy wasn't his forte.

But still, it did beg the question.

Was this all really worth it?

For over half a million dollars, you're damn right it was.

CHAPTER 12

KNOX

You may be wondering how this all got started.

Well, let me tell you.

I'd first heard the name Roger Theus when I was moving out of my raggedy apartment in West Hollywood. Yes, the same Hollywood that makes money hand over fist. There are two distinct segments of that city. The opulent, over-the-top Hollywood and the people one step from Skid Row. I was the latter.

"Have you found a new place to live yet?" Kitty, my landlord asked.

"No. I'm going to be looking today."

I'd just given my one-month notice, figuring this was L.A., and finding some shitty apartment would be easy. Shitty would be an improvement on Kitty's complex, even though I'd grown to like her personally.

"If you're not against living in Santa Monica, go check out this apartment complex on Wilshire and 15th. The guy who owns it is a friend of mine named Roger Theus. I think you two would get along famously."

Kitty was in her late fifties, and despite being thirty years older than me, she wasn't shy about hitting on me. There were a few times I'd considered sleeping with her, hoping my rent would get overlooked, but I couldn't bring myself to do it. I'd imagine the old landlady from the movie *Kingpin* and just couldn't pull the trigger.

Despite never having slept together, she liked to get involved in my business and I pretty much let her. She knew I was a bit of a grifter, moving from job to job and occasionally, con to con.

I think she enjoyed it.

My resume would have been comical.

I'd worked as a for-hire bartender at events like weddings or birthdays. That was actually the lone legit job I'd had. I'd been a middleman for drug deals. I'd referred people to a bookie and collected off their losses. And that same bookie hired me as a collector, so not only would I refer my "friends" to him, but then I'd go collect from them. Although no knees were broken, it was still shady.

Kitty didn't know the particulars, but she knew I was up to no good and usually on the grift.

One could argue that the charging of exorbitant rent in Los Angeles was a grift all its own. Maybe she saw a little of me in her. Just not the part she wanted.

I took her up on her offer and met Roger Theus on a Friday afternoon in mid-May. The complex was known as The Premier.

The exterior of the complex was painted white and brown and the paint job looked like it was from the 10s. And I mean the 1910s.

I'd soured on Hollywood and some of the people there had soured on me. Starting anew in Santa Monica seemed like the right move. Despite this place being another dump.

Sure, it was only ten or fifteen miles away, but it was like a whole different world. People were generally East of the 405 people (Hollywood) or West of the 405 people (Santa Monica/Brentwood/Venice/Malibu.) There wasn't nearly as much crossover as you'd think.

I knew people who lived in Santa Monica who might only hit Hollywood once or twice a year.

And that's what I was counting on. People on the Westside wouldn't know my reputation.

Roger Theus was a big guy, bordering on sloppy. When I met him outside of his apartment complex, his Tommy Bahama shirt was two times too big. And that's saying something considering he probably weighed between two hundred and fifty and three hundred pounds. He was also tall, somewhere around 6'4". I felt like he was trying to look younger than his fifty-something years. His long, wavy hair and tanned face partially helped do the trick, although Father Time is undefeated. He had a scowl and reminded me of a not-so-friendly, younger John Goodman.

"Thanks for meeting with me. I'm Knox," I said.

"Call me Roger."

"You come recommended by my previous landlady, Kitty."

His eyes looked skyward, obviously deep in thought.

"Ah, Kitty. We had some fun together back in the mid-90s."

I'd never felt younger, having been born in the mid-90s.

"We were up to no good, really," he added.

"Tell me more."

"Maybe when I know you better."

He smiled, insinuating there were stories to come. I could sense Roger's stories weren't going to be about milk and cookies. There was a definite menace to him.

"Do you have any units available?" I asked, getting down to brass tacks.

Roger hadn't asked why Kitty had recommended me. He'd probably guessed I wasn't always on the up and up. I had a feeling Kitty knew where a few of Roger's skeletons were hidden.

My guess was that Roger had seen and experienced a lot of less-than-stellar behavior over the years. Shit, he'd probably partaken in it himself. He's the type of guy you'd rob a bank with. He'd know how to keep his mouth shut.

I'd known him for all of two minutes and that's already the impression I'd got.

"I have someone moving out in two weeks. When do you need a place by?"

"I'm moving out of Kitty's complex in one month."

"That's perfect. Probably take about two weeks to clean the place up."

"Then I'll take it."

I was that impulsive. I knew I liked Roger Theus. Probably for all the wrong reasons, but what can I say? Shady characters seem to find each other and I felt like I'd found my much older doppelgänger.

"Glad to hear it. Call me in two weeks and we can do a walkthrough."

"Sure, we can do that, but I've already committed. I'm going to take the place."

He laughed.

"I think we are going to get along just fine."

Roger Theus was right. We became fast friends.

And it was our connection that eventually brought Shane Doyle into the mix.

CHAPTER 13

SHANE

The week that followed was packed with equal parts excitement and boredom.

The time I spent with Lexi was phenomenal. It was only a few weeks in, but we were more or less a couple. After the drink at The Belly Flop, we went to two more dinners of which I paid for both.

She'd offered to split both times which was all I really wanted. I had no problem paying. I just didn't want to feel like I was being taken advantage of, and her offering to pay put that to rest.

She didn't appear to be the gold digger I'd worried about the week previous.

We ate at an Italian place called Guido's on Santa Monica Boulevard. The food was great and I just loved the name. Can you get any more Italian-sounding than Guido's?

Two days later, we ate at a place called The Water Grill. It was on Ocean Avenue and was right next to - you guessed it - the ocean. It was primarily a seafood restaurant and I got an excellent piece of salmon. Lexi opted for the crab cakes. Don't get me wrong, I love crab cakes, but they are a slight cop-out at a good seafood restaurant. The breading, etc. overshadows the true state of the fish. It would be like lathering a great steak with a pint of A-1 sauce.

But I digress...

The more boring aspects were all related to my upcoming case.

Although, in fairness, it was going to be a lot more entertaining than my recently completed DUI case. He was convicted, at least.

It wasn't the case itself that was going to be boring, but the research sure was. There were four huge binders of evidence that I'd collected. Over thirty interviews. I had two other brand-new ADAs that were helping me out, but I was doing the lion's share.

I was going up against a very well-regarded defense attorney in Hilton Lund. Yes, his first name was Hilton.

I'd gone mano-y-mano with him in one other trial and he'd managed to get a hung jury in that case. It was one in which his client should have been convicted.

So yes, I was scared of Hilton Lund.

I had the facts in my favor, however.

A Los Angeles slumlord found out someone stole his drug money and killed him. With extreme prejudice. The Medical Examiner said the victim, Billy Aybar, had been punched in the face over thirty times. I'd seen the autopsy photos and they were extremely disturbing. I'd make sure that the jury saw them as well.

I also had the next-door neighbor to Billy Aybar in my back pocket. He was going to testify that he was 100% sure that he saw the slumlord leaving Aybar's apartment in the minutes after the neighbor heard a scuffle.

This guy was bad news and I couldn't wait to put him away.

Roger Theus was his name.

CHAPTER 14

LEXI

By the time the last week of August came around, I'd been with Shane for over two weeks.

We were having dinner a few times a week and usually, I'd end up at his place. We had sex every night. The more time we spent together, the closer I could feel Shane was getting to me.

I'd done everything Knox had asked, except for one thing. He'd wanted me to send an incriminating email from Shane to myself. It was going to be sexist, racist, and a few other things that would make Shane look terrible.

Knox was calling it our backup plan.

The problem was that Shane had yet to leave his phone or laptop open long enough for me to make my move. One time he went to the bathroom in a hurry, but once I got the courage to check his phone, I needed a password to unlock it.

I bided my time, knowing the upcoming trial was still a few weeks out.

At some point, I'm sure I'd have the opportunity.

And then I'd pounce.

CHAPTER 15

KNOX

Roger Theus served as a father figure of sorts during my first several months at his apartment complex, The Premier. The most misnamed complex in history. There was nothing premier about The Premier. No premiers (as in leaders) would be staying there. No premiers (as in movie openings) would be held there.

But for the twenty-seven-year-old me, it was perfect.

The Premier was two stories with six apartments on both the bottom and top floors. There was a communal pool in the center of it and while people occasionally used it, my guess was that some undiscovered, mutant algae may have lived in it. I stayed away.

When I'd originally been referred to this place by Kitty the landlord, I'd assumed it was because Roger was a bit of a troublemaker like me. I wasn't wrong.

At his heart, Roger Theus was a hustler. If he could raise your rent a hundred dollars and get away with it, he would. It may not sound like much, but when you own two apartment complexes, you're talking quite a bit of money.

He was disarmingly up front when we talked.

He'd evict people for all the wrong reasons. A young woman wouldn't sleep with him. He didn't like the ethnicity of one of his tenants. Obviously, he was more subtle than that and found bullshit reasons to evict them, but he'd basically admitted all of this to me.

And he'd allude to a bigger business he was immersed in, although he hadn't told me just what yet.

You get the point, though. Roger was a pretty despicable human.

But so am I, so we got along great.

And within a few months, he trusted me implicitly.

~

Above all else, Roger loved to party.

He owned another Los Angeles apartment complex, the other being just as contemptible as The Premier. So Roger was undoubtedly well off, but these bashes were fit for someone more like Hugh Hefner.

It had me wonder about the other business he was involved in. It surely wasn't knitting.

Roger had an all-time bachelor pad in Malibu. That's where the parties took place.

It was on the mountainside of the Pacific Coast Highway. The house itself was nice, very modern looking with three bedrooms and three baths.

But no one cared about the inside. People came for the massive backyard and the patio that looked out on the Pacific Ocean.

There was a pool, a giant deck with upwards of twenty recliners, and the biggest personal bar I'd ever seen. The bigger the better was Roger's MO. Whenever he held parties there, which was usually about twice a month, there were enough bottles of Dom Perignon for a party of a thousand, even though these parties usually had around a hundred people. Making things even better, three-quarters of the guests were usually hot women in their twenties.

Roger could have gotten laid if there'd only ten women there. He was the owner of the house and throwing the party, after all. Like it or not, that goes a long way. But Roger wanted to show all the pretty girls off to the guys lucky enough to be invited.

Of which, I was usually one.

Roger's parties further confirmed that he liked hanging out with me. He'd introduce me to way more women than any of the other guys there. I felt like he was serving young women up on a platter to me.

I wasn't complaining.

~

I'd been living at The Premier for about five months when Roger abruptly knocked on my door. We were damn good friends at this point. The parties, obviously, but we also spent time going to movies and hitting up bars. He'd also come by the complex a lot and he'd inevitably swing by my apartment.

He'd pawn it off as looking after his own property, but I think he just liked schmoozing with his tenants. He could have afforded to hire someone to manage the property full-time, but Roger liked being hands-on. No one was going to tell him how to run his apartment buildings.

When I opened the door on this occasion, he had a stern look on his face. I could tell this wasn't a courtesy visit.

"Hey, Roger. What's up?"

"If I ask you to do something for me, are you up for it? We will never mention it again as long as we live."

"What's in it for me?" I asked.

I didn't ask what we were doing or if it was illegal. All I wanted to know was how it would benefit me.

I'm sure a psychiatrist would say that pretty much sums me up. I was a narcissist who was only out for himself.

"I'll abate your next two months of rent," he said.

I didn't know exactly what abate meant, but I got the gist of it. And considering rent was $1500, I'd be saving $3000. There wasn't much I wouldn't do for that kind of money.

That was a lot of bartending shifts, bookie payoffs, or makeshift drug deals.

"I'm in," I said.

"Good. Follow me out to my car."

CHAPTER 16

SHANE

In a moment of manic lunacy (are they the same thing?), I decided that
Lexi was using me.

I'd been vacillating back and forth over whether it could be true.

And while I had zero evidence to support my theory, I woke up this
morning and felt like it was all a sham.

It was hard to believe a girl as beautiful as Lexi would fall for me so
quickly.

Even under the circumstances.

So I decided to make a phone call.

～

"Hello?"

"Bruce, this is Shane Doyle. How have you been?"

"Been good, Shane. You got a case for me or are you just calling out of
the blue?"

Bruce Palmer was a private investigator I used from time to time. I'd
been warned that he was a bit cutthroat, even for the already cutthroat
private investigator business, but he'd always come through for me.

"I've got a job, but it's a little different than one of your usual gigs."

"I'm listening."

"You won't be working a case per se."

"Come out and say what you want, Shane. I know how to keep a secret."

That he did. Palmer was a rugged, seasoned vet of the P.I. business and he knew you kept your mouth shut if you wanted repeat business.

"I've been dating this exceptionally beautiful woman."

"And you want me to teach you a few things?"

I laughed, in spite of myself.

"That was a joke, Shane. Don't take it the wrong way."

"Don't joke yourself out of a job," I said.

He laughed.

"Mr. Serious from here on in."

This had gotten off to an awkward start.

"So, I met her under suspicious circumstances, and I just want to make sure she doesn't have any ulterior motives."

"You're a successful, good-looking guy, Shane. Are you sure she doesn't just like you for that?"

I didn't bother telling him that money was tight for me at the moment. And was he being a bit tongue-in-cheek when he called me good-looking? I didn't think so, but I wasn't exactly Brad Pitt either.

"Well, that's what I want you to find out."

"Which is what exactly?"

"I want you to follow her around for several days. If you don't find anything suspicious, that will be the end of the gig."

"That's it?"

"That's it."

"I'll take it."

"Good."

"Couple of questions, though," Bruce said.

"Shoot."

"Do you only want to know if she's fooling around? Or do you want to know if she pays for her coffee in pennies?"

"Not sure I get the reference."

"I'm asking if you care about any of her peculiarities or merely whether she's exclusive with you?"

"Mostly, the latter, but I'll let you be the judge of what is important."

"When do I start?" Bruce asked.

"You already have."

"Where do I start?"

"I'll text you her address and name."

"I'll call you in a few days."

With that, I hung up and texted Lexi's information to Bruce.

I immediately felt like the biggest asshole in the world.

No wonder I didn't get gorgeous girls like Lexi. I sent private investigators after them.

CHAPTER 17

BRUCE THE P.I.

S hane wasn't wrong.

Lexi Grant was quite the looker.

A pretty face to be sure, but she was more than just that. She walked and strutted in a way that would immediately grab a man's attention. It's as if you couldn't take your eyes off of her.

And this was all following her from afar. I imagine she was even sexier with her eyes fixated on you.

Shane was a solid attorney and a nice guy. I'd always liked him. I don't think he was quite Johnny Cochran or Melvin Belli, but he was just fine for a Los Angeles ADA. If he had bigger hopes than that, I think he was mistaken. He didn't have the confidence - nor the swagger - to be a great defense attorney.

Similar to his attorney skills, he was middle of the road when it came to attracting the fairer sex. I'd known his soon-to-be ex-wife Christie for years, and while she was a nice woman who bordered on being attractive, she was hardly what you'd consider a catch. She was more homely than pretty.

I'd seen Shane try to flirt at the Santa Monica Courthouse and let's just say, I wasn't blown away.

So, I'll admit, after seeing Lexi in person, I was suspicious she would choose to be with Shane. Call me a judgmental asshole if you must, but that's what we do in my field, and I had some serious doubts that a mid-twenties bombshell like Lexi would fall for an average-looking guy ten years older than her.

Despite all this, I vowed not to jump to any conclusions. At least, no more than I already had.

～

I followed Lexi from her apartment to the bar she worked at, The Belly Flop, for two straight days. I figured it was better if she didn't see me in person, so I never entered the bar. Instead, I'd call the bar and - acting like an old friend - ask when Lexi's shift ended that night. Obviously, I'd hang up if a woman answered.

And then, when Lexi's shift ended, I followed her home.

On the first night she entered her apartment, I lingered outside in my car, waiting to see if a man other than Shane showed up. Once fifteen minutes passed, I crept within eyesight of the apartment to see if I could hear or see anyone else in the apartment. Nothing. It was just Lexi.

On the second night, she left about ten minutes after arriving, but Shane had told me she was going to his house that night. So nothing had aroused my suspicions.

Until the third night.

After finishing her third straight night shift at The Belly Flop, this time at two a.m., she didn't drive straight home. She continued down Wilshire about five more blocks, heading towards the ocean. She didn't make it that far, taking a right on 4th street and parking outside of an apartment complex.

What happened next was very dubious.

She knocked on the door, and a tall, wiry-strong guy with an arm sleeve tattoo leaned his head out of the front door. He looked to his left and right and then whisked Lexi into the apartment, quickly shutting the door behind him.

Something was amiss.

～

Instead of telling Shane straight away, I decided to investigate another day. I wanted to find out more. My spidey senses were telling me that there was a lot more to this.

I decided to take a huge chance. It was idiotic. Asinine. Foolish.

And despite knowing all that, there was no doubt I was going through with it.

~

Lexi had the next night off so I had to wait two days.

Shane had asked me if I'd learned anything yet. I lied and told him no, but I thought he should give me a few more days.

He conceded two more days, and I could tell he was mad at himself for allowing me/this to continue. His curiosity was getting the better of him.

Lexi's shift was a closing shift, from eight p.m. until two a.m. which was ideal for me.

After she left her apartment, I waited around for the sun to go down. It was late August and the sun was still out to almost nine p.m. in Los Angeles.

Finally, at 9:25, I took my big chance.

I approached her apartment with an old-school tool that I'd used probably fifty times during my career. It was a shimmying device that would help me get into cars and apartments that had less than stellar locks. Lexi's apartment complex wasn't exactly high end and I figured I could break in pretty easily. It helped that her closest neighbor was a good distance away. This wasn't one of those condensed apartment complexes that dominated LA.

I looked to my right and left and saw no one. I had a few makeshift fliers in my hand. If someone quickly appeared, I was going to slide the flier into the door jam. Sure, 9:30 p.m. isn't exactly the time that people are leaving fliers, but I figured it would buy me enough time to get the hell out of there.

That didn't prove necessary.

Lexi's lock was child's play and I got it unlocked in something like twenty seconds. I quickly shut the door behind me and entered the apartment.

I took out the second little gadget I'd brought for this adventure. It was what is most commonly known as a bug. That's right, I was going to listen in on Lexi's apartment.

Actually, I'd brought two bugging devices. They could pick up anything from about fifteen feet and in and I figured two would be enough to cover her smallish apartment.

I grabbed the first "bug" which was about the size of my finger and set it against her bed frame. The second one I attached to the side of a table leg in the "family" room.

I had them connected to my phone. I said a few quiet words and listened in. The bugs picked them up fine.

Mission accomplished.

I opened the door to the apartment and peaked to my left and right. Nothing to be seen.

I quietly exited Lexi's apartment, locked it behind me, and briskly walked down the street.

~

Lexi arrived home at 2:30 that morning.

The bugs only picked up her moving around and I heard her snoring less than twenty minutes later.

The next morning, just after eight a.m., I struck gold.

I could only hear Lexi's side of the conversation, but that was enough.

"Hey, Knox," Lexi said.

Pause.

"I stayed at his house two nights ago. I had a closing shift last night."

Pause.

"He doesn't suspect a thing. I think he might be in love with me."

Pause.

"Well, shit, for over half a million dollars, I'd sleep with a man uglier than Shane Doyle."

Pause.

"I haven't had the chance yet. We are going for a jog in a few hours. If he hits the shower when we return, I might have a chance to hit his laptop or cell phone."

Pause.

"Yeah, that would give me enough time."

Pause.

"That's the hope. Maybe he'll just say yes without the bribe. Be a lot easier for both of us."

Pause.

"We're still splitting the lion's share of the two million. I'll tell Shane his share is only 500k. What he doesn't know won't hurt him."

Pause.

"If I try to go as low as 250k, I'm afraid he'd be more likely to turn us in."

Pause.

"You're right, 250k is a lot of money, but he's an ADA in Los Angeles. He's not selling his soul without a huge payday. If we go too low we risk losing him."

Pause.

"I'm glad you agree."

Pause.

"And who knows, maybe your buddy Roger Theus will give us a little bonus once he gets out of jail."

Pause.

I was in complete and utter shock.

"Actually, I'm off today. I've worked four of the last five days."

Pause.

"Probably not."

Pause.

"Because after the workout, I'm just going to decompress. This is stressful stuff, Knox. I know this was all your idea, but I'm the one who has to do the day-to-day stuff with Shane."

Pause.

"Alright, thanks. I'll call you tomorrow."

Pause.

"Bye."

～

I was in a state of euphoria.

The first thing I did was to google Roger Theus. I knew the name rang a bell, but I couldn't place exactly how. As soon as his picture appeared, I remembered. The drug-dealing slumlord who had allegedly killed someone.

What the hell did Lexi and this Knox guy have planned?

Obviously, the goal was to keep Theus out of jail. And it appeared they wanted to bribe Shane in the process.

Jesus.

What had I walked into?

I had to assume that Shane was going to be the ADA for Theus's upcoming trial. Why else would they have picked him?

I googled Shane Doyle and Roger Theus together, but nothing popped up. I wasn't surprised. It was often hard to find the district attorney of record until after the trial started. Defense attorneys were a whole different thing and I saw that Hilton Lund was defending Theus.

He was good. Very good.

Shane would have been up against it, even if he was trying his hardest to convict Roger Theus. Which is what Lexi and Knox were seemingly trying to prevent.

"This is fucking crazy!" I yelled aloud.

I didn't know all the details just yet, but there was obviously a lot of money involved.

And I planned on getting my share.

Some people in our business considered me a bit of a rotten person.

It was time to live up to that reputation.

CHAPTER 18

LEXI

Something hadn't felt right the last few days.

I couldn't exactly place my finger on it. I just knew it.

The texts with Shane - even the nights with him - had changed. It was a subtle change, but a change nonetheless. It's possible it was his upcoming trial with Roger Theus and that's what I was counting on.

Hopefully, it had nothing to do with me.

And it wasn't just Shane.

When I left *The Belly Flop* the last few nights, I had a feeling of uneasiness.

Call it intuition.

Maybe it was all because of what I had to do in the coming days. I'd be lying if I said I wasn't nervous as hell.

I'd just got off the phone with Knox and was about to go for a run with Shane. I still hadn't sent an incriminating email from Shane to me.

Today was the day to make that happen.

I couldn't let him catch me in the act. I wouldn't have time to explain the long-term plan and he'd likely just call the cops on me. If that happened, everything would be over in the blink of an eye.

Even if today went off without a hitch, I was only a few days away from telling Shane why I'd seduced him. That was going to be a brutal confrontation.

Sure, Shane wasn't the most intimidating guy, but you never know how someone might react in a situation like that.

I was dreading the next few days.

CHAPTER 19

KNOX

"This was just a test," Roger Theus said.

We'd arrived at his car and I didn't know if we were going to be busting some heads, dropping off some drugs, or something worse. Anything was on the table.

And there wasn't much I wasn't going to be game for.

$3,000 was $3,000.

And it felt more like 30k, considering my economic prospects at the time.

I'd like to think if he asked me to commit a murder I would have said no. But who knows? I was an immoral prick. Scratch that. I am an immoral prick.

"Just a test?" I asked.

"Yup."

"Did I pass?"

"You most certainly did. I asked you if you'd be up for anything and you said yes, without even a second thought."

"I'm guessing there might be something like this in the future?"

"Very likely. And I had to make sure you'd be up for it if push came to shove."

"I'm up for it," I said.

"I know that now," Roger said sternly.

He then ripped two crisp, clean hundred-dollar bills out of his alligator skin wallet - at least, it looked like it - and handed me the money.

"Thank you, Roger."

"You're welcome, Knox."

"I think I made the right decision in moving to The Premier."

"You sure did," he said matter-of-factly.

"Is that it for today?"

"Yes. Now you can go back to doing whatever it is that you do."

Roger laughed, but there was a tinge of *I'm much more successful than you*. He wasn't wrong. He owned two apartment buildings. I could barely afford the rent for one of those units.

"I'm willing to do anything," I said.

In the wrong circumstances, he might have taken it as an advance, but he knew I wasn't referring to that.

"You'll get another opportunity quite soon," he said.

Roger was being evasive and I had a million questions. What was his side business? Was it drugs? He certainly wouldn't need the money, but that doesn't always stop people. Pablo Escobar could have stopped at any time, but he liked the action it entailed.

Maybe Roger was the same way.

Or, maybe he was just looking for me to babysit his nephew.

But I didn't think it was anything that benevolent.

It turns out I didn't have to wait long.

He was back knocking at my door a week later.

∼

"This one is not a test."

I'd opened my door to find Roger Theus standing outside of my apartment, obviously in a state of panic. If I had to guess, I'd say he was on a little cocaine. Or a lot.

"I'm ready," I said.

He shuffled me out of my apartment and led me to his light blue, brand-new, Corvette.

"Get in," he said.

He'd said all of eight words to me and yet I knew this was a serious situation.

He sped off way too quickly, leaving some rubber on the asphalt.

Once we got on the freeway, Roger finally spoke.

"You understand that everything I'm about to tell you is just between us."

"Of course," I said.

"I have a side business that makes me as much as my apartment complexes. In fact, it provided me with the money to buy these complexes. And there is someone very low on the totem pole who is threatening to take me down. You said you are willing to do anything, correct?"

"Do I still get two months rent-free?" I asked.

"Yes."

"Then yes."

He reached into his left pocket and produced a little pistol.

You'd think I would have been shocked, but I wasn't. Roger was in a state of panic. I knew we weren't going to a knitting class.

"Do you know how to use one of these things?" he asked.

"I didn't know I was signing up for this," I said, momentarily coming to my senses.

"You won't have to use it. I promise."

"Then why have it?"

"I need to scare this guy. Having an associate with a gun might do the trick."

"You couldn't just hold it yourself?"

Roger took his eyes off the freeway and stared over at me.

"Listen, fucker, do you want the 3k or not?"

I was a tough guy who didn't scare easily, but Roger Theus was an intimidating dude. Especially all coked up with a gun in his hand.

"Yeah, I want it," I said and grabbed the gun from his hand. I made sure the safety was on and put it in my pants. My momentary sense of right and wrong had vanished as quickly as it had come.

"Good. That's better. Now, you're not to do any talking. Just stand at the front door. If something goes down - and it probably won't - come inside the apartment and point the gun at the man in question. That should settle things down."

I wasn't sure pointing a gun at someone would help calm things down, but I didn't bother saying it. I was part of this now. No matter what happened.

"I understand," I said.

A minute later, Roger took an exit off of the 405 freeway.

He grabbed something from his pocket and put it to his nose. I was right about the cocaine.

"Want some?" he asked.

Even though I liked to dabble in cocaine, these weren't exactly the right circumstances. A smart person would know that. Newsflash, I wasn't.

"Fuck it, give me a bump," I said.

Roger handed over a little baggie and some coke. I knew how to do the rest.

"We're a minute away," he said. "I'm going to knock on the door. When he sees it's only me, he'll open the door. At that point, I'll push the door open and I want you to step in with me, but stay at the door. You don't need to take the gun out. They will assume you are packing."

"They?"

"Who knows? Maybe it will just be him. Maybe a few others. Don't worry about it though. I'm their money tree. They don't want to off me."

It was hardly reassuring.

I should have been scared as shit, but I wasn't. I was excited.

My mind was thinking ahead to more $3,000 paydays. $6,000 paydays. $10k paydays!

"I won't take the gun out unless they make a move."

I sounded like a character in a movie.

"Slow down a little bit, Knox. They are not going to make a move. Maybe you're a bit excited from the coke."

Roger was the one high as fuck, not me. Not that I was going to voice that.

"We're here," he said.

We got out of the car and I saw three apartment complexes, two restaurants, and one tattoo parlor.

The few people walking the streets were Hispanic.

Roger slammed his front door as if driving a brand new Corvette didn't bring enough attention. Was he trying to get us fucking caught?

I opened and quietly shut my door like a reasonable human being.

"Follow behind me," he said.

We walked right through the entrance of the closest apartment complex.

There was a little foyer in the middle of the complex with around seven or eight apartments on the lone bottom floor.

Roger bypassed the first few apartments before sneaking around the corner. There was a single apartment there, tucked away from the others.

We were in no way subtle, but at least we weren't out in the middle of the apartment complex.

Roger grabbed my arm and moved me right behind him. He knocked on the door, but there was no answer.

Then a second time. And a third.

"Fernando, I know you're there. Open up."

Nothing.

"If you don't open up, you're done forever. If you open the door and we talk, maybe we can salvage this."

I looked over at Roger whose eyes looked like they wanted to jump out of his head.

And then I saw the door slowly start to open. As it did, Roger used his shoulder and his monster frame to slam the door inward.

I saw the man fall back and stumble to the floor. Roger was on him in a second. He moved swiftly for a man his size. I entered the room and shut the door behind me. I know I was supposed to stand at the door, but I wanted to drown out the noise from the apartment.

"You made a smart decision, Fernando," Roger said.

Not the way it was going, he hadn't.

"I'm sorry, boss."

"Where's the money?"

Roger picked him up and pushed him up against a wall while grabbing him by the neck.

"I got robbed. I'm not kidding."

"By who?"

"I think I know, but I'm not sure."

I could tell Fernando didn't want to say who.

"I'm only going to ask you once, Fernando. Who robbed you?"

"Billy Aybar."

"Who the fuck is Billy Aybar?"

"I've been fucking his sister. And I think that bitch told him that I had cash lying around my place sometimes."

"How the fuck did Billy's sister know that?"

Fernando looked like he'd have preferred being waterboarded. He was petrified of Roger. I told myself, then and there, that I should never cross Roger Theus.

"Uh. Uh. She must have just assumed," Fernando said.

I saw Roger's grip on his throat tighten.

"You have one last chance to tell the truth."

"I showed her one time after a big score."

"That's what I thought. So this is on you, Fernando. If you don't get me back my money within one week, not only will we not work together again, but you will be in a world of pain. Do you understand?"

"Yes," a barely audible voice said.

Roger released his grip and Fernando fell to the floor.

"One week!" Roger yelled and then kicked Fernando in the sternum.

I was becoming more petrified of Roger by the second.

"Let's go," he said.

I followed him outside and shut the door behind me.

We walked through the foyer without saying a word, but once we got out to the street, Roger spoke.

"Fuck, that was fun! Exhilarating."

I just nodded, not sharing his enjoyment of choking and kicking people.

Although, I had just made $3,000, so there was that.

We got to his car and he drove off at a reasonable speed this time.

"You did a great job, Knox."

"Thank you, Roger."

"Listen, once I drop you off at The Premier, I don't think we should see each other for a few weeks. If Fernando knows what's good for him, he won't say a fucking word. But just in case he calls the cops or does something stupid, it's better we aren't seen together."

"I understand."

"And hey, you really don't have to see me for two months. Living rent-free during that time."

He grabbed my shoulders as he said that. I could tell that he looked upon me as a project. He knew I wasn't as cutthroat as him, but that the criminal life was something I wasn't opposed to. I imagine he envisioned toughening me up as this partnership went along.

We stayed quiet for the rest of the ride home.

He dropped me off at The Premier.

"Take care, Knox. Is it something you could imagine doing again?"

"For $3k?"

"Maybe we'll give you a little more next time."

"Fuck it. I'm in."

"There you go. We'll make something out of you yet."

He smiled and I exited the Corvette.

"See you soon," Roger said.

But I didn't see him for a month.

And by then, Billy Aybar was dead and Roger needed a much bigger favor.

CHAPTER 20

SHANE

"You ready for this?" I asked Lexi when she arrived at my place.

We were going on a run and she'd arrived at my house dressed in a white tank top, orange leggings, and bright yellow shoes. She certainly looked the part.

The Los Angeles weather was doing its part as well. A cloudless day in the eighties as we he headed toward the end of summer.

"I'm going to leave you in the dust," she said and laughed.

I doubted it.

While I might not have been the best basketball or football player, one thing I could do was run. Very few of my guy friends could keep up and I certainly didn't expect Lexi to stand a chance.

Not that that was my goal. This was a bonding experience. We'd had enough sex and dinners the last several weeks. Not that I didn't enjoy both. What we hadn't done was the other stuff that makes a relationship worthwhile. The small stuff.

Bruce hadn't found anything and my earlier suspicions were in the rearview mirror.

"This will be fun. Something new, getting in a workout together."

Lexi winked.

"We've had a few workouts together."

I laughed, knowing exactly what she meant.

She had a little bag with her.

"In case I take a shower later."

I grabbed it and set it on the couch.

"Let's do this."

She followed me outside and I locked the door behind us.

"We'll start by jogging," I said. "If you get tired, just tell me, and we can walk for a while."

Before I had a chance to finish, she'd started sprinting towards Wilshire Boulevard. I laughed and took off after her.

Lexi had been a faster runner than I could have guessed. We'd made it to the ocean and after taking a left at the Santa Monica Pier, ran another half-mile or so before she raised her hands.

"Alright, let's walk for a bit."

I was slightly winded, but never in danger of stopping. I don't think my pride would have let me even if my lungs had pleaded differently.

We walked along the beach for a good fifteen minutes more, taking time to look out on the beautiful Pacific Ocean.

If we'd been wearing flip-flops, I'd have suggested going to the water, but this was a running excursion. We'd hit up the ocean again soon.

"This is nice, Shane."

"We should make this a weekly occurrence. Work off all these meals we've been having."

"Sounds good to me," she said.

"Do you want to walk some mo…"

Once again, she'd started sprinting before I could finish my sentence. And there was no more stopping this time. She ran along the ocean, veered east on Wilshire, and sprinted the remaining blocks to my house.

I was always within five or ten feet behind her, and yes, I could have passed her if I wanted. But why lose the view?

She read my mind when we arrived back at my place.

"Enjoy the view of my butt?"

"Hard not to."

She laughed.

"How long was that run?"

"I'd guess around two miles. Maybe a little less. Not bad for our first."

"I feel good. Sticky, but good."

"Do you want to shower together?" I asked.

"As much as I appreciate the offer, I'm a little tired. I think I'll let you shower first and then I'll follow."

I might have been a little disappointed, but I couldn't blame her. I was a little tired myself.

Not that I'd admit that to her.

CHAPTER 21

LEXI

The chance presented itself in the blink of an eye.

"Fine, if you won't join me, I'll take the first shower," Shane said.

"Alright. I'll be here waiting when you get out," I said.

He set his wallet, keys, and cell phone down on the coffee table in front of the couch and walked briskly to the bathroom.

As soon as the door shut, I lunged towards the table, immediately pressing a button on his cell phone. I looked down. I'd made it!

The phone hadn't locked and no password was necessary.

As I heard the water start to stream, I clicked on his phone and found his Gmail.

I went to compose a message and put my email address as the recipient.

I then started typing my message. I'd outlined what I was going to say and it hit home just how brutal it was.

"Lexi,

I'm so sorry I hit you last night. That isn't me.

It's just that you make me jealous when you flirt with other guys.

I can't handle it.

Here's hoping that you never decide to leave me. I don't think I'd take it very well and I'd probably do something else that I'd regret.

Luckily, I don't think that will ever happen. I know you really do love me and would never intentionally do anything to hurt me. Right?

I tried calling and texting you, but you wouldn't answer, so I had to resort to emailing you.

Feel free to call or text me back. I hate coordinating like this.

I hope you can find a way to accept my apology.

I'll try not to ever hit you again.

Love,

Shane."

I pressed send and then immediately went to "Sent" messages and deleted it from Shane's history. I couldn't risk him coming across it.

While it may have been deleted on his end, it certainly wasn't on mine.

I'd be saving that email. It was Knox and my backup plan in case our initial idea didn't work as expected.

I almost exited Gmail.

It was then that my inner bitch kicked into another gear.

I started composing another message.

"And another thing, Lexi. I could almost understand if you left me for a white guy. But when I saw both black and Hispanic guys hitting on you, my blood began to boil. You know what I think about people like that!

Don't let me see that again.

Shane."

I once again deleted the email from his end and set his phone back down on the coffee table.

I was the devil incarnate.

Luckily, I didn't believe in heaven and hell, because if they existed, I knew I'd be going south.

Ten minutes later, Shane emerged from the shower. I put on my best smile. He didn't seem to notice anything. How could he?

"How was your shower?" I asked.

"Would have been better with you in it."

"Rain check."

"Sure, we can make love in the rain too. Any old liquid will do."

I laughed, probably harder than was warranted. I was still a little preoccupied with what I'd done.

"Did you want to shower now?" Shane asked.

"Yeah, thanks," I said.

Ten minutes later, I emerged from the shower, changed, and saw him sitting on the couch. I joined.

"When are you coming over next?" Shane asked.

"You won't have to wait too long."

"Good. Let's enjoy this while we can."

"What does that mean?"

"Jury selection starts in around a week. I'm going to be pretty darn busy once that starts."

"Too busy to fit in a love-making session?" I asked, using a phrase I'd likely never used.

Shane smiled.

"I'm sure we'll find a way to fit in a few. I really will be busy, though."

I knew I shouldn't say anything, but I couldn't resist.

"How's the case coming along?"

"My research is going well, although none of that really matters until we start the trial."

"You said a landlord killed a tenant, right?"

Knox would wring my freaking neck if he knew I was doing this.

"Not exactly. The guy killed someone who stole his drug money. And he wasn't just a landlord, he owned two apartment complexes."

"Jesus. You'd think a guy who owned apartment buildings in LA wouldn't have to get involved in drugs."

"You can say that again."

"Why did he?"

Knox had only told me a little about the case. He said it was for the best. The more I knew, the more likely I'd blurt something out that would make Shane suspicious. It made sense. It was too late now, I guess. I was asking question after question.

"From what I can gather, he was just an adrenaline junky. He partied like a rockstar. The guy jumped out of planes at 250 pounds. He probably considered drug-dealing just another risk worth taking."

"Sounds pretty dumb if you ask me."

"No question."

"So, will he get convicted?"

He looked over at me.

"This is definitely the most you've asked about one of my cases."

Panic filled me. I'd said too much. He was wary of me now. I had to think of something. And quick!

"Well, since we started dating, you've had two cases. And, no offense, but a DUI case isn't all that interesting."

Shane laughed.

"That's a solid point. Not much to talk about with the last one."

"Exactly. Hey, you don't have to talk about it if you don't want to. I just like learning everything I can about you."

He smiled and I knew I'd dodged a bullet. He doubled back to my earlier question.

"I hope we can convict him. Most people in the media seem to think it's a slam dunk, but they are mistaken. He's been convicted in the court of public opinion, but a court of law is much tougher and I don't have any concrete evidence. A lot of it is circumstantial. I've got one eyewitness but if he's lousy on the stand, who the hell knows? If I make a mistake or two, he could easily go free."

That was music to my ears. I wanted to hear more, but this would be a good time to exit stage left.

"Sounds fascinating. I'm sure I'll have some more questions once the case starts."

"You can be my co-counsel," Shane said and laughed.

"Lawyer Lexi," I said.

He laughed again.

I'd escaped from a potentially disastrous situation.

Knox would have been proud, even though I could never tell him it had progressed that far.

A few minutes later, I left Shane's apartment with plans on meeting again the following evening.

Depending on what Knox said, Shane's and my next visit might be a lot more combative.

The rubber was about to meet the road.

CHAPTER 22

KNOX

It took a few seconds to register.

I had the T.V. on in my apartment and some local reporter was talking.

"The deceased's name is Billy Aybar. He was thirty-one years old. Sources close to the investigation believe he was beaten to death in a savage manner."

I looked up for a second and something clicked. I rewound for about fifteen seconds and heard the name I thought I'd heard.

Billy Aybar.

There was no question that Billy Aybar was the name that Fernando had used.

Had it been Roger who killed him? I prayed it wasn't.

If it had been, he might give me up as the accomplice who helped him when he confronted Fernando.

Roger had convinced me to tag along, but that was no excuse with regard to the law. I was present when a man was choked, kicked, and threatened, all while I held a gun at him.

I'd be facing jail time.

Please don't be Roger who killed him!

～

He showed up at my house the next day. Technically.

The knock actually came at 12:25 a.m., barely five hours after I'd heard the name Billy Aybar on the news. I looked through the peephole and saw a clearly coked-out Roger. I'd seen what he did to people who didn't open the door so I reluctantly opened it.

"Hey, Knox," he said and barged in, clutching at his nose as he did.

"I saw the news," I said.

"I figured you had. It led every local news station at four p.m., five p.m., seven p.m., and eleven p.m."

His mind was racing. I'm not sure the four p.m.'s were necessary.

"Did you do it?" I blurted out, quickly regretting it.

He didn't erupt at me, much to my surprise.

"I hadn't planned on it. Fernando is worthless and I knew he wouldn't have the balls to confront this guy, so I went myself. No one steals from me. He made a move and being much bigger, I punched him, but he wouldn't stop coming, so I kept hitting him. And hitting him. And hitting him. And hitting him."

"I get the point," I said.

The owner of my apartment complex, a fairly well-known guy around town, was admitting that he'd beaten a man to death. I felt like I was in a dream. Or, more precisely, a nightmare.

"I wish you were there," he added.

That made one of us. I was already immersed in this. It would have been much worse if I'd been there when Billy Aybar had been bludgeoned to death.

"Sounds like self-defense," I said, not quite believing it myself.

"It was. That's not what the jury will decide though. Especially when they find out that I was a drug dealer on the side."

I rarely had nothing to say, but this was one of those times. I could tell he wanted to hear something, so finally, I said, "What are you going to do?"

"No, it's about what you're going to do."

Jesus. He'd come here to get me more involved?

I'm sure he was about to bribe me.

I won't mention your name if you do this for me.

Or something similar.

"What I'm going to do?" I asked.

"Yes. Don't interrupt. Just listen. Okay?"

"Okay," I said.

"I'm going to be arrested soon, maybe as quickly as tomorrow. Or today. Fuck, what time is it? Anyway, there was a guy at the complex who saw me. I saw him look over at me from behind his half-opened blinds. I'm fucked. But if I try to fly out of the country, who knows if I'd even make the plane? They might already have a hold on my passport. And if not, maybe they'd arrest me when my flight landed. Plus, I don't really want to live my life on the lam. So I've ruled that out."

His words were basically just one big stream of consciousness.

"So what's your plan?" I asked.

It was then I received his death stare.

"I told you to fucking listen," he yelled.

I wanted to tell him to keep it down, that my neighbors might recognize his voice. I decided saying nothing was the smarter - and safer - move.

What Roger said next changed my life forever.

"How would you like to make two million dollars?"

I didn't say anything.

"You can answer," he said.

"How, exactly?"

I should have been worried about a multitude of other things, but here I was, taking the bait.

"Once I'm arrested, I'm going to ask for a speedy trial. It should commence in about three to six months, If I had to guess. Now, once they pick the DA and the jury, you will go to work. I want you to do anything and everything in your power to help earn my acquittal. I don't care if you have to bribe a juror, offer the DA a million bucks, or blow the judge. Whatever you can do within your power to make sure that I'm not convicted. Come to think of it, going after the DA or the judge is preferable. Bribing a juror would just force a hung jury. They'd keep my ass in jail for sure. And that's what I'm trying to avoid. I need a full acquittal."

I jumped in, at the risk of getting another death stare.

"Maybe they'll give you bail," I said.

He glared back but didn't yell.

"No chance. They'll know I'm a flight risk. Plus, once they see the autopsy photos of Billy Aybar, no judge would give me bail."

I didn't ask for details. He continued.

"So, this is going to be on you. And before you decide yes or no, I just want to remind you that you broke the law when you entered Fernando's house with my gun. Come to think of it, you might have been with me at Billy Aybar's when I killed him. Yeah, that sounds right."

I was floored. Roger was pure evil.

"So what do you say? Are you going to do everything in your power to secure my acquittal?"

What choice did I have?

"Of course," I said.

"Good. Because if you don't, you're going to end up in prison with me."

Roger then slapped my cheek with unnecessary force. I took a step backward, but didn't say anything.

He turned to leave my apartment but swirled around at my front door.

"And I wasn't kidding about the two million dollars. I have four million in a secured area that the cops will never find. If you get me out... Excuse me, when you get me out, half of that is yours."

"I'll do everything I can," I said.

"For your sake, you better hope that's enough."

With that, he left my apartment and I stood there, shellshocked.

~

The first few months after Roger's "proposal" were excruciating.

Part of me - no, most of me - wanted to get the fuck out of Los Angeles. Rid my hands of Roger Theus and start over somewhere quieter. Maybe Topeka, Kansas. Or Toledo, Ohio. Somewhere very unlike Los Angeles.

There were two things preventing me from doing that.

The first was the fear that Roger Theus would drop my name to the authorities. I knew he'd exaggerate how big a part I played at Fernando's house. He'd also lie and say I was there when Billy Aybar was killed. I'd be in a shitload of trouble. Shit, he might say I killed Aybar and try to get a deal from the DA.

The second was the allure of the two million dollars. If I could somehow pull this miracle off and keep him out of jail, I'd be a rich man. Something I'd been longing for my whole life.

Those two factors ensured that I wouldn't be leaving Los Angeles. I was either going to get rich by earning Roger Theus acquittal, die trying, or end up in jail. Those were the only three possibilities.

~

Four months after Roger was arrested, the slick-looking man came up to me on the street.

"Shane Doyle should be your mark. He'll be confirmed soon as the

ADA assigned to prosecuting Roger Theus. He's going through a divorce and likes to gamble a bit too much. Go after him. That comes from our mutual friend."

The man didn't mention Roger Theus. It was unnecessary. I immediately knew this order had come from him.

How the hell had Roger found out this information from jail? I was reminded once again that he was more than just a brawny party animal. He was clever, shrewd, and perceptive. Even when he was coked up.

I went home and started doing a deep dive into everything I could find out about Shane Doyle.

He was thirty-five years old and a native Angeleno. He'd gone to UCLA for both undergrad and law school and now worked as a DA in West LA. Santa Monica, specifically. I'm sure the dude was smart, but he sounded pretty fucking boring. Going to the same law school where you completed your undergrad? Go exploring, you jackass. Not that I'd ever done more than one semester at junior college.

He had been married to a woman named Christie Connors. I couldn't find whether their divorce had been finalized or if they were still going through it.

I'd Googled, *Shane Doyle gambling* but as I expected, nothing came up.

I tried to think of the easiest way to get at a guy down on his luck.

My thoughts promptly turned to Lexi.

We'd dated for about a year back when I still lived in Hollywood. She was as close to the female equivalent of me as you could get. No, she wasn't quite as much of a deadbeat, but she was also a bit of a grifter looking for her big score. That usually meant dating a rich guy who she didn't give one shit about. I was the outlier of men she dated, being the only one with no money. Made me think she actually might have liked me.

Our relationship didn't end well. You know how they say opposites attract? I think Lexi and I were just too similar. Oil and oil. No water to throw in the mix.

Despite our break-up, we kept in touch, and I knew she'd started bartending. She wasn't too happy about it, having to smile at guys who just wanted to jump her bones.

I thought maybe it was time to use her innate sexiness to my benefit.

No down-on-their-luck guy like Shane Doyle - especially one who'd just got dumped by his wife - would have a chance of saying no to a girl like Lexi.

I dialed a number.

"Hello?"

"Lexi, this is Knox. I need to see you."

"Yeah, you missing me?"

"Maybe I am, but that's not why."

"Sounds serious."

"It is. You still know how to keep a secret, right?"

"I'm still the same girl who convinced people you were the stunt double for Chris Pine."

I laughed, remembering some good times with Lexi.

"When can I see you? The sooner the better."

"Let's make it tonight."

I drove to Lexi's apartment that night.

I pitched her my idea but didn't go into detail about who Roger Theus was. I didn't even mention him by name, just in case this all blew up in my face. I trusted Lexi, but we were talking two million dollars and trying to bribe an assistant district attorney.

Being elusive was the right move.

I could tell her if she agreed to join the team.

I waited for her response.

She began talking aloud, mainly for her own benefit, as she repeated what I'd told her.

"So, you want me to seduce a guy and then use my relationship with him in order to get him to throw a trial? And when that criminal gets released, he will give us two million dollars, of which you will give half to me?"

"Close," I said. "However, unless you have this ADA completely wrapped around your finger, we're probably going to be splitting some of the money with him."

Lexi took a few seconds mulling something over.

"We'll offer him less than one-third. Give us a little more."

"I love how your mind works," I said.

"Do you really think we can pull this off?"

"I'm sure there will be bumps along the road, but I have no doubt you will get this guy to fall for you. From there, I've got a few ideas on how we can pass go and collect our $200. Er, two million dollars."

"And if the criminal whose name you won't mention is acquitted, you're positive he will pay."

"I have no doubt."

Lexi raised her big beautiful eyes to meet mine.

"Fuck it, I'm in," she said.

"I knew you would be."

She leaned in and kissed me.

"Do you want to stay the night?" she asked.

"You know it."

CHAPTER 23

LEXI

The moment of truth had arrived.

Shane was just over a week away from starting the trial. It was now or never. I was back at his place, two days after our run and my "indiscretion" with his Gmail account.

We'd had sex twenty minutes previously and were now standing in his kitchen. I hoped the sex had weakened his knees. And his resolve.

"Why are you looking at me like that?" Shane asked.

He knew something was up. I'd been such a phenomenal actress up to this point, fooling him from that opening night at his house, but this time my face had betrayed me.

"You're scaring me, Lexi."

"Can you promise me to be a grown-up for the next five minutes?" I asked.

He waited a few seconds before responding.

"You're breaking up with me, aren't you?"

"No, I'm not breaking up with you. Sit down."

"Then what is it?"

"Sit, Shane!" I yelled.

My emotions had gotten the best of me and Shane looked at me like I was an alien. I'd never gotten that bent out of shape around him.

"Okay."

He sat down at the kitchen table where this had all started. Him making me a coffee. Me making him my doe-eyed face.

For the 50th time, I went over what I was going to say. I was hoping to convince him to throw the Roger Theus case for $500,000. I knew by now that Shane was far from a saint and we were talking about life-changing money. Especially for someone who had some financial issues. Hopefully, the money would be enough.

If not, I had my trump card. The sexist and racist emails that he'd "sent" me.

He'd probably want to kill me when I brought those up and I hoped it didn't come to that.

Time would tell.

"I don't like this," he said.

I'd been quiet for almost fifteen seconds, collecting my thoughts.

"You're really not going to like what I say next."

"Fuck, just get on with it, Lexi."

I had to move slowly, knowing if I dropped the bomb on him right away, he'd freak out.

"I'd first off like to say that I truly love you," I said, starting off with a whopper of a lie. I'd enjoyed some of my time with Shane, but this was all a scam and I wasn't in love. I wasn't even in like.

"Sure sounds like you're breaking up with me."

"I'm not. This whole thing is complicated, though, so I think you should just listen."

"Alright, I'll shut up."

"As I said, I love you. But, to be completely honest, our meeting each other wasn't by chance."

I looked at him and he nodded, signifying the floor was now mine.

"Your door wasn't just a random one that I decided to knock on. You were chosen. Let me start a little further back. An old friend of mine came to me several months ago. He knew I'd been down on my luck and asked me if I'd like to make some money. I was skeptical but decided to hear him out and it's what led me to you. He wanted me to knock on your door, get to know you, and find out if you were our type of people."

Shane looked like he'd seen a ghost.

"And what kind of people is that?" he asked.

"The type of people who think money is pretty damn important."

"That's pretty cryptic, Lexi. What exactly do you mean?"

"Let me go back a little further. My friend had a friend of his own. And this friend of his had a huge temper that would get him in trouble from time to time. And he recently let his temper get the best of him and it landed him in jail on a murder charge. The thing is, my friend's friend also has a great deal of money and offered my friend a lot of money to keep him out of jail."

Shane only got whiter.

"What the fuck?" Shane said. His voice was intense, but he didn't yell.

I ignored him, wanting to get the full story out before he peppered me with questions. Or his fists.

"And when I say a great deal of money, I'm not lying. He promised my friend 1.5 million dollars to keep him out of jail."

For obvious reasons, I wouldn't be telling him that two million was the actual number.

I was intentionally not mentioning Roger Theus's name, just in case this all went sideways. I could claim I was just referring to a nondescript, random person.

"Anyway," I continued. "My friend knew that he couldn't keep a guy out of jail all by himself, so he concocted a plan. And some might say my friend was extremely magnanimous because he brought on two people, taking his share from $1.5 million all the way down to 500k. He was sacrificing a lot of money."

"Let me guess. The other million gets split by you and me?"

Shane said it with a condescending tone, but he hadn't called the police or run for the hills yet. I considered that a win.

"Yes," I said.

"And he thought I'd throw this Roger Theus trial for $500k?"

So much for not mentioning the guy's name. Not that it was some great accomplishment to figure out who I'd been talking about.

"As I said earlier, he hired me to see if you were our type of people. The plan wasn't even to sleep with you. That just happened organically."

That was another whopper of a lie, but Shane didn't flinch. Maybe he was too proud to believe that this was all a scam. At the very least he wanted to believe that sleeping with a beautiful, sexy girl had been due to him.

I continued.

"But I've come to discover, and don't take this the wrong way, that you are like us. You've got some jump in your game. You're not opposed to taking some shortcuts. Just like us."

Shane looked me over.

"You keep mentioning us," he said. "Are you referring to you and John? Was there ever even a you and John? Did this John really hit you? My guess is no and that you thought I'd be more likely to fall for you if you knocked on my door with a bruise."

There was no point in lying about this. The answer was obvious.

"You're correct," I said.

I wasn't ready to tell him that Knox was the name of my real co-conspirator.

Shane was learning enough. He didn't need to know everything.

"Pull your shirt up. I'd also like to see your cell phone," Shane said.

I grabbed my cell phone from my pocket and handed it to him. He made sure nothing was recording.

When he was confident of that, he said, "Now pull up your shirt."

I stood up and pulled my shirt up to the edge of my bra. Shane wasn't being creepy. He just wanted to make sure I wasn't wearing a wire or some recording device.

"You can sit down now," he said, seemingly satisfied.

I could tell he was deep in thought, so I left him time to think.

Finally, he said, "And just to verify, if I throw this case for you, I get five hundred thousand dollars?"

"Yes."

"How will I be paid?"

"Roger Theus has 1.5 million dollars in a secured spot. He won't tell my friend where it is until he is released from jail."

Since Shane had brought up Roger's name, there was no use in avoiding it any longer.

"And you believe him?" Shane asked.

"My friend does. Do you think he'd risk all this if he didn't think he'd get paid? And this Theus guy - who I've never met - owned two big apartment complexes and apparently was a drug dealer as well. It wouldn't take that long to acquire that kind of money."

That connected. Shane nodded.

"You're right about that."

"So, what do you think?"

He looked me over once again. I'd avoided being attacked or having the police called. I was cautiously optimistic.

"I'm going to need some more time to think about this. This is easy from your end. I have to find a way to throw a trial that I'm expected to win."

"So, you're considering it?" I asked.

Shane thought about it for almost a minute. Finally, he shook his head like this was all some dream he'd just woken up from.

"This is insane. Maybe I should just call the cops. Have them lock you and this John character up and throw away the key. You can join Roger Theus in jail."

I couldn't tell if he was bluffing or not.

He reached for his phone and picked it up.

I saw him press a number.

I started to panic.

Was it time to bring out my ace in the hole?

Shane moved the phone closer to his face.

"Before you call the police, I need to tell you something. You're going to hate this as well."

Shane eyed me suspiciously.

"What the fuck more could you possibly tell me?"

He was furious.

"I wasn't supposed to tell you just yet."

"I wasn't actually going to call the cops, but if you don't tell me right now, I will."

He stood up and was towering over me. Shane was not the loose cannon that Knox was, but he could easily kill me if he wanted.

"This part wasn't my idea," I said, stalling.

"Tell me right fucking now."

Shane was dropping an f-bomb every other sentence. Not that you could blame him.

"One day when you were in the shower, I emailed something from your account to mine."

His eyes turned steely. At that moment, I could tell he wanted to kill me.

"What did it say?" he asked, trying to remain calm.

I would have had no problem saying the horrible words I'd sent, but I thought it would hit home more if he read them. I grabbed my phone, pulled up the email, and handed my phone to him.

It wasn't a long email, but he had the phone in his hand for at least two minutes. He probably read it three or four times.

He peered down at me. A curious look on his face.

"Fuck you!" he said.

I didn't respond.

"Part of me wants to jump over the table and strangle you to death. Instead, I'm going to let you walk out of my place in one piece."

"Why?" I asked, my mouth blurting it out before I considered whether I should have.

"Because the other part of me is intrigued by the five-hundred thousand dollars."

We sat silent for a good fifteen seconds. No one seemed to know how to respond to that.

"So what's next?" I asked.

"I will let you know my decision by tomorrow night."

"Okay, thanks, Shane."

"Don't you dare 'thanks, Shane' me. You're a fucking whore!" he yelled.

When I didn't respond, I saw his face soften up ever so slightly.

"That doesn't mean we might not be able to work together," he said.

"We could get rich together," I said.

He glared at me.

"Don't make it out like we are all buddy-buddy. Get out of my house," he said. "Now!"

As I stood up and walked toward the front door, I was half-expecting Shane to hit me over the head with something, crushing my skull in the process.

But nothing happened.

I walked out of his house and into the warm Los Angeles air.

CHAPTER 24

SHANE

I took an even deeper dive into the Roger Theus murder case.

I should have been taking a deep dive into my soul.

When Lexi had given me her "pitch", I should have instantaneously called the cops, given up Lexi who, in turn, surely would have led the police to "John", whoever the fuck that was. Obviously, a made-up name.

But I didn't call the police.

The only factor convincing me I wasn't doing a treasonous act is that Billy Aybar was a vile human. He'd raped a woman at twenty-two and somehow only got four years. When he got out, he assaulted an old lady less than six months later. He served three years for that and was stealing drug money within two months of being released the second time.

This guy was going to be a career criminal. The world was better off without him in it.

Not that any of that excused me for what I was considering doing.

I was a traitor to my job - and worse - a traitor to any morality I previously possessed.

I tried telling myself I was going to be fired regardless thanks to the email that Lexi - that bitch! - sent to herself. And yet, if I was being honest, it was the five-hundred grand that was really pushing me forward.

I needed that money.

No, that's not true.

I wanted that money.

Which made it even worse.

And I hate to admit this, but within about two hours of Lexi leaving, my decision had been made up. I'd always put up this '*Aw, shucks*' front, but I'd never been the most righteous guy. This was all coming to light and even I was surprised by my own depravity.

Would I rather prosecute scumbags for 70k a year or let one scumbag go for 500k? That was the rationale I'd talked myself into.

Regardless of my reasons, I started immersing myself in the case like no other case I'd ever had.

All with the intention of losing it.

And it had to be believable.

Or I'd be joining Roger Theus in jail.

After spending thirty-six of the next forty-eight hours reviewing the case files, I found a few instances where I could turn the jury against me.

It was an odd phenomenon, trying to find a way to beat myself.

The most obvious chance I'd have was with my prime witness, Alfonso Reyes. He saw Roger Theus leaving Billy Aybar's apartment minutes after hearing a struggle. Allegedly saw, I corrected myself. I had to start thinking like a defense attorney.

I knew exactly what I had to do.

And I had a feeling it could work.

After throwing around the pros and cons - even though I knew in my heart what conclusion I'd come to - I decided it was worth the risk.

$500k was $500k.

I was pure scum. There was no avoiding it now.

At least I'd be rich scum.

I grabbed the phone to call Lexi when I realized I'd forgotten something.

Shit, Bruce.

Better get him off this case before he finds something out.

It's hard enough to keep a secret with two people, much less three. Adding a fourth would make it near impossible.

I called him.

CHAPTER 25

BRUCE THE P.I.

Shane's name popped up on my screen.

I'd decided my best plan of action was to play dumb and not mention anything I'd found out. The information I had was much more valuable than the shock value of telling Shane. Best to not put my cards face up on the table.

"How are you, Shane?"

"Been busy, Bruce. Look, I just wanted to tell you that I think I'm going to cut this job short. I think you had another day, but let's go ahead and end it early. I realize now that she really does like me. I'll still pay you for tomorrow."

I was beyond suspicious. Shane had done a complete 180. More than that, he sounded odd on the phone. As if he was hiding something.

Two could play at that game. I was hiding some information as well.

"I'm sorry to hear that," I said.

"It's not your fault. I never should have hired you in the first place. As you said, I'm a successful attorney, why wouldn't she want me?"

He was laying it on pretty thick. It was very unShane-like.

"See? I told you."

I continued to play dumb as we finished our mockery of a phone call.

I was almost certain that Shane had gotten wind of Lexi and Knox's plan in the last day or two. There's no way he would have initially hired me with that atomic bomb sitting out there.

Since he was playing it close to the vest, my guess was that Shane had joined the team. If he'd gone to the police, he would have told me all about Lexi. He would have gloated about how right he was. How he knew Lexi had been up to no good.

So, I'd just sit in the background as the trial proceeded. Shane wouldn't hear a peep from me. And if - fingers crossed! - Roger Theus was acquitted, I'd have the bombshell of all bombshells to drop on Shane. And Lexi. And Knox.

And then it would be payday for good old Bruce.

Fuck yeah!

CHAPTER 26

KNOX

Once Lexi agreed to come on board, it had been mostly smooth sailing.

I'd already done a lot of research on Shane before she joined, but I wanted to leave no stone unturned.

So Lexi and I started rotating shifts following him home from the Santa Monica Courthouse. Trying to get a read on the man he was. His office was located at the courthouse, so he'd stay there all day and then stop at Equinox gym every night on his way home.

What didn't change is that he was home by seven o'clock each night and his lights went off at 11:30. Give or take a few minutes. Honestly, it was that fucking close each night. What a boring little shit.

It became an easy decision to have Lexi knock on his door at eleven. We wanted him to be a little tired. Almost ready for bed. Maybe ruminating on his failed marriage. Make Lexi all the tougher to turn down.

The few times I saw Shane leave the courthouse early, I headed to where the criminal cases were tried and asked people what they thought of Shane. I'd make up some story about how a relative of mine had been beaten up and Shane was prosecuting the man in question.

They'd usually offer their condolences and say I was in good hands. Shane was a decent attorney. A few were more talkative and they'd heard Shane wasn't the most popular ADA at the moment and that maybe he wasn't quite as proficient as some thought. I loved hearing things like that. A man who was afraid to lose his job - or wasn't very good at it - was more likely to turn their back on their job. Or, in our case, fuck it completely over.

~

The night that Lexi knocked on his door was obviously stressful as hell. All of my work could have been undone in a matter of minutes. If it went correctly, though, the sky was the limit. And Lexi worked my plan to perfection. I'd picked the right girl.

The next three weeks went as well as I could have hoped. Shane fell for Lexi and Lexi turned on the charm. And the sexiness. Whatever it was, it worked. Shane was all-in on Lexi.

And it all climaxed with Lexi dropping the bomb on Shane. The reason she'd met him. I wasn't there, obviously, but I imagine he hit the roof. Here he was, thinking this one-in-a-million woman had fallen for him when in reality, he was being played from the beginning.

And then she dropped the second bomb, telling him of the gruesome emails she'd "received" from him.

I'd love to have seen his face at that point.

I'm morbid like that.

Lexi said he thought he might just go along with it. Time would tell.

~

I hadn't heard back from Lexi in almost two days when I looked down and saw an incoming call from her.

"Give me good news," I said.

CHAPTER 27

LEXI

"Give me good news," Knox said.

"He's in!" I screamed, sounding like a damn schoolgirl.

Although, let's be honest, I was never one of those girls who screamed about the latest boy band. I was a bit jaded for that. Even at a young age. Not much had changed over the years.

Now, a shit ton of money? That I would scream for.

"When did he call you?"

"Yesterday morning."

"Wait, you didn't fucking tell me?"

I laughed.

"I'm kidding, Knox. He just called."

It felt good to pull his leg one time. Probably wasn't a good idea to make a habit of it.

He laughed as well.

"I'll let you get away with it this time. What else did he say?"

"Not much. He thinks it's better if we don't contact him while the case is going on."

"Probably a good idea. He doesn't want to see you?"

"I'm sure he does. Maybe he got the idea that I was never in love with him."

"While that may be true, it doesn't mean he still doesn't want the pus…"

"Don't be crude, Knox."

"I'll refrain for today only. Look at what an upstanding human I'm being."

"You must be in a good mood."

"Well, I've got over a million reasons to be."

"Don't you mean, *'We've got?'*"

"But of course, Lexi."

I didn't like the way he said it. There was a condescending tone. I had a quick, darting worry that this was all for nothing. That Knox had never planned on cutting me in on the money.

I told myself to calm down.

This was a day of celebration.

If down the road, Knox tried something shady, I'd be ready for it.

First, we had to pray that Shane could throw this case.

If not, this was all for naught.

CHAPTER 28

SHANE

"Nice to see you again, Alfonso," I said.

Alfonso Reyes, the most important witness in the trial, was sitting in my office. Working for the county, my office was located on-site at the Santa Monica Courthouse. In many ways, things were easier for district attorneys. We worked off the county's dime, not our own. We didn't have to rent space and hustle to get clients like defense attorneys had to.

Of course, most people would say that defense attorneys had more balls than district attorneys. That they were generally the superior lawyers. That they had taken a risk by going out on their own and not just getting a guaranteed paycheck.

All of these things were pretty much true.

"You too, Mr. Doyle," Alfonso answered.

He was a Mexican-American but treated me with suspicion like some of the illegal immigrants I'd come across. I can't say I blamed him. Hispanics - and Mexican-Americans specifically - were treated differently by cops and the legal system. I was probably just another gringo in his eyes.

If things had been reversed - and Billy Aybar had killed the big white guy in Roger Theus - it wouldn't have been as easy to get Alfonso to testify. Call it a hunch.

I sat down on my desk, having a bird's eye view of him sitting in the chair below. I wanted him to be intimidated because I was about to sell out my profession and have a prosecution witness turn against me.

"As you know Alfonso, the trial begins on Monday. The prosecution goes first and I will be calling you as one of my last witnesses. Most likely it will be Friday. I think I've got around five days of witnesses lined up."

"I'm ready, Mr. Doyle."

"That's good to hear, Alfonso. I just wanted to go over your testimony one more time."

"Okay."

"I'll start with some easy questions. Your name, age, and where you live. Things like that."

"Okay."

"And then I'll ask who lived next to you in the complex and you'll say, Billy Aybar."

"Okay."

"I'll ask how well you knew him and how long you'd known him. Some boring questions like that."

"Okay."

"And eventually we'll get down to the nitty-gritty of the night Aybar was killed."

I saw Alfonso Reyes gulp. He was nervous and this was just the two of us in my office. It would be much worse in front of a judge, jury, and a courtroom full of onlookers. Good. The worse a witness he was, the better for me.

"That's the part I'm a little nervous about," he said.

I chose my next words wisely.

"The most important thing is that you tell the truth. Do you understand that?"

"Yes, sir. Of course."

"So, I'll ask about the night in question and how you happened to be outside at eleven p.m. smoking a cigarette."

"Okay."

"That's the truth, right?"

"Yes, sir."

"And you looked over and heard some noises coming from Billy Aybar's apartment?"

"Yes."

"And then you went back inside your apartment?"

"Yes."

"But you continued peeking out of your blinds?"

"Yes."

Once the trial started, Alfonso would have to elaborate more, but it wasn't necessary for this exercise.

"And you saw Roger Theus walk out of Billy Aybar's apartment a few minutes later?"

"Yes."

"Do you think he saw you?"

"Maybe. He looked in my direction. Maybe he heard the blinds rustle."

"Before I ask the next question, I just wanted to remind you that honesty is the most important aspect of your testimony."

"I understand, Mr. Doyle."

"Which brings me to my next question. How positive are you that it was Roger Theus that you saw?"

"I'm positive, sir."

"But you'd never seen him before the night in question, correct?"

"No."

"And you were peeking through some blinds right?"

"Yes."

"At two a.m."

"All that's correct, Mr. Doyle, but I got a good look at him and when the police showed me his mugshot two days later, I was still sure it was him."

"Like 90% sure?"

"You know it's higher, Mr. Doyle."

"93%?"

"Higher."

"95%?"

"Higher."

"I'm only asking this because it was eleven at night and dark out. And remember, the most important thing about your testimony is that you tell the truth."

Alfonso looked at me oddly.

"Isn't your job to prosecute the guy?" he asked me.

"It is, but not by having you lie on the stand."

"I'm not lying."

"I know you're not. I just don't want you to say you're 100% positive it was Roger Theus when we both know it's almost impossible to be that certain in the dark at night."

"I guess, Mr. Doyle. I was pretty sure, though."

"I'm sure you were. Shall we say 96%?"

He eyed me with curiosity. I don't think he could have guessed the depths I'd sunk to, but he definitely sensed something was amiss.

"I'd feel better if I said like 97%," Alfonso said.

That would work.

"That sounds good, Alfonso. Remember, the last thing we want is for you to be accused of committing perjury. That's a bad crime and you can go to jail for that."

I was turning into a terrible, horrible, no-good, very bad human being.

"I don't want to lie, Mr. Doyle."

"Good, Alfonso. That would be bad for you. I think 97% shows that you are almost positive it was Roger Theus that you saw, but it's not like you are saying 100% where perjury could come into play."

"Okay," he said quietly.

I jumped off my desk and patted him on the shoulder.

"You're going to do just fine, Alfonso."

"Can I go?" he asked.

"Of course," I said.

He walked out my door and there was no longer a question as to why he wouldn't trust a gringo like myself.

The trial was starting the next day and I had my first ever panic attack.

If someone said I deserved it, they wouldn't be wrong.

Whatever I had coming was warranted.

Disbarment. Jail Time. A shallow grave.

What I didn't deserve was a blended Pina Colada while lying on an exotic beach. That was my goal, however. A three-week vacation with some exotic woman tending to me. If I had to pay for her services, oh well. Better than being dragged along as I had been with Lexi.

I really wanted her to get a comeuppance, but that would have to wait until after I got my 500k. That took precedence. For now.

After my vacation, I'd return to being a DA. It's not like I could just quit after losing a high-profile case. That would be way too suspicious.

And as much as 500k was, it's not like it could last a lifetime. Unless I could do this maybe two or three times. Be a DA for hire.

Do you need your relative acquitted of some crime? Come to Shane Doyle!

No, that couldn't happen. I'd be caught for sure.

This had to be a one-time thing.

~

The trial opened on Monday, as is usually the case.

I made sure my opening statement was solid but unspectacular. I couldn't just bomb it. That would get people talking and put more eyes on me. I had to wait to "throw it" until later in the trial when no one was expecting it.

The first few days meandered along. I'd decided Alfonso Reyes was going to be my final witness and I'd call him on Friday. While there were a few important witnesses leading up to him, he was the make-or-break witness to secure Roger Theus's conviction.

And I was going to ensure his testimony was going to break my case.

I did manage to throw a few breadcrumbs out there for the defense. With the medical examiner on the stand, I said, "With injuries like the ones that Billy Aybar suffered, it would have to be a big man who committed them, correct?"

I knew the M.E. wouldn't paint with that broad of a brush.

His response was exactly what I was looking for.

"I wouldn't concede that, Mr. Doyle. I've seen young women kill men twice their size. If you get the first blow in - and can incapacitate your opponent - you've always got a chance. So I think you're jumping to conclusions. Aybar's injuries could have been inflicted by anybody."

I looked at the jury and saw a few looks of surprise. I'd walked right into it. By my own volition, of course.

I saw another opening with my first Thursday witness, Nikki Crawford. She was an off-and-on girlfriend of Roger Theus's. A booty call would probably be a more accurate description. It's not like they traveled together. They just screwed.

Nikki was dressed like she was attending the Met Gala. Making matters worse, when she was called as a witness, she took a full thirty seconds to walk fifty feet, strutting the whole way to the witness stand.

The women in the jury box undoubtedly had already turned on her. The men - after checking out her body - probably had done the same.

Roger had claimed that he arrived at Nikki's at eleven p.m. on the night that Billy Aybar was killed, which was the time that Alfonso Reyes claimed he saw Roger leaving Aybar's apartment.

She was an important witness because she claimed that Roger didn't arrive at her apartment until 11:30., which poked a major hole in his alibi because he claimed he arrived to her place a few minutes before eleven.

I had to be subtle. I was still afraid that a perceptive attorney might realize I was off my game a few times during the trial. Once might be acceptable. More than that would be suspicious.

I'd come up with my idea the night before. I'd heard rumors that Nikki liked to drink and decided to roll with it.

For my fifth question, I asked Nikki the following:

"So you were just sitting at home waiting for Roger to arrive?"

"That's right," she said, looking over at the jury box like it was some splendid answer.

"Were you watching T.V.?"

"I was, in fact."

"Do you remember what you were watching?"

"Real Housewives."

"Which one?"

"Do you know your Real Housewives?" she asked me.

"Not even a little bit," I said, and the jury and spectators got a quick laugh.

"I think it was Atlanta."

"And you were alone, just waiting on Roger? No friends, right?"

It was the last leading question I could ask. If she didn't take the bait this time, I was done. Luckily, she took the bait, hook, line, and sinker.

"Not unless you count my bottle of Chardonnay as a friend."

The assembled people laughed again, but I knew better. I'd left the door wide open for the defense.

And Hilton Lund took full advantage several minutes later, getting Nikki Crawford to admit she'd finished one bottle and started up on a second before Roger Theus arrived.

"I have one last question for you, Ms. Crawford. After four or five glasses of wine, can you be positive about the time that Mr. Theus arrived?"

The silence was deafening in the courtroom.

"I'm pretty sure it was 11:30," she said.

In the court of law, "pretty sure" meant jack squat. You certainly weren't going to convict someone on a few "pretty sures."

Or 97%s.

~

Friday came around and I honestly believed I'd already managed to lose the case. I'd been understated the whole trial. My mistakes - while extremely important - weren't obvious. I was pretty proud of myself.

And now it was time for the coup de grace. The testimony of Alfonso Reyes. It would be the cherry on the ice cream sundae I'd built all week. I didn't want a hung jury. He might remain in jail. I wanted a full acquittal.

I talked with Alfonso outside the courtroom before I called him. I didn't want to go point-by-point over what we'd discussed, so I just said "Remember what we talked about."

He looked up at me and his eyes said everything. He knew I was up to something quite unethical, possibly worse.

I guess there was a chance Alfonso could be a problem down the line, but I doubted it. Once his testimony was over, he'd want to get as far away from a courtroom as he could. He wouldn't raise a fuss.

I called him to the stand.

It was time to lose this case once and for all.

After a few softball questions, it was time to get down to it.

"And on the night in question, you were in your apartment, correct?"

"Yes."

"What were you doing?"

"Early on, I was reading, but then I went outside to have a cigarette."

"Describe what happened next, Mr. Reyes."

"I heard a few loud noises coming from Billy Aybar's apartment. It sounded like a fight."

"And what did you do next?" I asked.

"I was a little scared so I went back inside, but I opened the blinds and looked at Billy Aybar's apartment."

"How far is your apartment from Mr. Aybar's?"

"I'd say thirty yards. It's pretty close."

"And what did you see next?"

"I saw Roger Theus leaving his apartment."

"How long after the noises you heard?"

"A few minutes."

I pointed at the defendant.

"And the man you saw leaving the apartment was Roger Theus, the man who sits right there?"

"Yes."

"And the lighting is pretty good in your complex, right Mr. Reyes?"

"Pretty good, yes, even though it was late at night."

Here we go, I said to myself.

"And you were positive it was Mr. Theus?"

Alfonso Reyes stared at me for about three seconds before giving his answer.

"I'd say I'm like 97% sure."

You could hear a pin drop in the courtroom. Anyone who knew how the law worked, knew this was a death knell for my prosecution.

I had to go back at Alfonso Reyes. Any lawyer in my situation would. You couldn't let 97% stand. I just prayed he didn't rat me out.

"You identified him from a lineup, didn't you, Mr. Reyes?"

"Yes."

"So you must be pretty darn sure it was Roger Theus that you saw."

"I am pretty darn sure. Like I said, 97%. Maybe even 98%."

"You told the detectives you were positive," I said.

He stared at me and at that moment, I thought I was a dead man.

"As I said, it was late at night. I'm still 97% or 98% sure though."

I put on the best version of my exasperated face.

"No more questions," I said.

I couldn't risk asking him anything else. He was a millimeter from telling the truth about how I'd perverted the law.

Hilton Lund put Alfonso Reyes through the wringer. I couldn't help but feel bad for the guy, even though it was my actions that had left him out to dry.

When Reyes was finally excused from the witness stand, he gave me a glare as he walked by.

If looks could kill…

I'd done a phenomenal job. I really had to pat myself on the back. Amusingly, I think I was better on this case than I'd ever been on a case I was actually trying to win.

We reconvened on Monday and Hilton Lund presented his defense for the next four days. He was great - as usual - but honestly, Roger Theus's acquittal had already been cemented with Alfonso Reyes's testimony.

And that was confirmed a few days later.

"Will the defendant please rise," the judge said.

Roger Theus stood up.

"Would Madam Foreperson please read your verdict?"

Gladys Tince, a woman in her late sixties with an old-school haircut to match, stood up from the jury box and said the following:

"In the case of California vs. Roger Theus, the jury finds the defendant not guilty of murder."

The assembled crowd erupted. Almost all in anger.

Billy Aybar's family was furious.

I pretended to be as well.

In reality, I had to resist letting out a small little smirk.

CHAPTER 29

KNOX

I was told the jury had reached a verdict and I knew I had to be there. I drove over and spent the morning loitering outside the Santa Monica Courthouse, waiting for word.

At ten a.m., I was told they were going to announce it any minute.

Part of me wanted to go wait outside of Department #21. It's not like Shane Doyle (who didn't know what I looked like anyway) or Roger Theus would be the first one exiting the courtroom.

But I couldn't take the chance.

At 10:12, I started hearing a loud, visceral reaction as people approached the exit of the courthouse. I immediately knew he'd been acquitted. The venom was palpable. If he'd been convicted, there would have been joy and relief. This was the opposite.

Just to be sure, I asked the first person who walked in my direction.

"What was the verdict?" I asked.

"Not guilty on all counts. Our criminal justice system is bullshit."

She wasn't wrong there.

I wondered if she might have been a relative of Billy Aybar. If so, this must have been incredibly painful for her.

Not that I was going to pretend to care.

Roger Theus was a free man!

I'd done it. Well, me, Lexi, and Shane.

I headed back to my car, a huge smile on my face.

~

I called Lexi when I arrived home.

"Give me some good news," she said.

"We fucking did it!"

I heard her scream in joy on the other end.

"Holy shit!"

"I never could have done this without you, Lexi. You're a big part of it."

"No shit, Sherlock."

She was right. I had my doubts at the beginning but she passed with flying colors.

"Do you want to meet up?" I asked.

"Is that the best idea? I'm sure Shane is going to be calling me any minute."

"Think he'll want a courtesy fuck?"

"Why do I always have to tell you not to be crass? But yes, probably."

"Let's meet up later tonight then. My place. We can't risk Shane showing up at yours with me there."

"Alright. What time?"

"Ten. I'm going to ravage your body."

"Can we make it like the movie *Indecent Proposal*? Spread our money all over the bed and screw with tens of thousands surrounding us."

"Sorry, babe, but we won't be getting that money by tonight."

"Yeah, I know. It just sounded good. Raincheck. When are you guessing that will be?"

"I'm sure Roger will want to lay low for a week or so. I'll wait till he approaches me. Don't worry, he knows what I did and won't forget me."

"Do I get to meet him?"

"Probably not."

"Why?"

"Because this isn't something you talk about and celebrate together. You go your separate ways and keep fucking silent."

"I guess. I just wish he could know how vital I was."

"I'll tell him," I lied.

"See you at ten."

"You did well, Lexi."

"Thanks, Knox. So did you."

I hung up the phone.

I remember thinking early on there might come a point where I might have to take Lexi and/or Shane out. And I didn't mean for dinner. I no longer thought that. This was a time for celebration.

Against all odds, I'd done it!

~

A week turned into ten days and I still hadn't heard from Roger Theus. I'd been tempted a few times to drop by the house in Malibu and ask when we were going to get our money but thought better of it. He'd know when the time was right.

CHAPTER 30

ROGER THEUS

There were a few points during my trial where I thought Shane Doyle made glaring mistakes, but it wasn't until Alfonso Reyes said 97% that I positively knew Doyle was in on it.

No prosecuting attorney would ever ask a witness if he could ID the defendant unless he knew the answer would be 100%. That whole "beyond a reasonable doubt" thing and all.

At that point, I knew this trial was in the bag.

But suddenly, on the day the verdict was to be read, I got nervous, something that was usually foreign to me. Had I been reading too much into Reyes's testimony? Had Shane Doyle really made the egregious errors I'd assumed?

And then, the moment of truth.

"In the case of California vs. Roger Theus, the jury finds the defendant not guilty of murder."

FUCK YEAH!

I'd done it. Well, that shitbag Knox had helped as well. He proved to be worth every penny.

Of course, there had been a helping hand behind the scenes. It was yours truly who - in jail - had heard the dirt on Shane Doyle and had my lawyer, Mason Croy III, relay that to Knox. I was the true mastermind. That doesn't mean Knox didn't deserve credit. He did.

As my attorney, Hilton Lund, patted me on the back, I looked in Shane

Doyle's direction. Nothing was said, but in that moment my suspicions were confirmed. His eyes told me all I needed to know.

He was in on it.

I wondered how Knox had gotten through to him. Was he giving Doyle half of the two million? Had someone else been involved?

Probably better I didn't know. Keeping a secret this big is hard enough. I'd rather not know the others involved.

I'd deal with Knox and he could deal with Doyle or anyone else.

What the fuck did I care? I'd been acquitted!

After a few hours of bureaucracy and paperwork, I was officially declared a free man and walked out of the Santa Monica Courthouse.

To my surprise, there were still at least twenty members of the media gathered out front.

A cute young Asian woman lobbed a microphone toward my face.

"How does it feel to be acquitted, Mr. Theus?"

I'd be lying if I said I hadn't thought about what I'd say.

"It's nice to know that the Criminal Justice System in America still works. You see all of these cases on T.V. where the wrong man is convicted and you start to lose faith. Today, however, is a shining light on how our system works. An innocent man was acquitted. It's a great day to be an American."

I was laying it on a little thick. And the ironic part was that as I made this saccharin speech, my mind was remembering beating Billy Aybar to death. That was a fun few minutes. I'm glad that fucker was dead.

I looked out at the media members and could tell they were eating up my little speech. I wondered if they really thought I was innocent. Really didn't matter. I was good for ratings, so they loved me.

"Anything else you'd like to say?" the young woman asked.

"The LAPD will be hearing from me," I said.

I almost added the DA's office as well and then realized that probably wasn't a good idea if Shane Doyle truly had been involved. Truth was, neither was going after the LAPD. I should just take my win and go quietly into the sunset. Not that I was that type of guy.

"Is your plan to sue them for your time spent in jail? Or unlawful arrest?"

I knew it was time to shut up.

"I have no other statement at this time," I said.

I walked down the steps and heard the flashes of the cameras.

It's like I was a celebrity.

Maybe it was time to endorse that. No more drug deals. No more murders.

Could I be a character actor in Hollywood? Sit courtside at Laker games?

The world was my oyster.

~

I waited to contact Knox.

Part of me worried that a relative or friend of Billy Aybar might follow me around. Make sure I wasn't getting into more trouble now that I was out of jail. And while I couldn't be tried twice for the same crime, giving someone two million dollars to throw a trial would be a new crime all its own.

After two weeks of freedom - and being certain I wasn't being followed - I decided it was time to pay Knox a visit.

On the day my lawyer relayed the message to Knox, he followed him home, so I had his address. He had moved out of my complex. A smart move, no doubt.

He was living in another of the long line of shady apartment complexes in LA. I knew something about them.

~

I showed up at Knox's apartment at nine p.m. on a Monday night. It had been fifteen days since I'd been acquitted.

He opened the door and merely said, "Roger."

"Meet me outside in one minute," I said.

He got the point and shut the door. I wasn't going to risk some nosy neighbor listening in on our conversation.

Any talking we'd be doing would be in my car.

Knox was outside less than a minute later.

"Get in the front," I said.

He sat down and no one said anything for a few seconds.

"Bring it in!" I yelled.

He unleashed a big smile and we shared a hug. Honor amongst thieves you might say.

"You fucking did it!" I said.

"Yeah, I did. Well, not just me."

"Stop right there," I said, deathly serious. "I don't want to know who else was involved. It's better that I don't know. Also, whoever you had to bring on, I don't want you ever talking to them again after you pay them. Do you understand?"

"Yes, Roger. I understand."

"One other thing and this is important."

"Shoot."

"Once you get the money, I want you and the others involved to destroy your cell phones. Nuke them in the microwave if you have to. If the cops somehow begin to suspect something is up, I can't risk them looking at old texts or phone calls between you. With all the money I'm giving you, you can afford to buy a new phone. This is non-negotiable. Do you understand?"

"I made sure to only talk on the phone - never text - but I understand."

"Good. I still need you to destroy them. Tell any others their money is contingent on that."

"I understand," he said a second time.

Knox was still scared of me. That much was obvious. And he wasn't your Caspar Milquetoast type. Knox was pretty jaded. If he was fearful of me, that probably said something about my vitriol. Not that I gave a fuck.

"Sorry to get so aggressive right off the bat," I said.

"I understand," he said, completing the trifecta. "You're trying to cover all your bases."

"But don't think I'll ever forget what you did for me, Knox. I'm forever in your debt. Literally," I said and he attempted to laugh. "About that. This Thursday, eleven p.m. Meet me outside just like tonight. I will have all the money. You can divvy it up as you see fit."

"Your'e giving me all the money at once?"

"Yes. I think the less we meet, the better. At least for a while."

"I understand. I'll be out here at eleven."

"See you then, Knox."

"You don't want to know any of it?"

"One of these days, I'll bring it up. For now, it's better I don't know."

"I get it. See you, Roger."

He opened the door to leave.

"Thank you, Knox. For everything."

I'd never been more appreciative of anything in my life. Thanks wasn't a verb I used very often.

Knox had just exited the car when I called him back.

"If I were you, I'd set up some sort of security deposit box before we meet again. Maybe two or three. Tell the others to do the same. Assuming there are others. If any of you are dumb enough to have the money stolen, you best not come crying to me."

"I'll relay the message, Roger."

"You can go now," I said.

He shut the car door and I sped off into the night.

~

I arrived home that night and thought about the night that had started this all: The death of Billy Aybar.

I'd long prided myself on my restraint.

Not with women. Not with food. Not with money. And not with my personal consumption of drugs.

I meant in my business enterprises. I'd sold drugs for approaching two decades. I'd owned my properties for about twelve. And the former had allowed me to purchase the latter.

The restraint that I speak of is when it came to my subordinates. Drugs were a dirty business and from time to time, people would steal from me. I don't want to say I took it as a badge of honor, but in a shady profession such as mine, it was inevitable, so I'd just turn the cheek if the amount of money involved was a drop in the bucket. Well, not exactly turn the cheek. I mean the guy would never work for me again, but I wouldn't bludgeon him to death.

For some reason, Billy Aybar had felt different. He was not a subsidiary of mine. I don't even think he was a user. He was merely the brother of a woman that Fernando was sleeping with.

It might be hard for people to understand, but this made it worse. If Fernando stole from me, I could almost understand. He could have thought he was underpaid - rightly so, I might add - and said, '*Fuck, Roger Theus' I'm getting my share.*'

That wouldn't have bothered me. Sure, I would have fired him to make an example that you can't steal from me, but at least it was a member of my own family. Not some stranger who didn't know me from Adam. And that's what Billy Aybar was.

He was just some guy who came and stole Fernando's money, which was really my money. I couldn't let that stand, which is what led me to his apartment that night.

All this being said, I didn't plan on it going down the way it had.

But I was furious as I approached his apartment, so it wasn't likely to end well.

It didn't help that I was a little coked up.

I was never very good at that whole, *'Don't get high on your own supply'* rule of thumb.

And on this night, it would prove catastrophic. Well, for Billy Aybar at least.

～

When I knocked on the door and Aybar answered, his expression was priceless. He thought I was a salesman or something.

"I'm not buying," he said.

"Good, I'm not selling," I said and pushed in the door.

I'd gotten a little information from Fernando leading up to me confronting Aybar. I learned his address, obviously, and also that he lived alone.

I'd considered asking Knox to come along, but he was still so green. I wasn't sure I could trust him for something this big. With Fernando, I just needed Knox there to represent that I meant business. With Billy Aybar, I had every intention of getting that money back and it might deteriorate into something more.

Maybe that was the exact reason I should have invited Knox along.

Looking back at what happened, obviously, I should have, but in the moment I figured I could handle it myself.

Once I got inside his apartment, I could tell Aybar was a bit surprised, but he didn't look scared. He wasn't some pushover, that much was obvious.

"Who the hell are you?"

"I'm Fernando's boss."

That's when it hit him.

"Oh, shit."

"Yeah, oh shit. You better have my money."

"About that."

"That's not the answer I want to hear."

"I'm sorry, Mr. Theus, I spent some of it."

I'd been hit by a double whammy. First, he'd spent some of my money which infuriated me. Second, and much more important, was that he knew who I was. I hadn't been expecting that. Fernando must have ratted me out. Was it in an effort to get his money back from Billy Aybar? Or, had they both been in on this from the beginning?

One thing was for sure. I'd be asking Fernando some serious questions next time I saw him.

"So you know who I am?" I asked.

He should have been rattled and realized it was a mistake to have mentioned my name. He wasn't. He was going to be a tough guy to the end.

"Yeah, I know who the fuck you are."

I ignored the obscenity. That doesn't mean it hadn't registered.

"We'll get back to that. How much of the money have you spent?"

"A bit of it...some of it...most of it."

"Shit, why stop there? Why don't you just tell me all of it?"

"I have some left."

"How much?"

"A few thousand."

Considering it was over forty grand, that wasn't going to cut it.

"I'll give you a week to get my money back."

He looked at me and a mocking smile made its way to his lips.

"You could give me a month and it won't be coming back. You see, I know who you are. Roger Theus. R-O-G-E-R T-H-E-U-S. And if you keep asking me for my money back, I'll go to the police. P-O-L-I-C-E."

Maybe he'd already sealed his fate when he first mentioned my name, but the act of spelling it out letter by letter certainly cemented it.

"You're a funny guy," I said and quickly took gloves out of my pocket and threw them on.

"What are you doing?" he asked.

For the first time, he looked scared.

He wasn't ready for what was to come. He'd probably thought he could bribe me for months to come. He was wrong. That's not how I rolled.

I unleashed a quick left jab. It connected flush with his nose. I didn't need to knock him out with the first punch, just put him on his back heel. And then I'd be going in for the kill. Literally. All I saw now was red. Billy Aybar had dug his own grave.

Billy was not a very big - nor tall - guy, and when he tried to punch me back, I swatted it away like a fly. I threw one more jab which again connected flush with his nose. I followed that with a right uppercut that sent him to the ground. I moved in his direction and proceeded to hit him in the nose again. This time it wasn't a jab, but a straight right. I kept hitting him. Over and over again. Repeatedly and with no remorse.

At one point, I felt his nose starting to turn from an outie to an innie as I pummeled it. He was probably dead by that point, but I still hit him five more times. Just for kicks.

At no point did I brush my skin on his with the exception of my gloved hands. I stood above him and hit from that elevated position. Although this was my first murder, I knew how they usually got you. DNA. I wasn't going to make that mistake.

Mercifully, Billy Aybar had stopped breathing.

And I'd committed my first murder.

I hadn't planned on killing him. It was bad business.

But he'd mentioned my name and I didn't have much choice at that point.

And yes, I'd brought gloves. So it was at least in the back of my mind that this could happen.

Maybe I thought Billy Aybar was an easy target.

Maybe I knew that Fernando would never say a word.

Maybe murder was just a natural progression for a scumbag like me.

Who knows? It had happened, though, and that's what mattered.

And I'll be honest, I enjoyed it.

Every. Single. Second.

'You think you're going to get away with stealing from Roger Theus?'

I don't think so.

And I probably would have gotten away with it if it weren't for Alfonso Reyes.

The fucker had seen me walking out of Billy Aybar's apartment.

But all is well that ends well, and Alfonso redeemed himself at the trial.

He was fantastic. An all-around Grade-A witness.

At least he was from my point of view.

Against all odds, my plan had worked.

I'm now out of jail and all is good with the world.

CHAPTER 31

BRUCE THE P.I.

When I heard about the acquittal, I wasn't sure whether it was me or Roger Theus who would be happier. Sure, he'd won his freedom, but I was about to win my financial freedom. Don't sleep on that.

I started to outline my plan. I'd wait a week. No, two weeks. No reason to rock the boat just yet. I'd ask Shane to meet for coffee. No, scratch that, we wouldn't be meeting in public. I had to be close to invisible from here on in.

I'd tell Shane there were a couple of loose ends in the Lexi case and I wanted to swing by his house. He'd grow immediately suspicious, but maybe that was a good thing. It would give him a little time to prepare for the bomb I was going to drop.

Now, as for how much I should ask for. From what I could gather, Shane was getting somewhere around $500k. Could I ask for half? That would be pretty aggressive. $200k? That was still 40% of what he received. Finally, I decided I'd ask for $150k.

Maybe that wasn't financial freedom, but it sure felt like it.

~

After a few days of thinking about it, my plan began to change.

Why go to a pawn like Shane when I could go straight to the top? I'd done some research on Roger Theus. The guy was involved in selling drugs and owned two Los Angeles apartment complexes. He obviously had a shit ton of money. If anyone is willing to give two million to keep himself out of jail - which is what Lexi alluded to - that means he's probably got at least five million or so. Shit, maybe ten.

I'd be able to get a lot more money from him than Shane.

$500k would be my asking price.

Maybe this would be my financial freedom after all.

～

Sixteen days after the trial ended, I decided to make my move.

I was able to find out that Theus had returned to a home of his in Malibu. While I didn't want to approach him at his house, it was the only logical place. Like I'd decided, it was better not to be seen with these people in public.

I'd been working on my pitch.

Give your man Bruce 500k and I'll walk away forever, taking your secret to my grave.

The man was free from jail and had money to burn. Paying off one last guy would be a no-brainer.

～

On a Friday morning at 9:15, I drove to Malibu and parked my car in front of Roger Theus's house. The views were breathtaking. No, I'd never own a house in Malibu ($500k might be a down payment), but this was no time to be jealous. I was about to reap a whirlwind of money. I think that's what that phrase meant.

There was only one other car parked in the open-air lot, a beautiful blue Corvette, and I hoped Theus was alone.

My hands were clammy, not that I should have been surprised.

Theus had killed a guy with his bare hands. I would treat him with the respect he deserved.

I knocked on the door.

A minute later, Roger Theus opened the door. He was even bigger than I imagined.

He was wearing a green bowling shirt with a Marlin and a boat.

It was like a big bear was looking down at me. Somewhere in the back of my mind, a little voice told me to use this chance to make an excuse and get the fuck out of there.

I didn't listen to that voice.

"Who are you?" he growled.

"Are you here alone, Mr. Theus?"

He stared menacingly.

"I'll ask you again," he said. "Who the fuck are you?"

I was already on my back foot.

"My name is Bruce Palmer and I work as a P.I."

"Do you want a medal?"

I'd met my share of tough guys over the years, but this man was truly frightening.

That little voice once again told me it was time to get out of there. Instead, my mind beelined towards frozen umbrella drinks, bikini-clad women, and the money to spend on both.

"No, I want to talk to you about some information I discovered," I said.

"What type of information?"

It was just time to come out and say it.

"I know why you were acquitted," I said.

I had to tell myself not to instinctively take a step backward. I was afraid this giant of a man might bum rush me.

Instead, I received a smile.

"Why don't you come inside?" he asked.

I followed Roger Theus inside his home. I looked out some bay windows and saw an even better view of the Pacific. It was gorgeous.

Pay attention!

I admonished myself. Roger Theus was not to be taken lightly. Stop admiring his home.

In what I assumed was the living room, there were two long, skinny couches that paralleled each other. He motioned to me to sit down on one, which I did. He sat across from me.

"Say your peace," he said.

I decided to just make it quick. No need for anything extraneous.

"I know that Shane Doyle threw your trial. And I know the other people involved."

He pondered my words.

"You said you're a P.I.?"

"Yes."

"Prove it."

I took out my PI's license and showed it to him.

"I'm not a cop or some member of the media," I said.

I continued to have a queasy feeling in the pit of my stomach.

"Why would you think such an absurd thing? I was acquitted by twelve impartial jurors."

"I won't patronize you, Mr. Theus, so I hope you'll grant me the same privilege."

He nodded and I continued.

"Alright, tell me what you think you know."

"I was hired by Shane Doyle to look into a woman he'd just started dating. It had nothing to do with you originally. However, I learned that this woman had seduced Shane and that he would be paid handsomely if he earned your release."

"How did you find this out?"

I decided to tell the truth.

"I bugged her apartment."

He gave me a slight smirk.

"Maybe we're more similar than I realized," he said. "I'm not conceding that what you say is true. If, hypothetically, it was, what do you want?"

"I'd like to say upfront, if you agree to my offer, you'll never hear from me again," I said. "That's a promise."

"What do you want?" Theus said more forcefully.

We'd hit the crucial moment.

"$500k."

He didn't laugh me off which I took as a good sign.

"As you may have guessed, I'm a little cash-poor at the moment thanks to your lawyer friend and the others."

"I understand. How long are we talking?"

"A week or two."

"That would be fine," I said.

"A few things first."

"Anything."

"Who have you told about this?"

"No one."

"Are you married?"

"Divorced and I live alone. I've told no one."

"Does Shane Doyle know what you are doing?"

"No."

"Why not?"

Once again, I saw no reason to lie.

"I figured why try and get a small portion from Shane when I could come to you."

Roger Theus laughed quite loudly.

"I appreciate the honesty."

"You're welcome."

"And if I decide to pay you, how will I know you won't ask for more money in six months?"

"Because I'll be drinking Margaritas on the beach in Mexico. With no plans on returning to the U.S."

Was that really going to happen? Who knew? I just wanted him to think I'd be far, far away.

"I want you to listen carefully," he said.

"Okay."

"You will not call me or try to contact me in any way. Two weeks from today, at nine a.m., you'll drive back here and I will give you $500k in cash. And then I will never see you again. Deal?"

"Deal, Mr. Theus. Thank you."

I'm sure he was livid, but he tried to remain stoic.

"You're welcome. Now you can show yourself out. And remember, you are not to tell a soul."

"My lips are sealed," I said.

We both stood up from the couches.

I walked outside, got in my car, drove down his driveway, and started pounding my roof in triumph.

I was on cloud nine in the twenty-four hours following my meeting with Roger Theus.

At fifty-six years old, I was ready to retire. Ready to travel. Ready to not have to deal with dirtbags on a daily basis.

Was I being a dirtbag myself by blackmailing Roger?

Of course, but it's not like I was blackmailing Mother Theresa. Roger, Lexi, Knox, and Shane had all put this massacre of justice together. They were the real villains. I was just taking advantage of a business opportunity.

A tremendous business opportunity.

I had $146,000 in my checking account, plus the $500k coming.

I Googled, *"Can you buy a house on a Mexican beach for $500,000."*

It turned out that was plenty.

I already had one foot out the door of Los Angeles.

~

Three days after my life-changing meeting, I went to my bank and asked if I could set up two safety deposit boxes, opting for the biggest they had. I knew they wouldn't hold $500k, but I'd leave the rest at my house and slowly deposit the money into my checking account. $3.8k here, $4.7k there.

That's how a criminal would think and I guess I was one now. Blackmail is still frowned upon by the State of California.

I drove home the fifteen miles from the bank to my house. LA being LA, it took me over an hour to get there.

I couldn't wait to get out of this shit hole. There were no homeless on Mexican beaches. Sure, there was killing and drugs and kidnapping in Mexico, but that didn't affect rich Americans. Of which, I was about to be one.

I'd be safe in my little bungalow on the Pacific.

"First-world problems in a third-world country," I said aloud.

And then laughed at my shitty joke.

~

I arrived home and parked my car in the driveway. I'd been living in a townhouse since my divorce eight years ago. Shelly - my witch of an ex-wife - had turned our two kids against me and they wanted nothing to do with me anymore. Not that I could blame them. I hadn't been the best father.

In *The Shawshank Redemption*, they say the Pacific Ocean has no memory. I was hoping that was the case. I just wanted to forget the first fifty-six years of my life and enjoy the last twenty-five or whatever God was willing to grant me.

I opened the front door, locked it behind me, and threw some of the paperwork from the safety deposit boxes on the desk next to me. I grabbed the remote and clicked the power button. ESPN roared to life, but it was some silly cornhole tournament. What the fuck, ESPN? Since when did throwing a bean bag into a hole become a sport?

My couch looked comfy, but I decided I was hungry and could use a bite to eat.

It was then, as I started towards the kitchen, that from around the corner, a man darted towards me.

It was Roger Theus. He had a Taser in his hands. I'd been a P.I. long enough to instantly recognize one. It sent me into a panic.

And there was something else that scared me even more. He was wearing gloves as well as a pair of blue, plastic disposable shoe covers.

There was only one reason he'd be wearing those things. And it meant I was in serious trouble. Without saying a word, Roger pressed a button on the Taser. My body started convulsing and I fell backward to the ground below me.

~

I awoke a few minutes later.

I wish I hadn't.

Why couldn't I have been one of those guys whose heart just gave out when tased?

It would have saved me a lot of pain. Unbearable pain.

When I came to, my mouth had been duct-taped shut.

Roger Theus was straddling me, his massive body giving me no possibility of escape.

I was in a horror film - only this was real - and my terror was magnified when I looked toward Roger's right hand. He was holding a hammer. And it wasn't one of those little seven-inch hammers that you used on nails.

This thing was approximately two feet long and more closely resembled a sledgehammer.

Roger spoke for the first time.

"I remember you saying you'd keep your mouth shut. My plan was to do it for you, but I'm not much of a seamstress. I'd imagined taking a needle and slowly making my way across your filthy mouth and sewing it shut. I would have enjoyed that, but alas, that's not in my repertoire. What is in my repertoire, however, is swinging a hammer. That's easy enough. And you know what, Bruce? I think it's going to have the same desired outcome. Your mouth will stay shut. Well, more like sunken, but hey, what's the difference at this point?"

Roger Theus paused and then said two more short sentences. They were the last two I'd ever hear.

"You fucked with the wrong guy. Sweet dreams."

He raised the hammer and I just hoped the end would come quickly.

CHAPTER 32

SHANE

I'd barely talked to Lexi in the days since Roger Theus was acquitted. She came over the day of the verdict and I hadn't seen her since. We'd had sex that first night, but I could tell she wasn't into it, and I lost interest after that. She'd probably never been into it. Her story about how the sex we had was purely organic was surely bullshit.

Instead, I started planning potential ways at getting back at her. I wanted to fuck her in a different kind of way. After we collected the money, obviously.

The next time I heard from her was around two weeks later and she said Roger was ready to pay up. He was going to give the money to Knox (she slipped and forgot to call him John) and then Knox would meet with Lexi and me individually and give us our share.

I'd expected that call. A surprising call came a day later.

Lexi told me plans had changed and Roger now wanted to meet all of us together at midnight on Thursday. At her apartment. I preferred that. I didn't know this Knox guy and he obviously didn't have A-plus scruples. Not that any of us did. Meeting Roger Theus face to face would ensure that I'd get the money directly.

"And another thing," Lexi said.

"What?" I'd become pretty curt with her on the phone.

"You won't be going home with your cell phone."

"Why?"

"Theus said he's going to incinerate each and every one of them. I told him we were smart and never texted each other about it. That includes me and you. And also me and Knox. I mean John."

"Stop with the charade, Lexi. I know his name is Knox."

She quickly changed the subject.

"Anyway, Theus doesn't want to take any risks so he's going to nuke our phones or something similar."

"Okay."

I had to admit, it was the smart thing to do.

"Did you get a safety deposit box as I suggested yesterday? Theus said if we lose the money on our own not to come begging to him."

"Yeah, I did."

I didn't like the way Lexi had to reiterate the safety deposit box. Would Roger give us the money and then have someone break into our respective houses and steal it back?

He wouldn't do that, I told myself.

The guy was a free man thanks to the three of us. He wouldn't risk it.

Then again, he knows we couldn't exactly turn him in, being complicit ourselves.

My head hurt. There was too much going on.

"Anything else, Lexi?"

"Yeah, don't knock on my door. It will be open. We want to keep this as quiet as we can."

"Got it. That's it?"

"That's it. Goodbye."

I hung up on my end. There was no love lost between us.

The day before we were to meet Roger Theus, things at work took a turn for the worse.

I went in around 8:15 a.m., parked my car at the usual spot, showed my badge at the entrance of the Santa Monica Courthouse, and made my way to my office on the third floor.

It was an ugly white building with awful blue awnings that greeted you as you entered. Ironically, we were mere hundreds of yards from the beautiful blue of the Pacific Ocean. No one had ever called referred to the Santa Monica Courthouse as beautiful.

I looked around my office. It wasn't very big and was messier than usual. Paper was sprawled all over my desk.

Assistant District Attorney of Los Angeles sounds like a big-time job, but they sure don't treat us like that. It's part of the reason I took the money to throw the case. That, and I was an asshole who'd sell out his own mother.

A few minutes after I'd entered, I got a knock at my door. Braxton Pue was at my door. He was a fellow ADA and a few years younger than me. By our peers, he was viewed as the better attorney. Rightfully so, I had to admit. He was a bulldog in court. I was more of a cocker spaniel. Braxton had prematurely gray hair which probably helped him look like a more seasoned ADA.

"Hey, Braxton. What do you need?"

I played nice.

"Can I come in?"

I didn't like where this was headed.

"Sure," I said.

He sat in one of the chairs that face my desk and I quickly tried to rearrange my desk to look presentable. As if fifteen seconds could clean up the mess it had become. Braxton may have been a good attorney, but most of our co-workers didn't like him. When he wasn't trying one of his own cases, he'd often sit in on other DA's cases, and sometimes give his unsolicited advice. Our fellow ADAs didn't take that well. Nor should they. Braxton was a pompous shit. I'd seen him sitting in on the Roger Theus case a few times. That's why I was worried.

"What is it?" I asked.

"What the hell happened in the Roger Theus case?"

Just like I'd feared.

I tried to quickly think of what to do. Saying I'd been great and the jury gave us a raw deal wouldn't cut it with Braxton. He was an intuitive guy and would see right through it.

"I wasn't on my A game."

"Or your B game," he said.

I had to remain calm and let him have his way. There was no need to squabble with him and make things worse. Even though I felt like giving him a quick jab to the face.

"That's fair," I said. "I'd met a new girl and was going through some things."

It sounded like the right thing to say, but mentioning Lexi by name would not be advisable.

"She fucked with your head?"

"Yes."

Braxton Pue looked around my office.

"I hate to say this Shane, but that's no excuse. You put a witness on the stand who said he was only 97% sure that Roger Theus had left the apartment. Who the hell does something that stupid?"

"I was as shocked as everyone else, Braxton."

"Explain."

"I really have to explain it to you? When we were prepping for the trial, Alfonso Reyes kept telling me he was 100% sure. I was as blindsided as anyone."

"Why would he do that?"

"I have no idea. You'd have to ask him."

I sure hope he didn't take me up on my offer. If Alfonso told him the truth, I'd soon be a former DA. And likely be finding myself in jail.

"And it wasn't just that witness. There were other points where you just didn't seem all there," Braxton said.

"I told you. My head was a little fucked up."

"And I told you, that's no excuse. You've now got a stone-cold killer out there walking free."

I wanted to tell him to 'Fuck Off' but I couldn't.

"You're right, Braxton. It's my fault. What else do you want?"

"Don't make this a habit or I'll go to Charlie and say you aren't cut out for this job."

Charlie Hunt was the District Attorney of Los Angeles. Not replaceable ADAs like Braxton and me.

"So you haven't told anybody else?" I asked.

"No, Shane, I haven't. Consider this your one mulligan."

"I'll be better next time. I promise."

"You better," he said and briskly walked out of my office.

I felt the walls closing in.

～

The day we were to meet Roger Theus (and get our money) had arrived.

The meeting with Braxton Pue had me on edge. I couldn't tell if he was calling me inept or whether he was alleging some malfeasance. I think he was only asserting the former, but I had to watch myself, knowing I was actually guilty of the latter.

I thought about my options.

I could ask for a few months off, saying I'd been under a lot of stress and wasn't being the best lawyer I could be. That could help explain away some of the Roger Theus trial.

I could suck it up and stay on for a few months, pretending that nothing suspicious had happened.

My third, and most intriguing option, was to get the hell out of the DA's office altogether and start my own practice as a defense attorney.

Shit, you already proved you could keep a defendant from getting convicted!

I laughed at my own joke as I was prone to do.

I wouldn't have Braxton's accusations looming over me if I was out on my own.

And while it's true that starting your own firm was a big risk, I now had a nest egg that could support me if I struggled for the first few years.

The more I thought about it, the more I wanted out of the DA's office.

That decision could wait.

I had more prescient decisions in the weeks to come.

Filet Mignon or Ribeye?

Do I eat at Maestro's or Nobu?

I wasn't going to be like Johnny Roastbeef in *Goodfellas* and buy a new Cadillac right after my big score, but I wasn't just going to sit at home either.

I was going to be out on the town, having $200 dinners and $500 bar tabs, all while screwing any girl who would let me.

Maybe it was because, in the back of my consciousness, where I'd tried to relegate it, I knew I'd done a horrible deed. Oh well. If I wasn't going to have fun with the money, then what the hell had been the purpose of this?

I couldn't wait to get my hands on the money later that night.

That would turn my mood around.

At 11:45 p.m., I grabbed my keys, wallet, and cell phone (like I'd been told.) I wondered if all my contacts would save to the cloud. If not, it would be a total pain in the ass trying to get them all back.

But I knew Roger Theus was right. Even though Lexi said she'd been careful about not texting Knox or me, if cops ever suspected us, they'd try to use our frequent calls as the groundwork for our conspiracy.

I looked down at my eighteen-month-old iPhone 13.

"We had a good run, buddy."

I sure was talking to myself a lot lately. I tallied it up to all the stress I'd been under.

~

It was a beautiful early September night in Los Angeles. It was still in the mid-seventies with a slight breeze as we approached midnight. There were several things you could complain about when it came to Los Angeles. The weather wasn't one of them.

If I didn't have to transport all the cash home with me, I'd have walked to Lexi's.

I wondered what Roger Theus would be like in person. Sure, I'd been in the same courtroom with him, but in my history, defendants act quite differently in person. They try to put on a loving, sympathetic face for the twelve jurors determining their future. For obvious reasons. And from my experience, most defendants don't have loving, sympathetic faces outside of a courtroom.

And how about Knox? I really had no feel for him other than that he'd probably dated Lexi. As in really dated, not like some schmo I know. I bet the whole black eye thing was probably bullshit too.

I was in the wrong mindset.

I arrived at Lexi's, parked the car, and took a deep breath.

You're about to be rich. Smile, fucker.

~

I made my way toward the front door.

As Lexi had mentioned, it was slightly ajar.

I walked in and quickly realized I was the last one to make it despite being ten minutes early.

Understandable. For something of this magnitude, being ten minutes early is basically being late.

The three of them were standing and talking quietly on the other side of the apartment.

Roger Theus stepped forward first. He was wearing a black Tommy Bahama shirt with two huge white and red dice. He looked ridiculous. Not that I'd be the one to tell him.

We shook hands. I had to refrain from shaking mine after. To get the feeling back. He had a vice-like grip.

"Nice to formally meet you, Shane. Your lawyering skills are second to none."

"It was interesting circumstances."

"That's what made it all the more impressive. You had to argue your case all while undercutting yourself at the same time. And that thing with Alfonso Reyes? Masterful."

I saw Knox look on with interest. He probably had no idea how I'd thrown the case. All that mattered to him was that I was successful.

"Thanks, Mr. Theus."

"Stop," he said. "My name is Roger."

"Okay, Roger."

I looked in Knox's direction.

"You must be Knox?"

He took a quick look at Lexi.

"Don't get mad at Lexi," I said. "She didn't slip until after Roger here was acquitted."

"That's not the fucking point. I don't want you to know my real name."

I'd met Knox twenty seconds ago and already hated him.

I saw Roger look at Knox with contempt.

"Keep it down, Knox. And that ain't your real name anyway. You trying to have a neighbor hear us?"

"I'm sorry, Roger."

It was readily apparent that Roger Theus was the alpha male in their friendship. I had no doubt that Knox was probably a tough guy, but he acted like a scared child when Roger reprimanded him.

I scanned the room looking for the duffle bags full of cash.

It's as if Roger could sense it.

"You ready to get down to business, Shane?"

I laughed awkwardly.

"I'm just looking forward to seeing what 500k looks like."

Roger made a peculiar expression. It most resembled curiosity. A few seconds later he laughed as if he'd just figured out an inside joke.

"What?" I said.

I looked at Lexi who hadn't said a word. I wondered if she was intimidated by all the testosterone in the room. Which, let's be honest, was mostly Roger's.

"Oh, it's nothing, Shane," Roger said.

I felt the tension ratchet up a tiny bit. It wasn't much, but I could sense it.

"Knox and Lexi, I think Shane wants to see the money."

I was ready to get the money and get out of there. I didn't like the feel of the room.

"Let's do it."

"First things first," Roger said.

"What?"

"Your phone."

"Oh, yeah."

I handed Roger my phone.

"Same goes for you two," Roger said.

Lexi and Knox handed theirs over.

Roger put them in a little plastic bag he'd brought.

"I also need your passwords," he said.

"Why?" I asked.

"If I just throw all three phones in the lake and the cops find them, they can still search the cloud for past texts and phone calls. I'm going to open your phones and do what's called a "mass extinction" of your phone where it deletes any and everything that's ever been on the phone. Trust me, you don't want this coming back to bite you down the road."

I'd never heard of anything called a "mass extinction" but who was I to argue? Plus, Roger was right. Just turning the phones off or destroying them wasn't enough.

Lexi spoke first.

"My password is Lexi69."

"It would be," Knox said.

She looked at him, almost blushing. I felt completely emasculated.

"And you, Knox?" Roger asked.

"123321."

"See that's why I need to thoroughly destroy these phones. Horrible passwords like that."

Knox once again looked like a dog with his tail between his legs.

"How about you, Shane?"

"SDLADA," I said.

Roger took a few seconds.

"Shane Doyle Los Angeles District Attorney?" he asked/answered.

"Impressive," I said.

It was. He may have looked like a buffoon, but I had a feeling he was a lot smarter than people realized.

No one said a word for a few seconds. Finally, Roger spoke up.

"Alright, I'm going to take Shane out to the car first and give him his duffle bag of cash. But first, let me say this. Thank you with all my heart. Because of you three, I'm a free man and I'm going to live a long and fruitful life. Knox, you were the ringleader and ran this to perfection. Lexi, it's probably better if I don't try to guess how you reeled Shane in, but you're obviously a beautiful woman so I have a few guesses. Shane, as I said earlier, you're a phenomenal attorney. Job well done."

We all quietly said thanks.

"Lexi, you and Knox stay where you are. I know Lexi's closest neighbor is a distance away, but we don't need them seeing four people leaving this apartment at once. Especially when you'll be carrying huge duffle bags in a matter of moments."

Roger paused and I hated how downbeat the room was. We were about to be rich and it felt like a damn funeral.

Fuck them! I'd celebrate on my own. I'd hit up a bar that was still open and buy every single person a drink and a shot. Enough of these freaking Debbie Downers. The only guy who seemed partially upbeat was Roger and he was about to be a lot poorer.

Screw Lexi and Knox. I'd be glad to be done with them.

Finally, Roger broke another silence.

"Knox, Lexi, I'll be back in a few minutes," Roger said. "You can say goodbye to Shane now."

Knox said nothing.

"We had some good times," was all Lexi could muster.

I didn't know what to say, so I said nothing. I was already looking forward to the smiles on the faces of the drunks whose drinks I'd be buying tonight. Screw it, I'd pick up everyone's tab for the rest of the night. It would be one a.m. by the time I hid the money and made it to a bar and how much damage could you actually cause in one hour? We'd be finding out soon.

Roger walked past me and was about to open the door. My financial windfall was about to take shape.

Instead, Roger swiveled around and as he did, I saw something coming from the back of his jeans. I thought it was a gun, but it was longer than any I'd ever seen. I soon realized a long silencer was attached to it.

Before anyone could do anything, he raised the gun and fired two shots into Knox's chest. A split second later, he fired two chest shots into Lexi. Her mouth was agape as she fell backward.

Everything was happening so quickly that I had no time to react.

I looked over at Roger to see if I was close enough to jump at the gun. He was too close to the door. I'd be shot if I leaped at him.

I was a dead man.

I said some quick bullshit prayer like I could absolve all my recent sins in one fell swoop.

But Roger didn't raise the gun at me.

Instead, he walked in my direction. He was still between me and the door so I had nowhere to run, but the fact that he hadn't pointed the gun in my direction gave me hope. It meant he didn't plan on killing me.

When Roger was two steps from me, he said, "You get to live. Come here and give me a hug."

It was such an odd request, but I couldn't exactly say no. The last thing I wanted to do was piss off a guy who'd just shot and killed two people.

I tried to avoid looking at Lexi and Knox's bodies. All I was thinking about was trying to stay alive.

And if that meant hugging the deranged psycho walking toward me, then so be it.

I put my arms forward and took a step in his direction.

When I got close, Roger moved behind me with a quickness I wasn't expecting. He instantly put me in a tight headlock with just his left hand. I tried to wriggle free, but he was entirely too strong. His grip was so powerful, I couldn't even scream. He was constricting my neck. I was going to pass out at any moment. Surely, never to regain consciousness.

Amongst a million other thoughts, I wondered, "Why is he going to strangle me to death when he could have just shot me?"

My answer came quickly.

"Oh, Shane," Roger said. "Sorry, it has to end this way for you. You see, I have to make this look like a murder/suicide. You're a spurned lover who came over and saw Lexi was still with Knox and killed them both. Beset with guilt, you killed yourself as well."

I tried to scream, but nothing came out. The blood making its way to my head was diminishing by the second.

I saw him raising the gun to the right side of my head.

"Don't worry," Roger said. "The bullet will go right through your head and miss me entirely. I'll be just fine in case you were worried about old Roger."

In the last few seconds of my life, I noticed a few things. Roger Theus was wearing gloves. How had I missed it? Or had I just ignored them since all I cared about getting the money? I guess it didn't really matter. Roger Theus would have had a built-in excuse that we'd be afraid to question. That's the kind of guy he was.

My neck couldn't move, but with my eyes, I took a quick look down and noticed the oddest thing. Roger had those little shoe covers over his shoes. Only, they were black and not the standard blue, which made them tough to discern with his black shoes.

There was no question as to why he was wearing gloves and shoe covers.

This had all been planned.

As I began to realize just how depraved Roger Theus was, the muzzle of his gun touched the side of my head.

"Consider this your suicide," Roger said.

And then everything turned black.

CHAPTER 33

KNOX

"I've changed my mind, Knox," Roger Theus said. "I'd rather meet you all together. Give everyone my thanks in person. Take your cell phones. And then give you each your own giant duffle bag."

This was only a few days after we'd agreed that only I would meet him. I didn't care. I thought it would be kind of fun to see all of our reactions to seeing the money. Even Shane. The man did his part, you had to give him credit for that.

"Sounds fine," I said. "When and where?"

"What's the living situation of the young lady who helped seduce Shane? I believe Lexi was her name."

"I thought you didn't want to know the details. How did you find out about her?"

"I know a great many people, Knox."

"I'm sure you do."

He didn't respond and I didn't like how close-mouthed he was.

"If I'm going to be giving you guys two million dollars, I'd rather not have twenty neighbors within earshot. And I'm sorry, but your apartment complex is just too condensed. That's why I'm asking about Lexi's living situation."

"Why don't we just meet somewhere else?" I asked.

"No, I'd like to do it at one of your apartments. Or Shane's house if absolutely necessary."

"You know about him too?"

"I was sitting front and center at the trial if you've forgotten, Knox. I'm not a dummy. I could tell he wasn't always giving it the old college try."

"Wish I could have been there for it."

"So, you haven't answered my question. What is Lexi's apartment like?"

"Her place isn't like the usual apartment complex. Each apartment is lined parallel along the same street. It's not like The Premier or my complex now. And there's a good distance between each place."

"Great. We'll hold this shindig at Lexi's."

"Okay. What day and time?"

"Thursday night, right around midnight."

Before I hung up, I remembered something.

"Roger, there's something I have to tell you."

"Fire away."

"We're not splitting the money evenly. Lexi only promised Shane $500k and then Lexi and I were going to split the remaining $1.5 million."

Roger laughed loudly on the other end.

"She sounds like a lovely young lady. Cunning. My favorite kind. Okay, I won't say anything. His bag will contain $500k and yours and Lexi's will contain $750k each. Is that what you're looking for?"

"That's perfect. Thanks, Roger."

"See you Thursday."

And then he hung up.

~

The meeting at Lexi's house was enjoyable until Shane showed up.

I had been regaling Roger with some Lexi stories and he genuinely seemed intrigued. He was smitten with her. As much as Roger Theus could be smitten by anything.

"Maybe the three of us should go into business together," Roger said and then laughed.

Lexi and I nodded, confirming that we'd be up for it, but Roger laughed a few seconds too long and we weren't sure why.

He was laughing a lot. Roger was - dare I say it - borderline jovial.

You wouldn't think a guy who was about to part with two million dollars would be so happy. Then again, any place is better than jail. And the more we talked, the more I thought his nest egg was bigger than I'd first assumed. He might have had ten or twenty million. Who knew?

Despite Roger's laughing, Lexi wasn't putting to bed the idea of us all working together.

"If you need me to seduce someone again, can it be Brad Pitt or some Hollywood star? Not some no dick, district atto…"

That's when we heard the door opening and Lexi rightfully cut her sentence short.

The mood seemed to change once Shane entered. Roger became more serious as if it was all business from here on in. If Roger hadn't been joking, and he wanted our help again, I hoped Shane wouldn't be part of it. He was a buzzkill. And I'd known the guy for maybe thirty seconds.

Shane introduced himself to me and I responded unenthusiastically.

The only levity was when Lexi said her password was "Lexi69." I looked over at Shane as if to say, *"She's my girl now and she always has been."*

He didn't look too happy, that's for sure.

We bullshitted for a few more minutes until Roger said it was time to start giving the money out. I figured he'd picked Shane first so he wasn't around to realize Lexi and my duffle bags were just a little fuller.

I was correct as he escorted Shane toward the door.

The next thing I knew, Roger raised his gun at me. I thought it was a joke.

An instant later, I felt hot lead burn through my body, and I knew this was all too real.

I didn't have time to question why this was happening.

I was still alive, that's all I knew.

Somehow he must have missed a vital organ.

As I saw him about to shoot again, I figured there was no way I'd survive the second shot.

I was right about that.

CHAPTER 34

LEXI

When I saw Roger raise the gun and then shoot Knox, I told myself to remember a happy thought.

I wasn't getting out of this alive. I might as well die smiling.

I thought back to when I was around nine years old. I was still an innocent girl who liked dressing up as a princess. It was before my family life went to shit and I became a rebellious pre-teen who made a series of bad choices for the rest of her life.

On the day in question, my best friend, Maribel, came over to my house after school. My parents, who were still married at the time, were both at work and I had a few hours after school each day to myself. Their fights were getting worse and my alone time was usually my favorite time of the day.

Maribel had brought something over called an easy-bake oven. I'd never seen one. My love of cookies was seemingly only surpassed by Maribel's. She brought chocolate chips, butter, flour, peanut butter, eggs, sugar, brown sugar, baking soda, and a few other ingredients.

She was prepared is what I'm saying.

We spent the next three hours baking cookies. Yes, we ate the cookies when they came out of the easy bake oven, but I felt like we devoured half the cookie batter before they even made it in.

We talked about princes, about us being future princesses, and how we hated our third-grade teacher, Ms. Teasdale. We did all this while having flour and chocolate chip stains all over our little clothes. I never remember laughing so hard in my entire life. Sure, we were laughing about stupid things, but that's what nine-year-olds do.

When my mother arrived home at six that night and sent Maribel home, I cried for two hours.

To this day, I think it may be the happiest I've ever been in my life.

I'm not sure how much of the Maribel story I was able to recollect in real time. Probably only a second or two.

When I looked down and saw two holes protruding from Knox's chest, I opened my mouth in terror. All of my terrible life choices had led me to this. I was going to die via gunshot on the floor of my apartment. I never even received the $500k. What a fucking waste of a life!

Roger Theus raised the gun at me and I wished I could go back to being that little girl cooking with the easy bake oven.

But it was too late…

CHAPTER 35

ROGER

I planned on giving the money to Knox, Lexi, and Shane until that shitfuck P.I. named Bruce showed up at my door.

I swear to God.

Do people still say that?

I used to tell my single mother that every time I got in trouble. *I swear to God I didn't do it, Mom.* Of course, I was lying a huge percentage of the time. Let's go with 97%. My forever favorite number from here on in.

Maybe my new best friend Alfonso Reyes should come into some money. I certainly have enough to spare. Now that Knox and his friends are gone.

Hahahaha.

So, once Bruce blackmailed me, I began going over my options. I didn't believe his bullshit story that this would be a one-time thing. That's not how this kind of thing worked. He'd skin me until I was dry.

Unless I got to him first.

And once I decided it was just going to be easier to kill that bastard, I started thinking about the other three. And because of Bruce, I learned about Lexi and Shane. Knox's cohorts.

I didn't blame Knox for that per se, but you have to know that every person you add brings new variables to the mix. In this case, Shane went to Bruce because he had reservations about Lexi. Lexi's hotness came back to bite all of them in the ass.

It doesn't appear any of the main three opened their mouths and things

still went sideways. That's why it's always better to keep your co-conspirators to a minimum. One other at the very most.

When I decided to kill Bruce, I considered hiring someone to do it.
However, due to the reasons I just outlined, I thought it better if I
hammered him to death myself.

As for the "murder/suicide" that I orchestrated for the other three, it
was a thing of beauty.

Let me outline it for you.

~

I knew I couldn't kill them all separately. First off, it's too many crime
scenes and each crime scene adds extra volatility, just as with Knox
bringing on others. Secondly, if dead bodies started turning up around
town, the LAPD was going to converge on the case.

I didn't want that. In fact, if I never dealt with the LAPD again, I'd be
fine with that.

I wracked my brain for a solid ten hours until I came up with a scheme.
Bruce - the deceased Bruce by this point - had made it clear that Shane was
infatuated with Lexi. Lovestruck at the bare minimum.

At that point, it hit me.

I'd use Shane as the scorned lover who took his revenge on Lexi and
her new (or old) lover. I wasn't sure of Lexi's history, but I got the sense
this wasn't her and Knox's first time around the block.

That's why, when I called Knox, I made it clear that Shane's house
would have to be a last resort. It would be hard to explain why Knox
would be at Shane's house.

Knox's apartment wouldn't work because of the proximity of the apartments. Even with my silencer, the neighbors might well hear the gunshots.
That type of condensed apartment complex was too risky.

That's why Lexi's place ended up being perfect. One, the neighbors
were far enough away that they wouldn't hear a silenced handgun. Especially at midnight, when most are likely asleep. Second, and almost as
important, is that it would make perfect sense that Shane would come to
Lexi's. And then when Knox was there, he went crazy.

At least, that's what I hoped the cops would think.

And I'd bought the gun years ago off of some street thug. The gun's
serial number had been sanded off.

There would be no tracing it back to me and the cops would assume
that Shane just bought it off the street.

~

I'd planned out everything in my head at least twenty times.

I tried to scheme for every possible contingency. I'd long considered myself a mastermind and now it was time to prove it. The Tommy Bahama bowling shirts were all a ruse to have people underestimate me. Hey, it had gotten me this far. And when you hear about the strings I was pulling from jail, you'll understand why I deserve the moniker of a mastermind.

Including having my attorney, Mason Croy III, go to Knox and tell him that Shane Doyle would be the weak link. You hear things in jail from other inmates. I just used them to my advantage.

I'll get back to that.

Before I knew it, the day had arrived. The small talk with Knox and Lexi went well. They didn't suspect a thing. When Shane arrived, things changed. I'll admit it. It was probably my fault. I knew what I'd soon have to do and the aura of the room had darkened.

When it came time to kill everyone, I had to make sure that Knox and Lexi were standing next to each other. I executed that perfectly. Them too. Hahaha.

The next part of my plan was not as easy.

I couldn't just shoot Shane from five feet away. Even the inept LAPD would realize that wasn't a suicide.

My idea - which ended out working flawlessly - was to tell Shane that I wasn't going to kill him. I'd be between him and the door so he couldn't just run and if I could get him within reach, I knew I was way too strong for him.

Once again, things transpired just as I'd imagined.

Maybe I should have been worried about the bullet taking a left turn somewhere inside of Shane's brain and ricocheting out and hitting me, but hey, there had to be some risk involved.

Shane's limp body immediately fell to the floor and I knew I'd accomplished the impossible.

Well, almost.

I couldn't leave the house just yet. There was something else I had to do.

In retrospect, it was probably a good thing I didn't leave right away.

If the neighbors happened to hear the silenced gunshot or the body hitting the floor, they might wake up and look toward Lexi's apartment. If someone (me) was leaving the apartment at that moment, they'd know it was no coincidence. If they saw or heard nothing coming from her place, they'd figure their ears had deceived them.

That was all hindsight. In the moment, as I sat in the room with the three dead bodies, I half-expected the police to show up and I was dying to get out of there.

Dying. I crack myself up.

So, why did I have to stay?

For the coup de grace.

I'd collected all three phones and, remember, I'd asked for their passwords as well. Knox had insisted that they never corresponded via text, but I had to make sure. I spent a good ten minutes going over their conversations and Knox wasn't lying. They hadn't texted one word about Shane Doyle or my trial.

They did text each other about the occasional booty call. Perfect! That would just play into my hand of Shane being the scorned lover.

I delicately put their phones back in their pants pockets.

I was wearing gloves, obviously.

And shoe covers.

Knox, Lexi, and Shane may have helped pull off the crime of the century, but they hadn't noticed my gloves or my shoe covers. Some criminals they were. Then again, maybe they were just too intimidated by me to ask.

Also, I'd intentionally made the gloves and the shoe covers black. I had black shoes on and a black shirt. They almost looked like part of the outfit.

I went over and grabbed Shane's phone. I scrolled through his texts with Lexi. Lots and lots of horny texts, but nothing mentioning my trial or their plan. Perfect.

I searched for Knox on his phone and found nothing. They introduced themselves less than ten minutes before they died, so I was pretty sure they'd never met, but I had to make sure.

I considered using Shane's phone to text Lexi and say that he was coming over. The timestamp could potentially cause problems so I tossed that idea out.

What I decided to do was have Shane text himself. If you were going to leave a rushed suicide note, it made some sense. The cops would obviously find it.

I typed the following:

"To whoever reads this, I'm sorry for what I've just done. Yes, I brought the gun, so it's my fault. I promise you, though, I hadn't intended on killing her. Or him. It was only once I arrived and that asshole said that Lexi was his now. Then I

snapped. There's no other way to explain it. Tell my family and friends I love them and I hope they won't judge me for one horrible decision. Now, I will be joining the other two in death. Goodbye."

It was impeccable if I don't say so myself.

I'd stayed long enough.

I looked out the blinds and no one was loitering around the outside of Lexi's apartment. I quietly slinked out, leaving the door unlocked. It's unlikely Lexi would have locked the door behind Shane, so it made it more believable if I kept it unlocked. Obviously, my gloves were still on.

I got to my car and drove out of the driveway, not turning my lights on until I was out on the main street.

I'm sure there is no such thing, but I felt I'd just committed the perfect murder(s).

The Mastermind was getting good at this shit!

PART TWO: NOBLE DUNN

CHAPTER 36

NOBLE

I remember the exact moment when I wanted to become a police officer. It wasn't some grandiose moment where my grandmother was mugged and I decided I wanted to save the world. No, mine was a lot more subtle.

It was 1982, and I was playing with my friends. As usual, I was the only black kid. Growing up in Santa Monica wasn't unheard of for young black kids, they just weren't in the part of the city where I grew up.

My four or five good friends all happened to be white. We were a pretty close-knit group, despite my pigmentation standing out.

On this day we decided to play a game of cops and robbers as we were prone to do. We were thirteen years old. Too young to know any better.

Randall, the leader of our group, started picking sides. Everett and John were selected as cops. Ethan was a robber. And then he looked at me and selected me as a robber. It wasn't malicious - Randall wasn't that type of guy - but it still hit home.

"Why am I always a robber?" I asked.

He thought about it and answered as eloquently as a twelve-year-old could.

"I'm sorry, Noble. I'm just not sure I've ever seen a black cop. Even on T.V."

Now, I'm sure there had been black cops on T.V. by the early '80s, but there certainly weren't many of them.

That didn't matter to me. I was pissed.

"I'll show you that we can be cops."

I remember Randall smiling.

"Alright, you can start now. You're a cop. Everett, you're now a robber."

Randall probably forgot about this a day later, but for a young black kid, it was a seminal moment. I remember thinking: *'I'll show them that I can be a cop!'*

I'm still friends with Randall to this day. It was a different time and he didn't mean anything by it.

That doesn't mean it didn't mean something to me.

It meant everything.

~

My plan came to fruition.

I became a rockstar cop in the early to mid-90s. I handled some of the biggest murder cases that Los Angeles had to offer. I was always the first one they called when a bonafide celebrity or even a D-lister was killed. They knew those were the cases that would garner the most attention.

And for those, they wanted their number one detective: Noble Dunn. Me.

You're probably asking yourself why I was named Noble. Wasn't that a bit presumptuous of my parents? Trust me, I was asking them the same question when I found out what the word meant.

'Mom and Dad, why'd you name me Noble?'

Their stock answer was that they thought names meant more than people realized. That, for better or worse, a little bit of your name seeps into you. And to them, being noble was the greatest trait someone could possess.

I used to laugh at the notion of names meaning so much, but I now believe there's some truth to it. If I'd been named Chester, things might have been different.

I've tried to live up to my name. I've tried to be a noble human being. While doing a job (police officer) where that wasn't always the easiest thing to be. Trust me, I've seen the worst of human existence. Murder, rape, kidnapping. And fifty other things I won't bother mentioning.

And sadly, some of my fellow cops have committed those crimes as well.

Luckily, there are a few good cops left. And I'm one of them. That's not being cocky, I'm just telling it like it is. I don't lie, cheat, steal drugs, beat up suspects, etc., etc. I play by the rules and treat my arrestees with respect, even when they don't deserve it.

Maybe I stood out because they weren't used to a cop who played by the rules. Or maybe I stood out because I was black. Whatever the reason, it allowed me to rise fast and become a star in the 90s, which feels like two lifetimes ago.

Now, at fifty-three, I'm just the old man on the force. I'm no longer that cute, shiny object that everyone desired. I was the wrinkled vet with a bit of a gut - and too much gray in my hair - that no one wanted to deal with. At least, not the ones who were guilty of something. I was still known as the straight shooter, which to my fellow cops, basically meant I was a goody-two-shoes. And that can wear on people after a while.

I could count on one hand the number of cops I considered close friends.

Oh, well. I'd had a good run. And with both thirty years on the force and retirement staring me in the face, I knew I wasn't going to be a police officer much longer. I'd given it a damn good run, but as we know, all good things must end.

∼

I first heard about the murder/suicide in Santa Monica on a Sunday.

The female victim, Lexi Grant, hadn't shown up to her bartending shifts on Friday or Saturday night. People had tried to reach her but her phone had been dead. So eventually, on Sunday morning, they alerted the police. When they went to do a wellness check, they discovered it wasn't only her phone that was dead.

It was a horrific scene.

Three dead bodies. In one corner of the room were Lexi Grant and a man whose ID said his name was Ben Hartley. In the other corner of the apartment was a man by the name of Shane Doyle.

Lexi and Ben were shot from a distance and Shane had been killed by what looked like a gunshot to the head. In all likelihood, a suicide. In fact, the way the crime scene had been described sounded very much like a murder/suicide.

I got the call a few minutes before ten a.m. Apparently, my fellow cops and the Medical Examiner had already been there for almost an hour. It made me wonder if I hadn't been the third or fourth officer they'd called.

'No one wants this case. Well, then *call Noble. He's got nothing to do on a Sunday morning.*'

Oh well. As I said, I didn't have much time left on the force anyway.

~

I drove from the Santa Monica police headquarters on Olympic Avenue and arrived on the cross streets of 10th and Wilshire about eight minutes after ten. We were that close to the crime scene.

I parked my undercover cop car out front and walked in. I was wearing civilian clothes as I was prone to do. Being a detective did have its advantages.

There was a Santa Monica police officer acting as a bouncer, deciding who got let into the crime scene.

"Detective Dunn," I said.

I flashed my badge.

"Come on in, Detective. Just a heads up. It's pretty gruesome."

I could have told this young cop that I'd seen it all, but what was the point of sounding like a know-it-all?

"Thanks," I said instead.

I walked in and damn if the cop wasn't right.

The first thing I saw was the brain splatter of Shane Doyle. He was by himself, about ten feet to the right of the front door. His facial expression was one I wouldn't soon forget. It was fear, anger, disgust, and resignation all rolled into one.

I'd seen many dead bodies, and let me tell you, the last expression your face ever makes is rarely a good one.

I walked over to the other side of the apartment. The bodies of Lexi Grant and Ben Hartley were both on their back, their eyes looking skyward.

Ben Hartley was basically expressionless. Lexi Grant had her mouth open as if she was seeing the most shocking thing of her life. Which, sadly, she had.

A bald Santa Monica cop in his thirties walked over to me.

"We just found out that the guy in the corner is an ADA out of Santa Monica. Shane Doyle is his name."

I wasn't expecting to hear that.

"Really?" I said.

Maybe this case was going to be bigger than I'd suspected.

"Yeah. And it looks like he was the perpetrator of this murder/suicide."

"It certainly looks that way" I conceded. "But how can you be sure?"

"We talked to the manager of The Belly Flop, the bar where the deceased woman worked. He confirmed that she'd been dating a guy named Shane."

"That doesn't mean he killed her."

It was a line I'd said a thousand times, but it came up a bit empty this time.

"No offense, Detective Dunn, but it sure seems that way. Shane Doyle was on the other side of the room as the girl and the guy. And he died from a gunshot to the side of the head."

"You're probably right, officer. I'm just saying that things aren't always what they appear to be."

"I get it. And it's a great honor working with you, by the way. I know all about the cases you've worked on. The Phil Spector murder. The Robert Blake murder. OJ."

"And a thousand more murders where the offender wasn't a celebrity," I said.

"Understood, but you don't really hear about cases like that, do you?"

"You're right about that."

Maybe I was making a new friend on the force. He seemed to be a straight shooter. Then again, they all seemed that way at the beginning.

"What's your name, officer?" I asked.

"Michael Towles."

"Good to meet you, Michael. I'm Noble."

We shook hands.

"Yeah, I know," he said.

I excused myself and made my way back to the front door of the apartment. It gave me the best view to take everything in. I started asking myself a few questions.

Had Shane Doyle surprised them? It didn't look that way. He didn't shoot through the door. He was obviously let in and the door remained unlocked.

Why were they standing when he shot them? There was a couch only a few feet away.

Did Shane just come in firing? Doubtful, because Lexi would be by the front door to let him in. So they must have talked for a while. Maybe Lexi walked back to be close to Ben because she was fearful of Shane. Or maybe he brandished the gun and had them stand on the other side of the apartment.

You may wonder why I use their first names. It's something I've done since I became a cop. It helps me to put myself in their mindset. Or, at least I've always felt it does and I'm too old to change now.

Something felt wrong about the room, but I couldn't place exactly why.

Officer Towles came back over to talk. I asked him if I could have a minute.

I looked back down at the three deceased. The M.E. was doing all the work he could before taking them away. You'd never have that time back once the bodies were removed. And as we've all heard a million times, sometimes first impressions are the most important.

That being said, some of the assembled officers would have preferred they took the bodies out a little quicker. The stench was formidable.

Not as bad as some cases I'd worked on. When you find a body after a week or two, it's downright nauseating.

By the looks of the bodies, and when Lexi went missing, this had only been a few days.

I looked out at the room again.

The bodies of Lexi and Ben gave me pause, but I still wasn't sure why.

Finally, something clicked.

The two bodies had fallen to their left sides. Usually - but not always - when you are shot from your right, your body falls to the left. The problem was that Shane's body was on their left. If Shane had shot them from there, Lexi and Ben would have likely fallen to their right. But they hadn't.

Obviously, Shane Doyle could have walked from the front door to his right before committing suicide. He could have been in a stupor and pacing back and forth. Who knew? There were definitely explanations, but it was still an odd crime scene.

I walked to the M.E.

"Can I ask one question?"

"Yes, detective."

Lexi and Ben were laying on their backs, so I could see the entrance wound. What I wanted to know was where the bullets had exited.

"Where are the exit wounds?"

The M.E. didn't flip the bodies over. He just looked at his notes.

His name was Arthur Zhang and we'd worked the same crime scene quite a few times, but we'd never gotten to know each other well. Once he was done with his part of the job, he'd quickly exit stage left. A crime scene wasn't exactly the time to get chummy.

He looked up at me and spoke.

"Both of the deceased were shot two times. All four bullets entered them slightly on the right side of their chests. And all four bullets either exited just to the left of their chest or dead center.

I was right.

The bullets had been shot from their right side. Closer to where the front door was than where Shane shot himself.

This wasn't some "gotcha" moment, but it did give me pause.

The one thing it did prove was that Shane Doyle didn't kill himself immediately after shooting them. If so, we'd have found his body by the front door. Maybe it meant nothing, but these small little finds were what made a good detective.

And despite me getting older, I was still a damn good one.

I left the crime scene a few minutes later.

I didn't tell any of my fellow officers about my discovery. If there was a fair criticism of my detective ways, it's that I wasn't always great about sharing my information with others. It was less being stubborn and more me wanting to make sure I was correct before running my mouth.

I'd never even have gotten this case if it weren't for the murder of Parker Brody.

He was a twenty-eight-year-old actor who had risen to superstardom. He'd been shot and killed outside of his plush, Brentwood mansion. He'd been ambushed in his car.

I wasn't exactly a movie buff, but it was near impossible not to know who Parker Brody was. He was in big superhero films and could be seen, at one time or another, on every billboard in LA.

I remember thinking one day, about three years ago, that Parker Brody was about the silliest, most made-up Hollywood name I'd ever heard. You had the trendy Parker. You had the trendy Brody. And you combined them to get the "perfect" trendy Hollywood name: Parker Brody.

I went on Wikipedia to confirm my suspicions. I was correct. The guy's real name was Nathaniel Cranch. He probably made the right decision. I couldn't see the last name C-R-A-N-C-H up in lights.

He'd been killed three days before I'd been assigned the murder/suicide in Santa Monica. The Hollywood gossip magazines, TMZ, and the national news were going nuts over the murder of Parker Brody.

Why it affected me was that my nemesis, Dax Everton, had been given the title of lead detective on the Parker Brody case. Dax was only a few years older than Parker Brody himself. Dax had arrived on the force at the ripe old age of twenty-two. His father had been a former chief of police in Los Angeles and Dax had basically been groomed to be a police officer since birth.

He was like an athlete whose father played in the big leagues. Great things were expected of him. And he wasn't bad. I'll give him that. He genuinely worked hard and would never give up. He'd turn over the last stone on earth to catch the killer he was after.

The thing was, I was still better. Every detective out of Santa Monica or Brentwood knew that was a fact, but I'd still been passed over. Dax was now the lead detective on the west side of LA. I hate to say it, but nepotism played a big factor.

His father still cast a tremendous shadow over law enforcement in Los Angeles which basically ensured that Dax Everton would rise quickly. And that he did. He became a detective by the time he was twenty-four, which was almost unheard of. At thirty, he was getting as many first-rate cases as I was. And now, at thirty-two, he was undoubtedly the number one guy.

It's why he was given the highest of high-profile Parker Brody case and I was given a murder/suicide that would probably be forgotten in a few days. Of course, when I was called to the scene, no one knew that the probable gunman was a Los Angeles Assistant District Attorney. That all but ensured my case would be getting some media attention as well.

Not Parker Brody level attention, mind you, but there were going to be a few news cameras in my future.

~

Two hours after leaving the crime scene, I was back at the headquarters on Olympic Avenue when my phone rang.

"Dunn speaking," I said.

"Hey, Noble, this is Javier down at evidence."

"How are you, Javier?"

"I'm good. Listen, I heard you were assigned this murder/suicide on 10th and Wilshire."

"I sure was."

"Well, we just came into some information that I'm sure you'd like to know."

"I'll come down and see you."

"I could tell you over the phone."

"I haven't seen you in a while. I'll make a quick road trip out of it."

~

The evidence room was located off our premises.

Smaller police departments have their evidence room where the officers are headquartered. Los Angeles is too big and they have a separate residence for the evidence room. Believe me, in LA, there's a lot of evidence that comes in and out.

Javier Botello was a good guy. I'd worked with him on and off for two decades and he'd always been a straight shooter. He was good at his job as well. Whenever I asked for something, you could be sure Javier got it to me.

He was meandering around when I walked into the evidence room.

"Javi!"

"Noble!"

We gave each other a quick hug.

"So, what the hell did you drag me down here for?"

He laughed.

"Nice try, Noble. I told you we could do this over the phone."

I shrugged.

"Well, I'm here now."

"Come with me."

Instead of leading me downstairs to the actual evidence room, he took me around the corner and into an office.

"Not going downstairs?" I asked.

"No. What I wanted to tell you came from Shane Doyle's cell phone, but it's now part of the evidence."

"What did it say?"

"Most of it was probably what you'd expect. Messages to Lexi Grant, the deceased woman. A lot of '*I want to jump your bones*' texts."

"You wouldn't have called me just for that."

"You're right. He also texted himself immediately after he murdered the other two."

"Oh, shit."

"Yeah, oh shit."

Javier grabbed his cell phone and held it up to me. It was a screenshot of the text that Shane Doyle sent himself.

"To whoever reads this, I'm sorry for what I've just done. Yes, I brought the gun, so it's my fault. I promise you, though, I hadn't intended on killing her. Or him. It was only once I arrived and that asshole said that Lexi was his now. Then I snapped. There's no other way to explain it. Tell my family and friends I love them

and I hope they won't judge me for one horrible decision. Now, I will be joining the other two in death. Goodbye."

I handed Javier the phone back.

Despite my misgivings, it had already been a pretty open-and-shut case. This just sealed it.

Shane Doyle was a disillusioned lover and he took it into his own hands.

Which cost Lexi Grant and Ben Hartley their lives.

I hated to admit it, but I was kind of disappointed. I was hoping this might be one last monster case before they sent me out to pasture.

But it wasn't meant to be.

I was jealous of Dax Everton.

He had a fascinating case with Parker Brody.

I had a case that would be wrapped up in two days.

Fuck me.

CHAPTER 37

ROGER

The murders I'd committed got far less media attention than I was expecting.

There were a few stories on the local LA news once the bodies were discovered. And then I saw a follow-up story once they discovered the purported gunman - Haha! - was an assistant district attorney. Finally, two days after the murders, the *Los Angeles Times* published a four-paragraph story about the murder.

And by day three, that's all I'd seen.

I had two separate incidents to thank for that.

First off, an A-list celebrity by the name of Parker Brody had been killed. I'd actually met him one time. At one of my Malibu parties. Some Instagram model who came to my parties now and then invited him over. Who knew that a few years later, he'd help keep my murders out of the headlines? Thank God for our country's fascination with celebrities.

The second incident was a train derailment in the San Fernando Valley that resulted in six deaths. This was usually the second lead after they spent a good five minutes on Parker Brody. Thank God for our country's crumbling infrastructure.

Things were looking up for yours truly.

The deaths of Knox/Lexi/Shane were a non-story and the rare times they were reported on, they were labeled a murder-suicide. I didn't want to count my chickens just yet, but things sure looked up for me.

Making things even sweeter, I didn't have to sacrifice the two million dollars. I was a free, rich man, who'd gotten away with murder.

Life is grand, ain't it?

CHAPTER 38

NOBLE

On the fourth - and possibly last - day of my investigation into the murder-suicide on 10th street, I got a visit from someone named Braxton Pue. He was a co-worker of Shane Doyle's; a fellow ADA. After calling the Santa Monica Police and asking to talk to the investigating detective on the Shane Doyle murders, they put him in touch with me, and he showed up at my office thirty minutes later.

He was young, probably two decades younger than me, and despite his prematurely gray hair, he was a good-looking guy. I'm sure he was going to go far in the district attorney's office where looks often mattered more than brains or character.

"Follow me," I said.

I led him to the closest interrogation room. Unlike in the movies and on T.V., not every person relegated to the interrogation room is a suspect. We talk to witnesses, friends of the deceased, and oftentimes have to listen to crackpot theories.

We each took a seat in the claustrophobic room, sitting across from each other, a small table in front of us.

"So, what brought you down here today, Mr. Pue?"

"I just wanted to give my two cents on the Shane Doyle murders."

Oh, great. This guy wants to give his two cents. Probably one of those crackpot theorists I despised.

I decided not to jump to conclusions and give him a chance. He was an ADA after all.

"Alright, what have you got?" I asked.

"I think I know why Shane did it."

"Let's hear it."

"First off. I just wanted to say that Shane was a good man and some-times a good ADA."

"Sometimes?"

"He wasn't his best on his latest case."

"Do you know why?"

"That's what I'm getting to," Braxton Pue said.

I'd pre-judged the guy and wasn't giving him room to breathe. I was a better detective than that.

"I apologize. Please continue."

Braxton Pue cleared his throat.

"I talked to Shane a week ago. It was about two weeks after he lost his latest case. I'd sat in on part of the trial and thought he was bad. After much debate, I decided to confront him on it. He told me that a woman had fucked up his brain and that he hadn't been able to concentrate."

"Did he give you the woman's name?"

"No, but it has to be the woman he killed."

"How can you be so sure?"

"Shane wasn't exactly the type to be dating multiple women if you know what I mean."

I did.

He'd all but confirmed that Shane Doyle was fixated on Lexi Grant, which would explain the murders.

"Did you ever meet the girl?"

"No, but I knew something was up. He was making some errors he wouldn't usually make."

"And you called him out?"

"Yeah, that's probably a fair assessment. I told him if he didn't clean up his act and I was going to talk to our superiors."

"And that's when he told you about being hung up on the woman?"

"Yeah."

"Did it ring true?"

"It did. As I said, Shane wasn't some lady killer. And from what I've heard after the fact, this Lexi woman was beautiful."

"I've heard the same," I said.

"He wouldn't be the first guy to lose his mind over a woman."

"No, but it shouldn't end in three deaths."

"Of course," Braxton Pue said. "That's not what I was trying to say. I meant he wouldn't be the first one whose work was affected by a woman."

"You're right about that. Was there anything else you wanted to say?"

"No, that's pretty much it. I'd debated for a few days whether it was even worth coming here. I know it's not much."

"That's not true. It helps us understand his motive."

He shook his head.

"I never would have expected it from Shane."

"That's what family and friends always say."

"Yeah, I guess."

"Trust me, I've been through hundreds of these. It's extremely rare where someone tells me they actually saw it coming," I said.

"Sure. If anyone would know, it's a detective like yourself."

It sounded like a compliment by the words he used, but it still felt like he was skeptical.

"Yes, I would know," I said.

He gave me an acerbic little grin.

⌐

As I led Mr. Pue out the door a few minutes later, our police captain, Captain Brendan Glanville turned the corner. Brendan had long considered himself quite the amateur chef and once the police force got wind of that, his nickname was inevitable: Captain Cook.

He could be a tough boss but had a good sense of humor about his nickname.

Captain Cook had a red beard and we all thought he looked like a middle-aged leprechaun. That was something we wouldn't bother telling him. He was a few years older than me and had been my boss for over twenty years. We both butted heads and had great respect for each other.

"Noble!" he yelled. "Who was that?"

"Hey, Captain Cook. He was a co-worker of Shane Doyle's."

"What did he have to say?"

"He said that Shane's head wasn't exactly right, due to Lexi."

"Just as I told you yesterday. An open and shut case."

"You're probably right," I said, my words just hovering there in the air.

"Explain yourself," Captain Cook said. "Don't just throw probably out there all nonchalantly."

There were a few other police officers and detectives mingling around the office, but no one was listening in on our conversation. I was fine with that. I didn't want people to think I was throwing crackpot theories out there. The very same ones that I so despised.

"There's one thing that's been bothering me."

"Spit it out, Noble."

"The location where Lexi and Knox were shot."

"Let me stop you right there. Who is Knox?"

"I found out over the last few days that Ben was called Knox by everyone who knew him."

"Okay. Continue."

"They were shot by someone standing near the front door of the apartment. And yet, Shane Doyle's body was found at the far right of the front entrance, probably eight to ten feet from the door."

"So…"

"So, after you murdered two people, wouldn't you just kill yourself right there, by the door? Why walk ten feet to your right and then off yourself?"

"Really? That's your big mic drop moment? Maybe he wanted to admire his murders. Maybe he wanted a few more minutes on earth. How the hell am I supposed to know why he walked ten feet away? And by the way, it's not like he was Cain from Kung Fu, walking to the ends of the earth. He walked ten fucking feet."

Captain Cook frequently had a temper and this was one of those times.

"I'm not saying this isn't the murder-suicide it looks like. I'm just not ready to wrap it up just yet."

"How long do you need?"

"Give me two more days."

"I shouldn't even give you that, but I will. All your fellow detectives think this is an open and shut case. So does the ME. And so do fucking I."

I felt no need to razz him up anymore. I should be happy he gave me more time.

"Thanks for the two days, Captain."

"Finish this up so you can join in on that Parker Brody mess."

Even if I was assigned to that case, I'd be the sixth or seventh lead on it and they'd already had a huge headstart. It was Dax Everton's case. I knew that. Captain Cook knew that. And most of all, Dax himself knew that.

"I'll update you in forty-eight hours, Captain."

"You'll be putting this baby to bed. That's the only update I'll need."

With that, he walked away.

∽

With less than two days to find anything to support my theory, I had to use my time wisely.

The first thing I did was head to Knox Hartley's apartment complex. He was no longer Ben to me. It went back to the whole *'thinking of them by their first names.'* And if people called him Knox, I was going to think of him as Knox.

Knox's apartment complex, Chateau Barry, was on Barry Street in the Brentwood section of Los Angeles. Calling it a Chateau was like calling a fat guy, Slim. The word Chateau gave off this French aristocracy vibe, rich people living in some castle outside of Paris. Chateau Barry was the polar opposite. If it was a bar, it would have been a dive bar with peanuts on the ground and a smell emanating from the bathroom. Chateau was about the last word you'd think of when you saw this dump.

I knew that Knox had lived in apartment #6 so I found the closest neighbor and knocked on their door. It was answered by a woman in her seventies with grayish-white hair. She had an oxygen tank by her side. I felt sad for an old woman in her shape having to spend her final years in a dump like Chateau Barry. I figure this conversation was unlikely to get me anything in the way of new evidence. Shit, maybe I was just an ageist.

"Hello," she said.

As a detective, I usually didn't wear my police uniform. Today was no different. I took out my badge and showed it to her.

"I'm with the police, Ma'am."

"What happened? Is it one of my grandchildren?"

My heart sank, feeling terrible for this old lady.

"No, nothing like that. I'm here about your next-door neighbor, Knox."

"Oh, thank God you're only here about him and not one of my relatives."

It was obvious that this old lady didn't think much of him.

"So you heard what happened to Knox?"

"I sure did. All of Chateau Barry knows."

"What did you think of him personally?"

"I didn't like him. Not one bit."

She took a deep breath and pressed a button on her oxygen tank.

"Why is that?"

"He was a hustler. A dirt ball. A slime."

"In what way?"

"In all ways. I don't think he ever had a real job. Always out there up to no good."

Her oxygen tank was a bit misleading. She was quick. At least, her mind was.

"How long had he been your neighbor?"

"Probably six months. I heard he moved from The Premier. Wish he'd stayed there."

I had no idea what The Premier was. Probably another shitty apartment complex in LA where people spent way too much of their hard-earned money on rent.

"Did he do anything to you personally?"

"He'd keep me up at all times with whatever lady friend he had that night."

"And that was pretty often?"

"Too often if you ask me. If I was going to give the guy one compliment, it's that he had an active sex life."

She took another deep breath. I didn't want to keep her much longer.

I grabbed a picture of Lexi from my pocket. I'd brought a picture of her, Knox, and Shane for instances just like this.

"Did you ever see Knox with this woman?"

She brought the picture to within an inch of her face.

"I'm not sure. There were so many, it's hard to know."

"I understand," I said.

I decided to take a shot in the dark, bringing out the picture of Shane.

"How about with this guy? Ever see him and Knox hanging out?"

She eyed it closely again.

"I don't think so. Never saw him hang out with guys."

I was about to bid adieu when she said something interesting.

"Come to think of it, there was a guy here late at night a few days before he died."

"How did you know it was a guy? Did you see him?"

"No, but there was a heavy knock on his door. Surely not from a woman."

"Did you hear a voice?"

"I think I heard a man's voice, but it was mainly the knock that told me it was a man."

"And how many days exactly was this before Knox was killed?"

"I'm not sure. As you can see, I'm an old lady. I'd say maybe four or five days. I can't be sure, though."

"I understand. You've been very helpful."

"I thought he was killed by a jealous lover of a girl he was with. Why are you still investigating?"

"Just tying up loose ends, Ma'am."

She gave me a quizzical look as I turned to go.

I headed from Chateau Barry down to the Santa Monica Courthouse.

Defense attorneys and the police have a very combative relationship for obvious reasons. They were trying to prove we lied or made mistakes during the course of our investigation. ADAs were different though. They put us on the stand to help support their cases. When I went to reach out to Shane's fellow ADAs, I figured they'd be helpful.

The first ADA I ran into at the Courthouse was Geoff Bonder. He was in his mid-fifties and one of the older ADAs. He had gray, slicked-back hair and thought he was either Pat Riley or Gordon Gecko. I'd testified in two of his cases and I'm pretty sure he'd won both of them. He seemed happy to see me. Probably because we were two old guys in young men's games.

"Detective Dunn," he said.

It was weird to be called by my last name. With a memorable first name like Noble, people usually call you by that.

"How are you, Mr. Bonder?" I asked.

"I've been well. Busy trying to put each and every last one of these criminals away."

He said it with a smile, but it came off as pretty vindictive.

"I had a few questions about Shane Doyle."

"Such a sad story. What did you want to know?"

"Were you friends with him?"

"We were friendly like I am with most of the other ADAs. I wouldn't quite call him a friend, though."

"What was he like in person?"

"He was a nice guy."

"Can you give me anything more than that?"

"I mean, I don't want to piss on the guy's grave."

That got my attention.

"This stays between you and me. What was he up to?"

"I don't know. He just kind of seemed disheveled these last several months. I know his wife was divorcing him. There were a few rumors that he liked to gamble."

My mind was rarely a calm one. This was no different. My thoughts immediately went to the idea that bookies could have killed Shane. But why would they kill two innocent people? How would they make it look like a suicide? And how or why would they follow him to Lexi's apartment? It didn't make any sense, but that doesn't mean I was ruling it out.

"Like betting $50 on an NFL game?" I asked, knowing that wasn't what he meant.

"A lot more than that."

"Was it affecting his work?"

"I don't know. I know he lost his last case."

Just like Braxton Pue had told me. Or had he? Maybe I'd just assumed he lost since Pue told me how bad he was.

"But hey," Bonder continued. "We can't win them all, right?"

I smiled.

"I seem to remember you went undefeated with me on the stand."

"That's right. Good memory, Detective Dunn."

"Anything else you can tell me about Shane?"

"Not really. I never met the girl he killed and was supposedly hung up on."

It was then that Bonder looked me straight in the face.

"Are you thinking there's more here to this? What's with all the questions?"

"You know how it is. I have to tie up all the loose ends before reporting back to my Captain."

"Good old Captain Cook."

"You know him?"

"I've been around the block a few times. We've run into each other over the years."

"Then you realize why I have to be thorough."

Geoff Bonder laughed.

"I do."

"I've got one last question," I said. "Was Shane Doyle a Romeo?"

"As in, got a lot of girls?"

I didn't know of any other meaning, but there was no reason to bring that up.

"Yeah."

"I mean, the guy was just going through a divorce."

"I know. You can still get a vibe from people, though. Was he good at talking with the ladies?"

"I'll put it this way. I wouldn't have been scared to leave Shane with my wife."

That was a no.

"Point taken," I said.

"Is there anything else?" Bonder asked. I could tell he was starting to get a little uncomfortable with our conversation.

"Not for now. Can I call you if I think of anything else?"

"Yeah, okay. Have a nice day, detective."

"You too, counselor."

It wasn't even noon and I'd knocked out an interview with Braxton Pue, dealt with Captain Cook, talked to Knox's neighbor, and got in a few words with Geoff Bonder.

It had been a pretty productive morning. My uneasiness over the murder hadn't subsided. Geoff Bonder's comments made sure of that. Even the conversation with the old woman had given me pause. If Knox was such a hustler, who's to say he wasn't mixed up in something?

I felt my mind begin to race again.

What if Shane was the innocent bystander? What if this was all a ploy to kill Knox? Then why would they show up at Lexi's apartment? And how would Shane let them get so close to shoot him at point-blank range in the head?

That whole scenario seemed unlikely as well.

The other piece that didn't fit was why Lexi Grant would date Shane Doyle. Sure, he had a solid job and wasn't bad looking from the pictures I'd seen, but there had now been two people telling me that he was hardly Don Juan. And from what I'd heard of Lexi, she was a knockout.

I'd talked to Lexi's neighbors about the night of the murders but they hadn't seen anything. Now I wanted to talk to them for a different reason. I wanted to know about her dating/sex life.

Why was she dating Shane Doyle?

I left the courthouse with plans to return to the crime scene where three young people had lost their lives. I was all over West Los Angeles this morning.

If I was being honest with myself, the most likely scenario was still a murder/suicide perpetrated by Shane Doyle. I had the better part of two days, though. And I was fascinated by what I still had to learn.

~

I'd returned to hundreds of crime scenes over the years. It was never easy. The prevailing feeling is the sadness that people's lives had ended needlessly. Crime scenes weren't a hospital. No relatives were saying goodbye. No priests were there to give last rites.

And it was always tougher when there were multiple people killed. I'd once been to the site of a school shooting where eleven teenagers were killed. Nothing will ever top that for sheer melancholia. I wanted to do something - anything - but it was too late.

So while not on that level, Knox/Lexi/Shane's deaths were bothering me quite a bit. The fact that I wasn't convinced it was a murder/suicide only exacerbated that feeling.

I parked my car outside of Lexi's apartment and knocked on the door of her neighbor to the left. After no answer for two minutes, I walked down to the apartment on the right.

A man in his twenties answered. I was happy to see he was young, thinking it more likely he'd notice the comings and goings of a pretty woman if he was twenty-five and not seventy-five.

"Can I help you?"

"I'm Detective Dunn and I'm here for a few follow-up questions about what happened next door."

His body told me he didn't want to do this, but his lips said, "Okay."

"What's your name?"

"Drew."

"Had you ever seen either of the men who died last Thursday?"

"No. Never."

"Had you ever seen Lexi with any man?"

"Come to think of it, no. She only moved in a few months ago though. My neighbor told me that the guy Shane came by once or twice, but I never saw him."

"Did you ever converse with Lexi?"

A slight blush appeared.

"A few times."

He had a crush on Lexi. I could tell that quickly. I'd become a good judge of character after almost three decades on the force. The truth was I'd always had a keen eye for human nature, dating back to when I was a kid, but being a police officer had certainly honed that.

"How did those go, Drew?" I asked.

"We were cordial. I never really got to know her well though. She was usually a little brief in our conversations."

The guy in front of me was a handsome guy in his mid-twenties and he'd had no chance with Lexi. Why/How had she fallen for Shane?

"I heard she was quite beautiful."

"Yeah, but it was more than that."

"In what way?"

"She was just so sexy. The way she walked. The way she talked. She was the complete package."

In my earlier days, I might have suspected the young man in front of me of having murdered her. Drew's was more like a high school crush, however. I could tell he was genuinely sad that she was gone. Probably liked living next to a hottie. His imagination would run wild with the notion that Lexi might fall for him.

"A girl that beautiful, and no guys on her arm. Kind of surprising."

"As I said, apparently that guy Shane came by. I'm just saying I never saw her with a guy."

Something clicked. If - and this was still a big if - Lexi wasn't dating Shane with honest intentions, then it would make sense that someone like Know would come over late at night. And Drew never would have seen him.

Even if this was true, and I was starting to suspect it might be, it still helped point the finger back at Shane. If he was dating Lexi - legit or not - and found out this guy Knox was coming over after dark, he'd be furious. And if he was spying on Lexi and saw Knox walk in one night, you could see how things could go sideways.

Especially if he'd brought a gun with him. Unfortunately, the murder weapon had been a dead end. The serial number had been filed off and anyone could have bought it from the streets.

Even if I jumped to the conclusion that Shane became jealous, there was still the big unanswered question: Why was Lexi dating Shane to begin with? And if it was for unscrupulous reasons, what were they?

"Maybe other men came later at night," I finally said.

"Yeah, that's possible, I guess. I mean, all these apartments are pretty far away. You can't hear much."

If you had to kill three people, it would be a good spot.

Part of being a cop was throwing everything at the ceiling and seeing what might stick. That's the mode I was in. I'm not even sure if I believed any of it.

"Is there anything else you can add that might be useful?"

Drew thought hard about it.

"I don't think so. I'm sorry. I'm just sad she's dead. Those guys too. I'm probably going to move out. Who wants to live next to a murder/suicide?"

I held my tongue. Drew hadn't asked why I was still investigating the case. No reason to bring up my doubts about it being a murder/suicide.

"I understand. That's a tough situation."

I'd seen it way too many times in my career.

"Are we done?" he asked.

"Yeah. Thanks for your help."

He walked back inside his apartment and shut the door behind him.

∼

It was now past noon and I had to get some food.

I was ready to hit one of my regular food spots around Santa Monica: O'Briens on Wilshire. Thunderbirds. The Brig.

But then I figured I could kill two birds with one stone.

I'd grab lunch at the bar where Lexi Grant used to work. The Belly Flop. I'd been by there once or twice. Their previous owner, a man named Barry Gant, was killed in a high-profile case in 2019. Sadly, it was my first extended vacation since joining the force and I was in Europe while it all went down.

That says all you need to know about me. I was lying on the beaches in Italy and having baguettes in France, but I still regretted not being in Los Angeles to help solve a murder.

I admonished myself. My beautiful wife was still alive at that point and we had a fantastic trip to Europe. I wouldn't change it for the world. Even if my thoughts still wandered back to my job in LA while we were there.

I love and miss you, Sherry.

Fuck cancer.

∼

I headed over to The Belly Flop and took a seat at the bar. This was a fact-finding mission so no reason to sit at some booth and talk to a bored waitress once every ten minutes.

I wanted to get this information from the horse's mouth. And Lexi was a bartender so I'd sit at the bar.

"What can I get you, sir?"

The bartender, a man with a serious five o'clock shadow and a hungover face, asked me. Sure, I was now in my early fifties, but I'm not sure I was ever going to get over being called sir. I still imagined myself as that vibrant guy in his twenties. I'm sure that's true of a great many people as they age.

Technically, I was on the clock, but I didn't think one beer was going to kill me. And I wouldn't look like some schlub drinking tonic water.

"I'll take a Sierra Nevada on tap if you've got it," I said.

The bartender made an ugly face.

"Don't have it on tap?" I asked.

"No, just thinking back to last night. I started with a few Sierras before it turned into shots every twenty minutes."

"Been there, done that," I said, even though I'd never been the biggest drinker. I was more of a few glasses of wine at home kind of guy. Being hungover as a detective wasn't advisable. That doesn't mean it had never happened. I'd certainly been through the wringer a time or two.

The bartender smiled. He must have liked my comment.

"Pint of Sierra coming right up."

Once he set the pint down, he asked, "So what brings you to The Belly Flop today?"

He was one of the talkative hungover types. Usually, they are either very quiet or overly talkative. There doesn't seem to be much middle ground.

"It's funny you should ask," I said.

"Oh no, this doesn't sound good."

"I'm actually an LAPD detective."

The bartender raised his arms.

"I didn't do it," he said.

This guy was a character. I gave him a courtesy smile.

"Actually, I had a few questions about your co-worker, Lexi."

His body sagged.

"Oh yeah, that. I've been trying not to think about it for the last several days."

"I'm sorry for your loss," I said. "Were you guys close?"

I did a cursory look around the bar. There were only two other people sitting at the bar and they both seemed to be in their own world.

"No, we weren't exactly close, but we were co-workers. Isn't that enough to make you feel sad?"

"Of course. How long had you worked with her?"

"I've been here a year, but Lexi only got here like three months ago. She just came in like a bat out of hell."

"What do you mean by that?"

He paused. One of the waitresses came over and put in an order. A minute later he was back.

"I used that phrase because she was like a tornado. Hot, sexy, hard-headed. Words like that. And then, a few months later she's dead."

"You almost sound like you're not surprised."

"I think you're always surprised if someone young dies. She did seem like a girl who couldn't just be mellow though. Do you know what I mean?"

He could have phrased it better, but I knew what he meant.

"She was a wild card?"

"Yeah, pretty much."

I decided on a shot in the dark.

"Did you ever meet Shane Doyle?"

"I did. I was working with Lexi the first time she brought him in. May have been the only time, actually. He seemed so mellow. Who would have thought he was a killer?"

As I'd done earlier with Drew, I held my tongue.

"Did they seem like a happy couple?"

"I'm not sure I'd go that far. He was like a kid in a candy store. Her, I'm not so sure. I remember him looking around the bar, almost like hoping that people would see that he and this hot bartender were together."

"Did Lexi come out and say they were?"

"No, but it was obvious from the moment he walked in that something was going on."

"Did they kiss when he walked in?"

I was trying to establish whether Lexi wanted people to know that they were a couple.

"I think they did. I don't know, I might have been doing stuff when he walked in."

"How long did he stay?"

"I think for only one drink."

I took a sip of my Sierra Nevada, having forgotten it was right there in front of me.

"Now, don't let this lead to shots and get all drunk like I did," the bartender said and laughed.

He was hard not to like, having a self-effacing nature.

"I'll try not to," I said.

Next, he asked the question that Drew never did.

"Why are you still investigating this if everyone knows the guy Shane did it?"

Usually, this is when I'd say we're just tying up loose ends, but I decided to play it differently, hoping he might open up.

"I've got my doubts that's exactly what happened."

"Wow," he said too loudly.

The two other patrons looked in our direction. This hadn't been my plan.

"What's your name?" I asked.

"Buddy."

"That info was just between us, Buddy. I don't want the word getting out that Shane may not have done it."

"Then why tell me that?"

"Because I was hoping you might have some information that might help support my hypothesis."

Buddy scratched his neck.

"Now I want a drink."

I didn't respond, allowing him to think about it.

"What am I supposed to know about what happened?"

"Do you think Lexi was in love with Shane?"

"How the hell do I know?"

He was getting a little flustered so I had to calm him down.

"This is just a casual conversation between two Sierra Nevada drinking guys. Lexi and Shane just seemed like an odd match. That's why I'm asking you, Buddy."

I was trying to use his first name a lot to build up a camaraderie. It was an old trick that everyone used, but I still felt it could be beneficial.

"Asking me what exactly?"

"In the short time you saw them together, did it seem like a loving relationship?"

"No," he said. "I guess not. It felt more like the guy Shane was in lust with Lexi."

That's what I'd been shooting for.

"Is there any reason you can think of as to why Lexi would have dated him?"

"I heard after the killings that he was a lawyer, so maybe that."

I didn't think so.

"Was Lexi a trustworthy person?"

I was now firing questions in rapid succession. Give him less time to opt out.

"She never stole from the till if that's what you mean."

"No, that's not what I mean."

"Yeah, I didn't think so. I don't know. I probably wouldn't have wanted to go into business with her."

"A bit devious?"

"Yeah, I think that's probably fair. I just felt like she always had the next thing on her mind. Like working here was just a means to an end."

I liked what he was saying. But a means to what end?

"Thanks for all of this, Buddy."

I took another sip of my beer. He was looking a bit nervous.

"Am I supposed to ask you for your badge or something?"

I took it out and subtly showed it to him, hoping the other customers didn't see it.

"I'm the real deal, I promise," I said.

"Ok, good. I was scared there for a second."

"Don't be."

I figured I'd gotten all the information I could have out of Buddy.

I took out a ten-dollar bill and laid it on the bar.

"You want another drink?"

"No, that's for you. Thanks for talking to me."

"You're not going to finish your Sierra Nevada?" Buddy asked.

"No, I'm afraid that would lead me to having shots."

He laughed quite loudly. Buddy didn't seem like the type who would stay nervous for long.

"You're funny."

"Have a nice day," I said and walked out of the bar.

As I drove back to police headquarters, the same question kept going through my mind.

Why would Lexi Grant date Shane Doyle?

It certainly wasn't his money. I'd received the financials on all three of the deceased's checking accounts. None of them were rich. Knox had $9,000 in his checking account. Lexi had $14,000. And Shane, the leader in the clubhouse, only had $21,000. You'd think an ADA in his mid-thirties would have accumulated more wealth than that. Maybe that gambling problem that Geoff Bonder alluded to had taken a chunk of change.

So if it wasn't for his money, there was only one other reason that I could think of: The fact that Shane Doyle was an ADA.

I knew what I had to do. Take a deep dive into Shane Doyle's recent cases.

One thing was for certain.

Captain Cook was going to be livid.

CHAPTER 39

ROGER

Five days after the murders, I'd started to relax. There hadn't been any articles in a few days nor had I seen a TV segment dedicated to it.

I'd even considered returning to my former life of crime. I mean my drug dealing days. I guess a triple murder would be considered a crime as well. Hahaha.

And there was a fourth if you counted Billy Aybar.

But I smartly decided against it. I didn't need the money that drug dealing gave me. Then again, I hadn't needed the money for years. Once I bought The Premier and The Red Carpet, I was set for life. At that point, it wasn't about the money. It was about the thrill. About getting one over on the police. About living life on the edge.

As they say in the movie *Heat*, "The action is the juice."

Which is a movie about Los Angeles criminals.

Seems apropos.

～

I visited a few rub and tug "massage" places in the first few weeks out, but it wasn't doing the trick.

I'd decided to get back to having my parties in Malibu. Like the good old days. I'd been acquitted. I was a free man. No need to sit in the corner and cower.

Shit, I'd probably get even more hot women to come over, now that I was a celebrity and all.

That idea was put to a halt one morning.

As had become customary, I went down to my local store and picked up the *Los Angeles Times*. As I flipped through the pages, assuming the murders were no longer part of the public consciousness, I came across a headline that shocked me.

"ADA murder/suicide not what it seems?"
by Paul Manger

The recent murder/suicide that was allegedly carried out by Los Angeles Assistant District Attorney Shane Doyle may not be an open and shut case after all. The well-known LAPD detective Noble Dunn is continuing to investigate the case.

I've talked to a neighbor of Lexi Grant's, where the murders occurred. I also interviewed a bartender at The Belly Flop, where Ms. Grant used to work.

Both men said it didn't sound like Noble Dunn was convinced Mr. Doyle had carried out the murders. They said he continually asked them about Ms. Grant's and Mr. Doyle's relationship, almost as if he didn't believe it was legitimate. This is a developing story and if you have any information about the murders, please contact me.

Editor's Note: This article went to print before we had time to reach out to the LAPD for their reaction.

"FUCK!!" I screamed.

If I was living at one of my garbage apartment complexes, I'd have woken up everyone in the building. In Malibu - where the rich people lived - neighbors were a good distance away.

I recognized the name, Noble Dunn.

I googled him.

Oh yeah, that fucking black cop who was all the rage back in the day. Fuck that old man. He had no chance of keeping up with me even if we were around the same age.

A few minutes later, my mind opened up to a new interpretation of this news.

Maybe this wasn't the worst thing.

After all, I was the guy who liked action.

What could be more fun than a formerly famous LA detective trying to chase you? A washed-up has-been detective on his first big case in years. And me, lying in wait.

This could be fun.

Detective Noble Dunn vs. the criminal mastermind, Roger Theus.

Noble vs. Evil.

This was perfect.

One thing's for sure: If he decided to come after me, it would be the biggest regret of his life.

Bring it on!

CHAPTER 40

NOBLE

I found out about the article in the *LA Times* the morning it was released. I got three texts, two emails, and one phone call. The call was from Captain Cook whom I'd planned on going to see anyway. I told him I'd meet him at his office.

We weren't going to get off on the right foot, that's for sure.

"What the fuck, Noble?" he said as I walked into his office.

"I had no idea, Captain."

"This is the last thing we want. We've got enough damn attention with the Hollywood actor getting whacked."

"Whacked? What is this, a mob movie?"

"Slow your roll, Noble. Remember who your boss is."

I held my tongue, something my younger self never would have done.

"I don't know how the story got leaked. I talked to Lexi's neighbor, her co-worker, and a few of Shane Doyle's fellow ADAs. One of them must have reached out to the *LA Times*."

"I don't care how it happened. I care that it did happen. We don't need this right now."

"What if I told you the *Times* is right?"

"What do you mean?"

"I have serious doubts that Shane Doyle carried out these murders."

"We're doing the whole 'He was found ten feet away from where he shot them' thing again?"

"There's more."

"More is good."

"I don't think Lexi Grant was dating Shane Doyle out of love."

"Okay. Say I concede that's true. Then that's all the more reason Shane would kill them when he found out."

I was tired of hearing that comeback. Probably because it did ring true.

"There's something more here, Captain."

I tried to avoid adding 'Cook' when we were having a serious conversation.

"Do you have any proof of that?"

"I'd like to ask a favor," I said.

He shook his head, more in exasperation than contempt. Deep down, I know he respected my skills as a detective.

"What do you want, Noble?"

"I want to do a deep dive on Shane Doyle's last several cases."

"What the hell?"

"If my theory is right, there's only one reason Lexi would want to date Shane."

"You know, I've always hated how you use the first names of the deceased. You never knew these people."

"But it helps me feel like I did."

He shook his head again.

"What exactly do you want? You can't read Doyle's notes. Attorney/client privilege and all that."

"I'll read the courtroom minutes. And I'm sure there are a few summations I could get my hands on."

I could tell he was considering it. He just needed a push in the right direction.

"You've always hated ADAs, Captain," I continued. "You think they fuck up our cases after we make solid arrests based on well-founded evidence. What if I was able to find out that something stinky was going on in the DA's office? Wouldn't you just love that?"

Captain Cook actually smiled.

"You always knew how to schmooze me, Noble."

"Is that a yes?"

"How long do you need?"

"Just a few more days."

"I'm pretty sure that's what you asked for last time."

I could tell he was about to cave so I stayed silent.

"But I guess two or three more days isn't the end of the world. You've got your wish."

"Thank you, Captain," I said.

"One thing. If there really is something going on in the DA's office, don't let anyone down there know that's what you're investigating. They'll shut ranks on you and you'll get a bunch of '*no comments.*'"

"I'll be subtle."

Captain Cook smiled.

"You might just be able to pull that off. The thirty-year-old you wouldn't have known what that word meant."

I smiled, knowing he was correct.

"Ain't that the truth," I said.

"Report only to me."

"Got it. Thanks for this, Captain."

"Good luck, Noble."

By day's end, I'd accumulated case files on Shane Doyle's last six trials, which took us back twelve months. Was it possible this dated to a case further back? I guess, but one year was a good start. He'd surely settled a case or two in the meantime, but I wasn't privy to the settlements. I'd concentrate on the cases that went to trial.

I lived in Santa Monica, about twenty-five blocks from the beach. The closer you were to the beach, the more expensive the rent or mortgage was. I'd been smart and bought a house twenty years ago. It was a small two-bedroom home that wasn't going to be featured in any magazine, but it had been perfect for me, Sherry, and Sherin.

Sherin was our only child. She was kind of a miracle baby because, after the fact, the doctors told us Sherry would never be able to give birth again. We didn't care. We were just so happy we had Sherin. It was pronounced Sha-rin, with a soft A. Too many people tried to vocalize it like her mother's name. We wanted the names close, not identical.

Sadly - no, horrifically - the same stomach that gave birth to Sherry's greatest joy later would prove to be her demise.

We'd had Sherin in our early twenties and when Sherry was diagnosed with stomach cancer, Sherin was in college. She was a senior at UCSD and she'd drive back from San Diego to Santa Monica every weekend.

As my wife got sicker and sicker, Sherin would drive back every few days. Finally, near the end, she dropped out of school for the quarter and came back home. She was by her mother's side for the last several weeks of her life. Obviously, it was a horrible time for our family, but Sherin and I grew closer than ever.

Sherry finally lost her battle with stomach cancer nine years ago. I still think about her several times a day. I haven't ruled it out, but I've never remarried or even seriously dated. She was my one.

Sherin was now a pediatrician in San Diego. She was married with a young daughter. And yes, I've heard a few 'Grandpa Nobles' around the office.

I remain very close to my daughter.

After Sherry died, could I have sold the house and downgraded to a townhouse or an apartment? Of course, but I couldn't let go of all of our family's memories here. If you put my hand on a stack of bibles, I'd swear that Sherry's smell still permeated the house.

I sat on my couch and poured myself a glass of red wine, trying to focus on the case and not Sherry. That wasn't easy to do.

I told myself I'd limit myself to two glasses of wine. After that, my mental acuity took a slight dip. This case was important and I knew better.

I quickly separated the information on each trial.

The six cases - starting with the most recent - went as follows:

Defendant: Roger Theus. Charged with murder. Acquitted.
Defendant: Carl Hillerman. Charged with DUI. Convicted.
Defendant: Henry Miles. Charged with Assault. Convicted.
Defendant: Andy Redding. Charged with Spousal Abuse. Convicted.
Defendant: Van Atwater. Charged with Fraud. Acquitted.

～

I read a brief synopsis of each case. My initial thought was that the three cases in which Shane earned a conviction were the cases to take a deep dive into. After all, if a person was acquitted of a crime, why would they come after Shane? If they were convicted, however, there would be a motive. Sure, the defendant was likely still in jail, but there'd been hitmen hired by inmates.

So I grabbed the file on Carl Hillerman, the most recent case in which Shane earned a conviction. It was only a DUI, but I still felt every case deserved my full attention. I didn't want to overlook anything.

After reading for a minute, something in the back of my mind told me to set the file down.

I was thinking about this the wrong way.

If Lexi seduced Shane, it wouldn't be to earn a conviction. What would be the point of that?

Now that we've had sex, you are going to do the best you can to prosecute this guy! Yea! Go, Shane!

No, that seemed pointless.

Now, trying to get Shane to throw a case? To be off his game in order to earn an acquittal? That seemed a lot more plausible.

So I set aside the file on Carl Hillman and grabbed the one for Roger Theus.

And then started reading.

Two hours later, it was nine p.m. and I was exhausted.

But I couldn't stop reading. I was also enthralled.

Shane had made a few monumental mistakes. The kind a first-year law student wouldn't make.

He put a guy on the stand who said that he was 97% certain that Roger Theus had left the apartment of the man whom he was accused of killing. No, I wasn't a lawyer, but I knew what the hell *'beyond a reasonable doubt'* meant and no lawyer worth his salt would put on a witness who would testify to 97%.

I wrote down the name of the defendant: Alfonso Reyes.

There were other examples of things that Shane missed.

Obvious follow-up questions. Clear chances to object. Very average opening and closing statements.

These were almost forgivable. If he was truly wrapped around the finger of Lexi - as Braxton Pue had alleged - you can understand making a few minor mistakes. What there was no excuse for was the interrogation of Alfonso Reyes. That was unforgivable.

Something was amiss. I felt it now more than ever.

I needed to meet up with Alfonso Reyes and get to the bottom of this.

CHAPTER 41

ALFONSO

I'd felt guilty during the weeks following my testimony.

Not only had I lied on the stand, I'd sold out my fellow Hispanic man. Roger Theus had killed Billy Aybar. And I'd sold out Billy for some murdering gringo. I disgusted myself.

Not that it was my idea. It was that asshole district attorney, Shane Doyle. He probably thought I was some dumb Mexican-American that he could lead along, but he was mistaken. I knew exactly what he was doing.

I shouldn't have played along - I know that now - but I didn't want to start up a fight with an ADA. He had more power than I'd ever have. I feared he might tell the police to start fucking with me. So I stayed quiet.

A few weeks after the trial ended with Theus getting acquitted, I started considering going to another ADA and telling him my story. Maybe even the police. I'd tell them that Shane Doyle had basically told me to say I was 97% sure it was Roger Theus. That he had made sure I perjured myself.

Yes, I'd gone along with it, but it was at the suggestion of Shane Doyle.

Maybe I could get him disbarred. I'd have to prove that he'd told me to say 97% which wasn't going to be tough. They were likely to believe his word over mine and he'd surely say that when I said 97% on the stand, he was as surprised as anyone.

I flip-flopped for a few days, not sure whether I should go to the authorities. I was leaning towards it until I realized that I might well be charged with perjury.

My mind had settled on telling someone when I saw the staggering news that Shane Doyle had committed two murders and then turned the gun on himself.

I was immediately suspicious. It seemed too much of a coincidence, especially after what he had me do.

I wasn't going to the cops or the courthouse anymore, though. That was for sure. Whoever these people were, if my suspicions were correct, they'd killed an assistant district attorney. What chance would I have? Zero.

So I decided to say nothing and keep on living.

And that's when I received a phone call from that detective.

"Hello?"

"Is this Alfonso Reyes?"

"Yes, it is."

"My name is Detective Noble Dunn and I'm a detective with the LAPD."

I knew this was pertaining to Shane Doyle's death. It had to be. I was a law-abiding citizen and there was no other reason a detective would be calling me.

"How can I help you?"

"You testified at the Roger Theus trial, didn't you?"

The detective sounded black. Good. I was sick of gringos.

"Yeah, I did."

"I was wondering if you'd be willing to come down to police head-quarters?"

"When?"

It was a Monday morning at eight a.m. and I had to leave for work in thirty minutes. I worked as a construction worker and this was a pretty busy week. We were helping pour the cement on a new apartment building going up in downtown LA. It was tough work and this week was no different.

Usually, I'd be at work at five a.m for this type of job, but they had different waves of workers for this gig. And my shift started at nine.

"You work as a construction worker, correct?"

He'd done his homework.

"Yeah."

"Are you working all week?"

"I am. And I have my kids tonight."

"How about tomorrow night, after work? I wouldn't ask for this if it wasn't important."

"We can't do this over the phone?" I asked.

"I'd rather make this official and have you come down to the station. Don't worry, you've done nothing wrong."

I wish that were true.

"Where are you located?" I asked.

"In Santa Monica."

Great. I get off work around five and the drive from downtown to Santa Monica at that time is brutal. Then again, what choice did I have?

"Yeah, I guess I could come after work tomorrow."

"Thank you, Mr. Reyes. Again, I wouldn't ask you to do this if it wasn't important."

I wanted to stay mad, but the truth was, I was starting to get interested.

What was he going to tell me about Shane Doyle? That he threw a case? That he was murdered?

Suddenly, I was almost looking forward to the meeting.

~

Work that day was exhausting.

It's like my meeting the following day hung over everything. That's not to say I regretted agreeing to meet him. I was still eager to hear what the detective had to say. And yet, I felt like I already knew. I'd known from the start. Shane Doyle was shady as hell and it had gotten him killed. Murder/suicide my ass.

I picked up my two kids - Sadie and Alfonso, Jr. - at my ex-wife's. Her name was Isabella and we'd been divorced for six years.

I took the kids to Olive Garden for dinner. Don't blame me. At eleven and nine years old, my children's food palettes weren't fully formed and they loved snacking on breadsticks. Whenever they were asked where they wanted to eat, it was always the same answer. So Olive Garden it was.

I took them to a local batting cage next. You'd have thought that my son would have been the one who loved it, but it was more my daughter. She had no fear. She asked for the batting cages to give her the fastest pitches they had. For her age group, that was fifty miles an hour. She'd have to wait for sixty, seventy, and eighty. Still, I had mad respect for my eleven-year-old daughter trying to hit a ball going that fast. I'm not sure I'd have been much better.

My son opted for the forty miles per hour pitch and even those scared him a little bit. He'd probably have selected a slow softball pitch if his sister wasn't there, upstaging him.

"She's two years older," he'd always say, ignoring the fact that it was technically only fourteen months.

I could have told him that boys were expected to hit higher speeds than girls, but that would have just fractured his already fragile ego so I said nothing. I let him hang with me after he finished his first round. He obviously wasn't that into it.

"What's next?" I asked him.

It was eight p.m. and they knew I had to have them home by nine so there wasn't much time. My ex-wife didn't like the apartment complex I lived at and preferred the kids sleep at her house. We'd gone back and forth on this since our divorce, but when Billy Aybar was killed at my complex, there was no use debating any longer. My ex-wife's fears were now justified. The kids would sleep at her house.

"Ice cream!" my son exclaimed.

Oh, to be a kid again. Dinner. Then a sport. Then dessert. Not even a consideration of what turmoil your stomach might be going through.

"Baskin Robbins?"

"Yes. I want to get mint chocolate chip."

Sadie had just finished her second round and was walking over to meet us.

"How about you, Sadie? What type of ice cream do you want?"

"I'll take strawberry."

She liked ice cream, but not with the aplomb that her brother did. To him, it was life-altering. To her, it was a pleasant diversion from baseball. Her true love.

"Let's go," I said, trying to sound into it.

The truth was I was exhausted. The phone call from the detective this morning felt like two days ago. A long day at work followed and then almost four hours with the kids. I'm not saying I didn't want to show them around. I loved them with all my heart.

It had just been a long day and tomorrow was only going to be worse.

After ice cream, I drove them back to their mother's. They seemed happy and Sadie regaled her mother with stories of hitting baseballs at fifty miles per hour.

"Most girls can only hit the softballs," she said.

"We've got an athlete on our hands," I said to Isabella.

She smiled. We rarely saw eye-to-eye, but we always tried to keep our vitriol to a minimum around the kids. We even managed a smile now and then.

"Maybe the first female major leaguer," she said.

"Maybe?" my daughter said and we all laughed. "It's a for sure."

"So, I'll see you next week?" Isabella asked me.

"Of course. Do you think I'd miss out on my time with these little buggers? Give Daddy a hug goodbye," I said.

They came and hugged me and it made everything all worthwhile. My kids were my world.

~

I drove back to my place, enjoying the quick ten-minute drive. I knew that wasn't going to be the case tomorrow.

It was 9:30 by the time I got home. I was in bed before 10:00. And I fell asleep barely a minute later. Those were the advantages of a long, fulfilling day. I could fall asleep as soon as my head hit the pillow.

~

I awoke the next morning at 8:10 and got dressed for work. There was going to be more filling cement today. I could complain, but who would listen? Better to just suck it up and do my job.

I was hopeful that having my meeting with the detective later in the day might speed the day along. I was genuinely interested in what questions he'd asked me. Were my suspicions true? Had Shane Doyle thrown this case? If he hadn't, then why the hell did he instruct me to answer in a way that would be hazardous to his case? There was no good answer for that last one.

I worried less and less about being charged with perjury. This guy Dunn was an LAPD detective. They had bigger fish to fry.

I took the stairs down to the parking garage which sat underneath the apartments. It was even more dilapidated than the complex itself. Tiny segments of concrete would routinely fall from overhead. If one day the apartment complex had pancaked the garage below, no tenants would have been shocked.

I pressed the fob on my car - a tan 2013 Honda Civic - and sat down in the driver's seat, throwing my hard hat on the passenger seat beside me.

As I moved the keys toward the ignition, I saw a figure rise in the seat behind me. Before I knew it, he'd thrown some sort of rope around my neck.

I looked in the rearview mirror and it was none other than Roger Theus. I'd helped him go free. What the fuck was he doing?!

"If you answer honestly, I'll let you go," he said. "Do you understand?"

I didn't believe him, but I had to hold on to some sliver of hope.

"Yes," I said.

Before he asked the next question, another piece of rope wrapped around my chest and arms pushing my arms in and restricting them from moving. I looked down at the horn on the steering wheel and figured he was trying to prevent me from pressing it.

He didn't ask his question for a few seconds because he was tying a knot. The rope around my sternum grew tighter. He'd now have both hands free to pull on the rope around my neck. I shuddered with fear. My only way out was to plead to his humanity. To reinforce to him that he was free because of my testimony.

"Did Shane Doyle have you commit perjury?"

"Yes."

"Who have you told about it?"

"No one."

"The police haven't contacted you yet?"

"They have, but I haven't told them what happened."

I instantly realized my colossal mistake. I was trying to convince him that I wouldn't say a word to the cops. Instead, I should have just claimed they hadn't contacted me.

"Who reached out to you?"

It was too late to backtrack at this point.

"Some detective named Noble Dunn."

"And you talked on the phone?"

When I didn't answer for a second, he tightened the rope around my neck.

"Yes. Yes. We did."

"What did you say?"

"Nothing. I was supposed to meet with him later today. But I won't be doing that now, Mr. Theus."

I'd made another mistake. By saying his name, I'd proven that I could positively identify him. Ironic, considering that's what I'd failed to do at his trial.

"Have you told anyone else?"

"No, I promise."

"Wife?"

"I'm divorced and I'd never tell her anything."

"Co-worker?"

"And admit I'd perjured myself? I'm not crazy."

"Okay, good."

Now that I'd said his name, there was no reason not to say it again. It was time to plead for my life.

"I helped you go free, Mr. Theus. I'm not the bad guy."

He loosened the rope ever so slightly. It was the first moment I thought I might get out of this alive.

Those hopes quickly faded.

"No, you're not the bad guy Alfonso. The police are. But they want to talk to you and because of that, you pose too big a risk for me."

He reached around me and put a piece of duct tape over my mouth. He wasn't going to allow me to scream.

With that, he tightened the rope around my neck. I tried to kick and resist, but I was no match for his strength. With my arms and chest restrained, there's very little I could do.

I tried some crazy behind-my-head kick with my leg, but all I did was hit the steering wheel with my knee. I tried to swing my arms around and break free from the other rope. To no avail. It was too tight.

My only hope was someone would descend to the parking garage and help save me. As I began to lose consciousness, I looked around and saw no one.

My life was going to end in this shitty, dilapidated parking garage.

Knowing I had seconds to live, I tried one last crazy backward kick.

It never had a chance.

I was dead seconds later.

CHAPTER 42

ROGER

Two days after reading the first article mentioning Noble Dunn, there was a follow-up.

'More questions than answers regarding murder/suicide.'

The article was basically a continuation of the first article, stating that Dunn was going around town, asking people about Shane Doyle, Lexi, and Knox.

This wasn't going to go away. I knew it.

I was sitting in the Brentwood section of Los Angeles, having a cappuccino on San Vicente Boulevard, admiring the hot women who'd walk by every few seconds. If this had been a year ago, I'd have approached them and asked them to attend one of my pool parties in Malibu.

As for now, I had other things on my mind. The women could wait.

I went over my options and I kept coming back to one thing.

The only man tying this all together was Alfonso Reyes. If he was gone, there was nothing that could prove Shane Doyle threw this case. Shane had told me himself.

Without Alfonso Reyes, Shane Doyle had still committed a murder/suicide. If the LAPD - and specifically Noble Dunn - heard from Alfonso, the house of cards would definitely come crashing down.

So I had to make sure he wouldn't be available to talk. It was that simple.

∾

I tailed him for less than twenty-four hours.

Once I saw him emerge from that disgusting parking garage on Monday morning at 8:30, I knew it would be the perfect place to do what was necessary. I'd get there at 6:30 the following morning just to be safe. Jimmying the lock to his car would be no problem.

I wore long gloves that would protect me from leaving any fingerprints behind. I picked up some clothes from Goodwill. Better not to take a chance that an old set of clothes might leave some DNA behind.

Alfonso Reyes was not a very big man. Once I got the rope around his neck he wouldn't stand a chance. I'd make sure to secure one around his chest and arms as well. That would prevent him from hitting the horn, one of the few things that could have derailed my plan. Luckily, I'd thought everything through. This wasn't some impulsive, imbecilic meeting like the one that had gone wrong with Billy Aybar.

I'd thought of everything.

I was the Mastermind, after all.

~

The murder of Alfonso Reyes went off without a hitch.

My one fear was someone walking into the garage as I garrotted him to death. That didn't happen.

The irony that I'd now killed two people at this complex wasn't lost on me. First, Billy Aybar. And now, Alfonso Reyes.

He gave me all the information that I'd asked for. And he'd yet to speak with Detective Dunn. Well, technically he'd talked to him, but he didn't give him anything of substance. That's all that really mattered. Everything was coming up roses for old Roger.

I guess one unexpected thing did occur. When I'd finally killed Alfonso Reyes, his eyes slightly popped out of his sockets which gave him this buggy-eyed look. It gave me a much-needed laugh as I exited the car.

Should I not be laughing about something like that?

Oh, I'm fucking sorry.

Maybe you didn't realize that I don't give a shit about anyone but myself. And a guy's eyes popping out of their sockets is funny to me.

Plus, who is going to stop me?

I'd committed another perfect murder.

~

A day after the murder, I started fearing his death probably wouldn't put an end to this.

If Noble Dunn was as dogged as everyone made him out to be, the death of Reyes would just motivate him further. It's not like I had a choice, though. If Reyes had talked to him, Dunn would have known that Shane had thrown my case. And then it was only a matter of time till he found his way to me.

At the very least, Reyes's murder delayed that. And maybe, by some miracle, this would derail the case.

Something else crossed my mind. What if Dunn found out that Knox had lived at one of my complexes? That could be troublesome.

There were a few things I could do. The first would be burning all the evidence of leases, signed contracts, etc. between Knox and The Premier. He'd have changed his mail to be delivered there, but The Premier was at least one address ago and maybe two. It's doubtful Detective Dunn would go digging up old addresses. It's just not something that a detective would assume to prove fruitful.

I was confident he wouldn't be able to tie Knox to me.

And if he did?

Then it would probably get to the point where I'd have to kill Dunn himself. Go ahead and cut the head off of the snake.

Time would tell if that would prove necessary.

PART THREE: MANO A MANO

CHAPTER 43

NOBLE

O nce Alfonso Reyes was thirty minutes late, I started to get a bad
feeling.

When he hadn't shown after an hour, my heart began to sink. I called
his phone and it was going straight to voice message. Maybe it had gone
dead while he was working and he was stuck in Los Angeles traffic. It
wouldn't be the first time someone was an hour late for that very reason.

When ninety minutes passed with no sign of Reyes, I couldn't wait any
longer. It was time to head home. I left him one more voice message asking
if we could reschedule this.

I woke up the next morning and immediately looked at my phone.
Nothing from Reyes. I tried his number and it once again went straight to
voicemail. It was still only 7:15. I'd give him until 9:00 to contact me. If I
didn't hear from him by then, I was sending a welfare check to his place.

9:00 a.m. came and went. By now, I was in the office and asked a
sergeant on duty if he'd send an LAPD squad car to check on Reyes.

"Is he in Santa Monica?"

"No, downtown."

"I'll have an officer contact you, Noble," he said.

"Thanks."

I got a call fifteen minutes later from Officer Overby of the LAPD.

"Hello."

"Is this Noble Dunn?"

"It is."

"We just did a welfare check on your guy."

"And?"

"No one was at the apartment."

"Did you go in?"

"Yeah, after there was no answer. We didn't see anything amiss. No flipped-over tables. No blood stains. Nothing."

"Okay, thanks, officer."

He hung up.

Maybe Alfonso Reyes had just gotten cold feet. It happened all the time. People didn't like dealing with the LAPD. Even innocent people who had nothing to hide.

Plus, there was no sign of a struggle in his apartment. I was suddenly optimistic.

I considered driving downtown later that night. Reyes would be more likely to talk to me if I showed up at his front door.

Unfortunately, the drive down wouldn't prove necessary.

At 1:45, I got a second call from Officer Overby.

"Hello?"

"Officer Dunn, this is Officer Overby again."

I didn't like the way his tone sounded.

"Did you find Mr. Reyes?"

"Yes, but not in the way you're thinking."

My heart sank.

"He's dead, isn't he?"

"Yes. Some neighbor saw him slumped over in his car. We got the call. Looks like he'd been strangled to death."

"Oh, Jesus," I said.

"Yeah, it was pretty nasty. His eyes were bug-eyed."

"You can spare me the gory details, Overby."

"You've been on the force so long, I figured you've seen it all."

Even though we were in different precincts, Overby knew who I was. I guess that's what being on the force for almost thirty years got you.

"I have seen it all. That's why I don't need to hear about it anymore."

"Understood. Do you want to come down to the crime scene?"

The real answer was no, I didn't want to, but I'd started investigating this Shane Doyle angle and now Reyes was dead. I wouldn't be doing my job if I didn't.

"I'll leave the Santa Monica office right now. Try to ask the Medical Examiner to keep his body there until I arrive."

"Will do. See you soon."

"Thanks, Overby."

~

The trip down to see Alfonso Reyes's body was probably unnecessary. I saw the bug-eyed look that Overby had referred to. It was sad. That shouldn't be anyone's final expression. It made me think back to the crime scene in Santa Monica and their expressions.

Besides that, I didn't gain much from the crime scene. It looked like a rope of some sort was used to strangle him. It was gone. Not that I expected the killer to have left it there.

They had DNA experts going over the backseat of the car, but I wasn't holding out much hope. I had a feeling this killer knew what they were doing. He'd probably been hiding out in Reyes's car, waiting for him. The guy had thought this through. He was surely wearing gloves. Maybe a full body suit to prevent any DNA.

I was once again reminded of the crime scene at Lexi Grant's apartment. If the killer had been someone besides Shane, they'd done a great job covering it up.

~

I went home that night and poured myself a large glass of wine.

I was now in the thick of this investigation. I'd brought it on myself. Captain Cook and others had pleaded with me to let it be.

It was too late for that.

I was about to go all in.

The case of California vs. Roger Theus seemed to be at the forefront.

Was Theus involved?

Shane Doyle certainly hadn't been at his best during his trial. Was it intentional or had Lexi really fucked with his mind? Were those two mutually exclusive? Maybe Lexi had fucked with his mind for that exact reason.

What the hell did Knox have to do with this? Was he an unlucky bystander? Possible, but unlikely. Lastly, who killed Alfonso Reyes? Was it the same person who killed Shane/Lexi/Knox?

Before I had a chance to answer all these questions, I'd poured myself another glass of wine.

I was going to break my rule tonight.

With all that was going on, this was going to be more than a two-glass of wine type of evening.

I looked in the direction of a family photo and saw my wife's beautiful brown eyes.

"I'll love you forever, baby," I said.

~

The next day I delved deeper into the Roger Theus case.

I arrived at the office by 8:00, my head not in tip-top shape due to the five glasses of wine. My hangovers - even minor ones - seemed to be getting worse with age. Oh, to be young again.

I'd already read most of the court reporter's minutes, but I now went over them with a fine-toothed comb. And about two and a half hours in, I hit gold.

Roger Theus's defense attorney, Hilton Lund, was asking questions to his client.

Lund: *"And what is your profession, Mr. Theus?"*

Theus: *"When I was younger, I flipped houses. With the money I made from those, I was able to buy two Los Angeles apartment complexes."*

Lund: *"Where were those located?"*

Theus: *"The Red Carpet was on Olympic Avenue in West Los Angeles. And The Premier was on Wilshire."*

Lund: *"You named them The Red Carpet and The Premier?"*

Theus: *"What can I say? I love the glitz and glamor of Los Angeles."*

~

It took a minute for it to register.

And then I remembered.

The Premier!

Someone had mentioned that complex. I tried to rack my brain. It took another minute and then it hit me.

The old lady. Knox's next-door neighbor. She'd mentioned that Knox had previously been living at the Premier.

Knox had lived in an apartment complex owned by Roger Theus.

Holy. Fucking. Shit.

CHAPTER 44

ROGER

I started going over my options in the twenty-four hours after killing Alfonso Reyes.

One, I could get the fuck out of Dodge. Fly to Europe or South America or Asia and just never come back. It wouldn't be my first choice. I wasn't a big fan of "Dodge." I didn't like running. I liked being in the middle of things.

Two, I could keep killing people that might have damning information on me. I was getting pretty good at these murders, I had to admit. I knew how to keep a clean crime scene. The problem was that eventually, my luck would run out. It's kind of amazing it had already lasted this long.

As much as I didn't like the idea of running, staying in LA and turning into Ted Bundy just wasn't a long-term plan.

I'd murdered the right people and as far as I knew, nothing could come back on me at this point. It was time to get out while I still could.

But god damn it would have felt good to kill Noble on my way out.

Maybe I could find a way.

It would have to be the last thing I did before catching a flight somewhere. Killing an LAPD detective would bring the kind of attention I was trying to avoid.

Of course, if I was a continent or two away, it wouldn't much matter.

CHAPTER 45

NOBLE

"There is zero evidence that Roger Theus was involved in either the Reyes murder or the murder/suicide off of Wilshire."

I'd walked directly to Captain Cook's office after I found out Knox lived in one of Roger Theus's apartment complexes. He wasn't taking it well.

"Will you stop calling it a murder/suicide?"

"Until proven otherwise, that's what the fuck it is, Noble."

We'd butted heads more in the last week than we had in years. I don't know if it was this case specifically or whether nearing my retirement had made me tougher to get along with. I want to think it was the former.

I was as pissed as the Captain was.

"Then I'd like for you to explain something to me," I said. "What are the odds that (1) Alfonso Reyes is killed on the day he's supposed to come to see me? (2) That he was the witness that likely caused Roger Theus to be acquitted? And (3) that Knox, one of the men killed in the triple murder, was a tenant at one of Roger Theus's apartment complexes?"

"Alfonso Reyes lived in a rough neighborhood and - who knows - he might have been tied up in drugs."

"Because he was Hispanic?"

"Watch yourself, Noble."

"I'm sorry, Captain. That was out of line."

"Apology accepted. And the answer to your question is no, it had nothing to do with his race. It's because that section of downtown LA and his complex specifically were both dangerous."

"That's fair, but his complex was dangerous because Roger Theus killed someone there. Actually, I now think he might have killed two people there."

"I didn't know you had your law license as well, Noble. Congrats on that. Must be nice. The state of California acquitted Roger Theus. You suddenly know more than the twelve jurors?"

Usually, there was some sort of give and take when we argued. There was none of that going on here.

"If you read the recap of Theus's trial, you'll see that I'm right."

"No, I will not be reading about the case. I have a job to do and it's not being a lawyer. It's looking after my subordinates. Especially the ones who think they've become lawyers."

"Screw you," I said and instantly regretted it.

"Get the fuck out of my office, Noble. You're off the case."

I was hoping for a biting comeback, but what came out was lame as hell.

"Everyone knows you're a shitty chef, Captain Cook."

Fifteen minutes later, I was still fuming.

At Captain Cook, yes, but mostly at myself. I was out of line with my remarks about Alfonso Reyes. And I'd also said, "Screw you" to the captain. He was my boss. I was 100% in the wrong even if he was being an asshole himself.

I considered going over his head to someone higher on the totem pole. It would be a very disrespectful thing to do and it would alienate me from him forever. Not that we had much time left together.

I decided that would only be a last resort.

And it proved to be unnecessary.

Thirty minutes later, Captain Cook knocked on my door.

I opened it, but didn't say a word. He did.

"I'm sorry, Noble, but in my defense, you said, 'Screw you' first."

He was right.

"I'm sorry too, Captain. For that and disparaging your abilities as a chef."

That got him to smile.

"That's more of an insult than screw you. And it's also patently false. I can cook my ass off."

"I know. Heat of the moment comment."

"I shouldn't have said you're off the case. There are obviously a few irregularities in this case. My problem is that you have zero evidence that Roger Theus killed Alfonso Reyes. And need I remind you that he was already acquitted of the Billy Aybar murder? If the LAPD is going to arrest someone who has already been acquitted of a murder, we have to be 1000% convinced he's guilty. Not 100%. 1000%. The media would have a field day with us and we'd look like some spiteful assholes who - if they don't get their way - just re-arrest the guy weeks later."

"I get your point, Captain. But this all leads back to Theus. I've got a feeling this guy is really bad news."

He looked at me and let out a small smirk.

"Then prove it."

"I'm back on the case?"

"Were you ever really off it?"

We both let his rhetorical question hang in the air.

There are some things that you know - even in the moment - are the wrong thing to do. And yet you do them anyway. I was about to do one of those things.

I left the precinct on Olympic Avenue and headed toward Malibu, assuming that Roger Theus still lived at his listed address.

As I drove along the Pacific Coast Highway, I tried to come up with a good rationale for my foolish decision. The negative side of the ledger was obvious. My appearance at Roger Theus's house would alert him to the fact that I was on to him. Most people would probably say that was game, set, and match. There was no positive that could overcome that negative.

As you may have guessed, I looked at it a little differently. To me, my appearance would put him on edge and hopefully, that would make him more likely to make a mistake. When people get pushed into a corner, they tend to fight back. That may sound dangerous, but it's also when they often make a fatal mistake.

He was also much less likely to kill if he knew he was on the police's radar. I only wish I'd confronted him before Alfonso Reyes was murdered.

I looked down at my notes for his address. I was only a few minutes away.

I drove up a small hill, all the while looking at the Pacific Ocean in my rear-view mirror. Did it piss me off that a thug like Roger Theus got to enjoy this view every day? In a word, yes.

I came upon a large, open, circular driveway. There were two cars parked that were probably worth more than I made in a year. First, the view. Now, the cars. As if I needed more reasons to despise this man.

I assumed I'd be knocking on his door, but that wouldn't prove necessary. Roger Theus was just getting out of a car himself. He stepped out of a gorgeous, brand-new blue Corvette and was wearing a bright as hell, yellow Tommy Bahama shirt. I had no idea the guy was going to be as big as he was. Sure, I'd seen 6'4, 250-something on the paperwork, but he was much bigger in person.

I had no plans on using the gun I had on me, but I'm glad I'd brought it.

I stepped out of my car and walked toward him.

He looked in my direction, a look of bemusement on his face.

"Roger Theus, I presume?" I said.

"Noble Dunn, I presume? Or is it Detective Dunn? Or Detective Noble? I can never figure out with you detectives. As for me, just call me Roger."

He was already trying to get the upper hand. That much was obvious.

"Any of those are fine," I said.

We shook hands. He was squeezing as hard as he could. I was stronger than people realized and he couldn't get the upper hand.

"Strong grip you got there, Noble."

I nodded and he released his grip.

"Would you rather talk inside?" he asked.

"Sure. I'm missing out on the view out here, Roger."

He smiled, albeit deviously.

"That you are. Here, follow me."

I followed Roger Theus - a man I presumed to be a multi-murderer - into his house. We weren't quite at surreal yet, but we were headed in that direction.

We walked inside and I was not disappointed. Huge bay windows led to a spectacular view of the Pacific below. My rearview mirror couldn't do it justice. I also saw his pool and what seemed like a million lounge chairs surrounding it. I wondered what went on down there.

"I went into the wrong line of business," I said.

Roger laughed.

"It's never too late to turn to the dark side," he said and laughed even louder.

He was a charismatic guy, but he didn't fool me. I wasn't going to let my guard down. I knew him for what he was. And his "dark side" comment told me that he was going to step close to the line, but not quite over it.

"Nah, I wouldn't be able to sleep at night," I said. "Those damn pesky morals my parents instilled in me."

"My mother instilled fear in me. Usually with a paddle. Sometimes a belt."

"And those are supposed to excuse your actions as an adult?"

He laughed again. This was all one big joke to him.

"Here, let's sit," he said.

He walked me back from the windows to two thin couches that sat opposite each other. We sat down and Roger laughed for what seemed like the 10th time.

"What's so funny?" I asked.

"Oh, I was just thinking about the last guy who sat on your couch."

"I'd like to meet him."

"That's going to be tough to arrange," Roger said.

"Is he dead?"

He sat there and didn't respond.

"I get it," I said. "I'm not here to get you to incriminate yourself."

"Then what are you here for, Noble?"

I used his first name because he asked me to call him Roger. He called me Noble to be snarky.

"Well, Roger, I just wanted to see what the devil looked like in person."

He snickered.

"He looks pretty damn good, don't you think?"

"I think he could lose a few pounds. Don't worry, you'll quickly sweat it off in that fiery hell you're headed to."

"You're a funny guy, Noblel. Maybe you did go into the wrong field. Stand-up comedy could have been your thing. There's actually some funny black guys these days."

I didn't want to take the racist bait, but I couldn't stop myself.

"You're right. We've come a long way since those no-talent hacks like Richard Pryor, Redd Foxx, and Eddie Murphy."

"Your people have come a long way. I'll give you that. It's Utopia in Compton these days."

I despised the man in front of me. He was despicable. This time I decided not to take the bait.

"Where is the name Theus from? Who are your people?"

"Germany. Although, there was a black basketball player named Reggie Theus. He's the black sheep of the Theus family."

He emphasized the word *black* in black sheep. Quite unnecessarily.

"You think you're a pretty smart guy, don't you, Roger?"

"I've been known to call myself the mastermind."

"Why am I not surprised?"

"Probably lets you know what I think about my own intellect. I easily could have been an undercover detective."

"Not with those clothes," I said.

Roger roared with laughter.

"Yeah, I guess bright yellow Tommy Bahama shirts wouldn't work well for coppers. Plus, someone like you has the built-in advantage of being hard to see at night. Ain't that right, Nobe?"

I wanted to plant a four-iron into Roger Theus's head. Instead, I decided to play nice and laughed.

"Maybe you should have been the stand-up comedian," I said. "Although racist jokes don't go over so well anymore."

"Bunch of woke pussies."

"Maybe. But making people laugh without going to the least common denominator is much tougher. Not sure you've got that in you, Rog."

I decided two of us could play the old "shorten their real name" game.

"Maybe you're right, Nobe. I think I'll stick to my day job."

"Which one? Property owner? Drug dealer? Murderer?"

"Right? My resume is so comprehensive these days."

"Was that an admission that murderer has a spot on there?"

"C'mon, Nobe. You've got to be better than that. You saw what happened last time you guys tried me in court."

"Yeah, people ended up dead."

"I was so saddened to hear about that DA. Sounds like he fell in lust with the wrong girl. And that poor third guy getting caught in the middle. I think his name was Ben if memory serves."

"You probably knew him as Knox."

"No, I'm sorry. That doesn't ring a bell."

Laying all my cards on the table probably wasn't the best strategy, but I detested the man in front of me and wanted to see him squirm.

"That's surprising. I figured you knew most people who lived in your complexes."

Most criminals would tell me to leave the premises at that point. Not Roger Theus.

"He must have lived at The Premier. I rarely visited that one. I preferred the Red Carpet."

"You've got an answer for everything, don't you, Rog?"

"I guess I do, Nobe. Or should it be Nob? Yeah, I think that sums up your personality better. Let's go with Nob."

I laughed.

"If you weren't such a vile scumbag, I'd almost be enjoying this back and forth."

He smiled devilishly.

"You're black and a cop - the two worst things in the world - and I'm managing to enjoy this. Just roll with it, Nob."

"I'm looking forward to rolling your ass into jail."

"I'm not buying that. I think you'd much rather kill me."

"You might be right there, Rog."

"So that makes this a battle to the death."

"But this isn't just mano a mano," I said.

"Oh, but it is. What do you think, your Captain Cook is going to help you?"

I was taken aback. Not for the first time. Roger Theus was disarming in that way.

"You know Captain Cook?"

"I know a lot of things, Nob. I know who Sherry is. Was sorry to hear the cancer got her."

"What did you say?"

"You heard what I said. Sherry, your deceased wife. The mother of Sherin, who I've heard is a beautiful young lady. I'd really like to meet her acquaintance. Have her spent some quality alone time with Rog."

Before I had a chance to reconsider what I was about to do, I stood up, took my gun out, and pointed it at Roger Theus. It took all my restraint not to shoot him. If I was a dirty cop, I would have shot him and found a way to frame him.

But that wasn't me.

Despite him insulting my race, my wife, and even my daughter, this would still be cold-blooded murder.

"You don't got the balls," Roger said.

"And you don't deserve an easy death," I said and slowly, painstakingly, put my gun away.

"This is fun. I'll be seeing you around. I like the idea of mano a mano. The cop vs. the criminal. Black vs. White. Good vs. evil. And any other boring old stereotype. Let's see who wins. Or, should I say, lives."

"Yes, you will be seeing me around," I said.

I turned to go.

"I really enjoyed this," he said. "Until next time. Oh, and to get out, just turn the Nob on the door. That's K-N-O-B."

As I walked away, I could hear Roger Theus laughing at his own joke.

CHAPTER 46

ROGER

I thoroughly enjoyed every minute of my visit with Noble Dunn. I'm not sure I'd ever laughed so much. Sure, some of it was mocking Noble, but still, I was laughing.

And yes, I ridiculed his race, his name, his ex-wife, and even his daughter, but he was a fun adversary. Not that he'd ever have a chance against yours truly, but I'd enjoyed the tit-for-tat.

I avoided using the N-word. I think he really might have shot me. Hahaha.

What a fucking coward he was. He could have shot me dead and ended this all. He knows I'm guilty, but he's never going to be able to prove it. That's why he came alone. He's got nothing on me except his own suspicions. That and six dollars will get you a small cappuccino.

If he had a spine, he would have taken the law into his own hands.

Shows you that having morals will get you nowhere.

Was I really a racist? You're damn right, but to be honest, with him it was just more to get under his skin. His charcoal skin. It worked. He pulled his gun on me.

Once he left, I debated whether I should try and kill him later that night.

That felt like it would be cheating. I had always enjoyed one-on-one battles and with this one, everything was on the line.

For now, Noble Dunn would remain alive.

He'd meet his demise soon enough, but it wasn't going to be on this day.

CHAPTER 47

NOBLE

After my face-off with Roger Theus, the rest of the day kind of just meandered by. Nothing was going to live up to the confrontation I'd just had. I saw Captain Cook but decided not to mention my trip to Malibu. He would have loathed my decision to confront a suspect, so I thought it best to keep him in the dark. At least, for now.

I got off around six and headed back home where I was greeted with a huge surprise. My daughter Sherin was waiting for me in the kitchen. I'd seen her car in the driveway, but it was still a shock to see her in the flesh as I walked in.

Sherin was now in her early thirties. She was tall and statuesque with a body fat percentage that I'd forever be jealous of. She'd recovered from her pregnancy quicker than any woman I'd ever known. She could have turned heads if she'd gone into modeling or show business, but that definitely wasn't her vibe. Despite her beauty, she was still shy and preferred wearing sweats to dresses.

On this day, it was her beloved sweats in some light yellow color that very few could pull off.

"We're having chicken piccata for dinner," she said.

"Nice to see you too."

"Oh, sorry. How are you, Dad?"

She walked over from the cutting board she was using and gave me a big hug.

"To what do I deserve this surprise?"

"I hadn't seen you in a while and Bobby is watching our little Ava."

"It's great to see you," I said and we hugged again.

"So, you're good with chicken piccata?"

"I'm good with anything my daughter is cooking."

"I'll have dinner ready in twenty minutes. Why don't you sit down and turn on CSI or whatever it is you cops do."

I laughed.

"Actually, I kind of like to get away from cop stuff once I get home."

"I hear ya. Any big cases going on right now?"

I thought back to my encounter earlier today. And then my heart sank.

'The mother of Sherin, who I've heard is a beautiful young lady. I'd really like to meet her acquaintance.'

The gift of having my daughter visit suddenly had me on edge. There's no way that Roger could have known, is there?

"What time did you get here today?" I asked.

"Just an hour ago. I figured you wouldn't be off of work yet. Looks like I timed it perfectly."

My heart reconvened its normal beating pattern. That doesn't mean everything was hunky dory, but at least Roger hadn't somehow known my daughter was in town. She'd arrived well after our face-off.

I hated that I was thinking of Roger Theus by his first name. I did that with the deceased, not with suspects. I hated to admit it, but the guy was in my head.

I looked up and saw my daughter studying me.

"Everything okay, Dad? You didn't answer my question about having any big cases."

"Sorry, honey. Just a long day at work."

She smiled in my direction.

"Then go sit down on the couch and turn on anything but CSI."

I smiled back, but my stomach was a little queasy.

I sat down on my couch and threw on the Discovery Channel. Maybe watching some animals would settle down my wandering mind.

Twenty minutes later, dinner was served.

Sherin had been a good cook since she was a teenager. I'm not sure she ever hit the heights that her mother did, but she was certainly a better cook than I ever was.

She served the chicken piccata over noodles with a side salad.

"It's delicious, Sherin."

"Thanks, Dad. I know you always liked this dish."

"Your mother used to make it a lot."

"Oh, trust me, I remember."

"I miss her every day."

"I know you do, Dad. You say that same line every time I see you."

It was true. And it was true.

"Is there something wrong with that?"

"Of course not, but have you thought more about trying to date again? Mom would have had no problem with that."

"You're probably right. I'm just not ready for it right now. Maybe when I retire."

"That's coming up next year, correct?"

"That's the plan."

"You'll have put in your thirty years. Now you can go travel the world instead of chasing after bad guys."

I thought back to the lone European vacation I'd taken with Sherry. We'd had a great time, but I kept worrying I was missing some great cases back in LA. I wish I could have focused more on our vacation at the time. I was never very good at that. Work was always front and center in my mind.

I'd now thought about that vacation twice. Maybe it was a subtle hint that I should start traveling again. Post-retirement, obviously.

"I'll become a globetrotter," I said.

"Just not the Harlem version. You're too old for that."

I laughed. My daughter had always had a keen sense of humor.

I took a few bites of my chicken. I'd had this dish enough to know the sauce consisted of wine, butter, lemon, and capers. It was superb.

"So, how are Bobby and Ava? And how'd you get time off work?"

"Even pediatricians are allowed a day off from time to time. And they are great."

"You picked a great husband."

"And you picked a great wife."

We both paused and reminisced for a minute about my wife/her mom. My eyes instinctively looked toward one of the pictures of our family.

"I'm currently working on a case, but when I'm done, I'll come down to San Diego for a day or two and see my granddaughter."

"That would be great. Bobby figured I could use twenty-four hours off from watching her. It's the first time I've been away from her since she was born three years ago."

"She's probably throwing a fit right now."

My daughter laughed.

"Good. Let Bobby know what I go through on a daily basis."

I smiled. I'd raised a smart, charismatic daughter. Well, really, my wife had, but I'd done my own little part as well.

"So you're only up here a day?" I asked.

"Yeah. But I won't head back until tomorrow night so we've got all day tomorrow to hang out."

I walked over and gave her another hug.

"It's great to have you here."

CHAPTER 48

ROGER

The more I thought about things, the more I realized getting out of Dodge was my only choice. I hated to run but I hated jail more. And even if Noble Dunn was the only one who knew I was guilty, he might be enough. The guy was tenacious. I'd met him one time and already knew that.

I talked to my accountant and my lawyer - both almost as big of scoundrels as I - and we started transferring my money to some offshore accounts, namely the Caymans and a couple of Swiss bank accounts. You gotta love the Swiss! Always neutral, and by neutral I mean allowing despots and scummy people around the world to hide their money.

I had my real estate agent put The Premier and The Red Carpet up for sale. I told him to keep it on the down low. I didn't want Noble Dunn driving by one of my complexes and seeing a big "For Sale" sign. That might give him pause.

Speaking of Noble, I hadn't forgotten about him.

I was still considering one last hoorah before I left town.

And by hoorah, I meant killing an LAPD detective.

It wasn't hard to find out his address. There are some hidden perks of owning apartment complexes in Los Angeles. You basically have carte blanche to search for anyone. I'm sure cops were supposed to be tougher to find online than a regular Joe. Not for me, it wasn't.

Noble Dunn. 1072 Montana Ave.

I'd take a little drive by his home the following morning. Put my thinking cap on and see what plan I could come up with.

It was time for my coup de grace.

CHAPTER 49

NOBLE

"Let's go out on the Santa Monica Pier."
Saturday came and even though it was technically my day off, I probably would have been working on the Roger Theus case. Not anymore. My daughter took precedent. And if she wanted to hit up the Santa Monica Pier, then doggone it, that's what we were going to do.

With my wife, I'd chosen my profession over her a few too many times for my liking. I wasn't going to make the same mistake with my daughter.

"That sounds fun. I'm in," I said.

It was nine a.m. I'd woken up that morning and my daughter once again had food waiting for me. This time it was French toast. I didn't like the fact that she was the one visiting and had already cooked twice. I'd take her out to dinner. No more cooking for her.

Not that I was complaining. The French Toast had been darn good.

~

A few hours later, we headed down Wilshire and toward the ocean.

Sherin tried to convince me to let her drive us down. I was in my early fifties, not my early nineties. I still did the driving when she visited. We arrived at the pier and walked around, taking in the sights. My daughter played a few of the carnival games while I watched. She was thirty-one years old and had just started her career as a pediatrician and yet, she looked like one of her young clients, enjoying games meant for children.

A young, white guy with sleeve tattoos covering both arms stared at me long and hard. It took me a minute and then I remembered. Lenny Roiling. A woman had been killed in a meth lab that he was running. He didn't do the killing, but he did get a few years for running the lab.

He continued staring and I almost wondered if he was going to make a charge at me. Finally, he just yelled, "Fuck pigs!"

People stared at the guy as he walked away. I played dumb.

A few minutes later - thank God she hadn't seen Lenny Roiling - Sherin brought over a huge stuffed animal she'd won. When I laughed, she deadpanned, "This is for Ava. Not for me."

"Are you sure?" I asked. "You looked to be having quite a bit of fun playing those carnival games."

"I'm sorry, I didn't know they made a law against that."

She was smiling as she said it.

"What's next?" I asked.

We'd been walking around the pier for almost two hours by this point.

"I'm kind of hungry again."

"Bubba Gump's shrimp?" I asked.

"You know it."

It had been one of our favorite spots when my wife was still alive. No, the food wasn't all that great, but you're sitting out on the Santa Monica Pier and looking out on the Pacific. For a location, you could do a lot worse.

We ate lunch with our monster stuffed animal looking on as the third member of our crew.

I got the coconut shrimp while my daughter ordered a chicken caesar wrap. I didn't bother mentioning that we were at a purported shrimp restaurant.

By the time we finished eating, it was approaching one, so we decided to head home.

~

"What if I played matchmaker, Dad?"

We were only a few blocks from home when she broached the subject.

"Oh, Sherin. Didn't we go over this last night?"

"There are some divorced women who come into my practice with their sons and daughters."

"They are probably in their early thirties."

"You'd be surprised. Lots of women in their early forties have young children these days."

"Well, I'm in my early fifties. Even forty sounds young to me."

Sherin laughed.

"So, you're just going to stay celibate for the rest of your life?"

"I'm not going there with you, but if you must know, I'm not celibate."

I wasn't lying. I'd been on some dates in recent years and there was one woman that I'd occasionally have over for the night to Netflix, then Chill. That's what the kids say, right?

But even with her, it had never gotten too serious. I certainly didn't want her or any other woman moving in with me. And who would want to? I still had pictures of Sherry all over the house.

"Well, at least I know you're not a monk," my daughter said.

"This conversation is over," I said and she laughed quite loudly.

I pulled into the driveway and parked behind Sherin's car.

I got out of the car and started walking toward the front door. I looked back and Sherin was putting the monster stuffed animal into her car. She was going to have a nice present to bring home to her daughter.

As I approached the door, I saw a piece of paper curled up and lying on the doormat. Damn salesmen. What was it this time? Solar paneling? A free window wash? Maybe some old-school Jehovah's Witness fliers? No, they'd probably have waited until we got home. They liked the whole in-person thing.

I grabbed the piece of paper from the ground, uncurled it, and started reading.

My stomach dropped. I'd never been more furious in my entire life.

It read:

"I told you I heard your daughter was a beautiful young lady. She's even more attractive in person. In the flesh, if you know what I mean."

CHAPTER 50

ROGER

I got the gift of a lifetime when I drove by Noble Dunn's house that morning.

A young, attractive black woman was walking with him toward a car. I immediately assumed it was his daughter. Not only did they look alike, but Noble Dunn didn't seem like the cradle-rocking type.

The moral bastard probably thought you should date a woman your own age. What a loser. I preferred my women barely legal, and when I was traveling abroad, I didn't care what age they were.

Which was going to come in handy considering my time in the United States was coming to an end.

I was watching from across the street when I first saw Noble and this mystery woman. I was driving my one inconspicuous car so as not to stand out. I was sandwiched between two other cars and wearing sunglasses. There was very little chance Noble would recognize me. And if he did? It's not like I was breaking the law.

I rolled my window down and that's when my suspicions were confirmed.

I was probably thirty yards away but was able to hear them pretty clearly.

"You sure you don't want me to drive?"

"I'm still your father. I'll do the driving."

It was his daughter, just as I'd assumed.

A devious smile enveloped my face.

I decided to follow them, but that plan was derailed pretty early on.

At the first light, I got stuck behind another car that stopped at a yellow light. Any real Angeleno would have driven through the intersection. By the time it turned green two minutes later, Noble and his daughter could have been anywhere.

I pulled over and ran through a few options.

The one I decided on was certainly going to ratchet things up.

Good. I was always one for ratcheting.

I found out where the closest Kinkos was and had them print up a letter and asked them to put it in an envelope.

You might call it a love letter to Noble's daughter. Hahaha.

I returned to Noble's home and put on my always-handy gloves as I removed it from the envelope. I curled up the letter and left it on his doorstep.

Fuck, I would have loved to see his reaction.

Even my unscrupulous mind knew that wasn't advisable.

Instead, I drove home, half-expecting the LAPD to make an appearance at my house that night.

But it never happened.

I had a feeling Noble was taking this mano a mano thing quite seriously.

CHAPTER 51

NOBLE

"What is it, Dad?"

I'd tried my best to put on a poker face, but my daughter knew me too well.

"I want you to go back to San Diego."

"What are you talking about? We've got half the day left."

"Please, Sherin. Do this one thing without asking me why."

"That's an impossibility. If I'm driving back early, at least I should be told why."

I didn't like that we were still standing outside of my house.

"Come inside," I said.

She followed me in and I locked the door behind me.

"What is going on?"

"When you asked earlier if I'm working on any interesting cases, I lied. I'm currently on a case where the guy is a madman."

"How bad could he be?"

"He's killed a bunch of people."

"Wow. Really?"

"Yes, really."

"Then why isn't he locked up?"

"He was acquitted of the first murder. I'm almost positive that a few people - including an assistant district attorney - conspired to throw his case."

"That would be a national story. Why isn't it?"

"Because he's been eliminating his fellow co-conspirators."

"You can't leave me hanging with that."

Sherin was right. If I was going to force her to drive home early, she deserved an explanation.

I spent the next five minutes telling her everything I knew about Roger Theus.

"And what does the note say?"

I hated showing it to her, but what choice did I have?

She read it but didn't wince as I did.

"It's a little disturbing," was all she said.

"A little? He's talking about my baby girl."

"I'm not your baby girl anymore."

"You know what I mean."

"He's not going to go after an LAPD detective's daughter."

"That's exactly something this asshole would do."

She could tell I was serious.

"Really?"

"Yes. He's a horrible human being. The scum of the earth."

I could feel her tense up a little bit.

"I hate doing this, Sherin, but can you please go back to San Diego? I'll owe you."

I could feel her weighing her options.

"Ava is probably missing me right about now," she said.

Good. She sounded willing to leave.

"Yes, I'm sure she is. I'll finish up this case soon. I'm sure of it. And then I'll come down and visit you without some maniac tailing me."

"Are you going to be alright?"

"I'm going to be fine. No bad guy has gotten me yet."

I said it, but there were a few doubts. My meeting with Roger Theus had been unlike any I'd ever had. It had shaken me more than I'd let on. He was genuinely scary.

"Are you going to tell Captain Cook about the letter?"

Usually, I'd enjoy the fact that even my daughter called him Captain Cook. Not today.

"It will be the first call I make after you're on the freeway."

I was serious. I'd intentionally avoided telling him about my visit to Malibu, but now the guy had either staked out my house or was following me around. Both were equally scary.

"You promise?"

"I promise, Sherin. Now, will you please - pretty please - drive back to San Diego."

"Alright, let me put my stuff together."

"Thank you."

~

I gave Sherin a huge hug and then followed behind her until I saw her get on the 405 freeway headed south. During the drive, my eyes kept looking back in my rearview mirror, making sure no one was following us.

No one was.

I arrived home and the first thing I did was call Captain Cook.

"It's a Saturday, Noble. What could you possibly want?"

"Roger Theus killed all these people," I said.

"Do you have evidence?"

"He followed me around earlier today."

"I'm not sure the courts will count that as evidence of murder."

He was being a sarcastic asshole as he was prone to be. I'd interrupted him on a Saturday - maybe during some family time - so I guess I couldn't blame him.

"He threatened my daughter."

"Sherin?"

He seemed genuinely disturbed by this. Sure, we often butted heads, but as a whole, we got along pretty well. He'd known Sherry and had seen Sherin grow up.

"Yeah."

"How did he threaten her?"

"I'd rather tell you in person."

"I'm in Ojai with the family. I'm back tomorrow morning. Can it wait until then?"

"Sure. Thanks, Captain."

"I'll be back by eleven or so."

"If you want, you could swing by my house. Don't have to get all dressed up and go to the precinct."

"Tomorrow is Sunday. I wasn't going to get dressed up for you, anyway."

I laughed. Deep down I liked the guy.

"Keep me posted. You can come here or I could meet you at the station."

"We'll talk tomorrow. Don't go dying tonight, you hear me, Noble?"

"I'll do my best."

I got off the phone and saw the letter sitting on my kitchen table.

My rage returned.

I met with Captain Cook the following day at noon.

He had surprised me and accepted my invitation to come to my place.

We sat at my kitchen table.

He'd bypassed my offer of coffee and taken a glass of red wine instead. I joined him.

"Hey, it's Sunday. It's like we're drinking from the chalice at Church," he said.

"It's not like I'm going to judge you. I'm having one too."

"Alright, let's hear what you've got, Noble."

"Take a big sip first," I said.

"That bad?"

He was referring to the threat to my daughter, which obviously was the worst of it. However, I was thinking about my decision to confront Roger Theus at his house in Malibu. He wasn't going to take that very well.

For the next ten minutes, I talked. I started at the beginning. He'd heard most of it already, but I thought it important to lead up to everything that he hadn't heard yet. He didn't interrupt once. He gave me an eye roll when I mentioned the distance from the door to where Shane Doyle's body was found, but he let me finish.

I finally got around to explaining why I went to the house in Malibu. I described how menacing - and yet, oddly cordial - Roger was to start. And how that deteriorated into a pissing contest in which he offended my race, my deceased wife, and my daughter.

I even told Captain Cook that Roger mentioned him by name. He wasn't impressed.

I closed by telling him about Sherin's visit and then showed him the letter that was waiting when we arrived back from the Santa Monica Pier.

"And that's about it," I said.

"You know what, I'll take a refill as I digest this all," he said.

I stood up, walked ten feet, grabbed the bottle, and topped him off. I left mine as it was. It was Sunday and I wasn't working, but just in case something came up, I decided a second glass of wine wasn't in my best interest.

Captain Cook stared at me.

"Before I get to the nuts and bolts, I just wanted to say I'm sorry, Noble. I can't imagine being with your daughter and seeing that note. Roger Theus sounds like a real scumbag."

"Thanks, Captain."

"But we can't let our emotions get the best of us, so I have to ask. Do you have any direct evidence that Theus killed any of these people? Shane Doyle, Lexi Grant, Ben/Knox, Alfonso Reyes? Any of them?"

"Direct evidence? No. But I've got a shitload of circumstantial evidence. Don't you find it odd that the guy whose testimony helped acquit Roger Theus was killed less than a month after he got out? Or that the DA who threw the case ended up dead in a triple murder?"

He didn't bother correcting me and saying murder/suicide. I took it as a small win.

I thought he was about to say something, but instead, he looked at me quizzically.

"You ever heard of a guy named Bruce Palmer?"

"The name rings a bell, yeah. Is he a PI?"

"Was."

"What happened?"

"Met a brutal end."

"Not the biggest surprise in that line of business."

"Agreed, but your little spiel here got me thinking. Maybe, just maybe, it's related."

"I like where your head is at. Do you know if he worked for any of the deceased?"

"Do I have to explain the hierarchy again? I'm the Captain. You're the detective."

I laughed.

"Mission accepted. I'll look into it tomorrow."

"I have no doubt you will."

"Does this mean you are starting to believe me?"

"I never said I didn't believe you. We need evidence, though. Especially against a guy who just got acquitted of murder."

"True," I admitted. "But let's be honest, there were a few times you were doubting me. Call it a hunch."

Captain Cook laughed.

"You'll make a good detective yet. And I saw you had a tiny bit left in that bottle. You might as well top me off."

"Coming right up."

∾

By 10:30 Monday morning, I'd confirmed that Shane Doyle had used Bruce Palmer as his P.I. at different times over the years. Quite a few DAs at the courthouse were able to confirm that.

This case was getting weirder and weirder.

If my suspicions were correct and Lexi, Knox, and Shane had collectively tried to throw the trial of Roger Theus, then where did Bruce Palmer fit in?

Why would you need a P.I. to investigate a case that you were trying to lose?

I tried to come up with a reason that he'd be involved. If anything, you'd want fewer people, not more. Why include Bruce Palmer?

To follow around Alfonso Reyes and make sure he was still going to sabotage his testimony?

That seemed possible.

And then, when Roger was acquitted, he decided to go full-on scorched-earth policy and kill anyone involved in the conspiracy? That also seemed possible. Shit, with the body count we had, it was more like probable.

You'd think most people would want to lay low after being given a 'Get out of jail free' card. Then again, Roger Theus wasn't like most people.

∾

I returned from the courthouse and knocked on Captain Cook's office door. He was rehanging some pictures on the wall as I walked in.

"Hey, Noble."

He left a picture dangling from the wall and walked back to his desk.

"How are you feeling today?" I asked.

"Perfect. I think 2.5 glasses of wine is my sweet spot. No more. And usually, no less."

"It was nice to have you over."

"I'll make sure next time it's not so long between visits. What can I do you for?"

"Bruce Palmer worked as Shane Doyle's P.I."

"Jesus."

"Yeah. Your intuition was right."

"Kind of hoped I was going to be wrong."

"Do you think all these coincidences would be enough to get us a warrant on Roger Theus?"

"I'm not sure. As I've said multiple times, we have to be positive when it comes to this guy. I can't imagine a judge is going to think any differently. He'll know Theus was just acquitted and probably won't be likely to give out a search warrant unless the evidence is irrefutable."

"I think if we laid everything on the table, a judge would listen."

"It sounds like you think Theus is a really smart guy. Do you think he'd have left any evidence at his house?"

"No, probably not."

"Then why get the warrant? Is it getting personal to you? You want to shake him up a little bit?"

"First off, yes, this is personal to me. He's intervened with my family. That makes this personal. But that's not why I want to do this. What if we could get his phone and check his GPS? It might show if he was at the scene of the triple murder that night. Or Alfonso Reyes's house. Or Bruce Palmer's."

"If he's as cunning as you say, wouldn't he know to turn his phone off?"

"I said he's smart. He's not the Michael Jordan of criminals. He easily could have made a mistake and kept his phone on at one of these crime scenes."

"I'll ask around. See if people think it's enough. Also, maybe I can find a judge who is police friendly. There are still a few of those left. Why don't we meet again tomorrow morning?"

"Okay. Thanks, Captain. For this and for believing in me."

"How long have we worked together, Noble?"

"Shit, over twenty years now."

"Exactly. And I've always believed in you. Don't make it out like this is some new occurrence."

"That's true. I just haven't been feeling the love lately."

The captain smiled deviously and I knew what was coming next.

"Is that what you need? To feel the love?"

"Fuck off," I said, but I was laughing too.

"You're just a little butt hurt that Dax Everton is now the '*It Guy*' of the LAPD."

There was no use denying it.

"You're right. Being a detective is now a young man's game."

"Hasn't it always been?"

"Maybe. But it's not as fun when you're the old guy."

Captain Cook laughed.

"We're all getting older, Noble."

"Yeah, but you can just sit around the office. I've got to be out in the field."

"Then get the fuck out there and stop talking to me. Go talk to some friends of Bruce Palmer."

"That's not a bad idea for a Captain."

"I've got my moments."

"I'll see you tomorrow."

"Come here for one second, Noble."

He motioned me over. I walked around the desk and he leaned in to whisper something in my ear.

"Even at your age, you're ten times the detective that Dax Everton is."

I patted him on the shoulder. He knew that meant a lot to me.

"You're alright, Captain."

"Now get the fuck out of here. This mutual admiration society of the last few days ends right now."

I smiled.

"Bout damn time," I said and walked out of his office.

The Bruce Palmer angle turned out to be a dead end.

I found out he was estranged from his ex-wife and children. She hung up on me within twenty seconds of calling. I talked to a couple of his private investigator friends, but they had no suspicions of how or why he had been killed. Nor had they heard if he might be working a recent case for Shane Doyle.

I still thought that his death was likely related to Roger Theus. I just wasn't sure how. The fact that Bruce Palmer had worked with Shane was just too coincidental if not. The problem was I couldn't prove Roger was involved which would hurt our chances of getting a warrant.

I called the Captain and told him no luck connecting Bruce Palmer to Roger Theus.

An hour later, l called Sherin.

"Hi, Dad."

"Everything okay?"

"Yes, we're all fine. Just like Saturday when you made sure I arrived home safe and just like when you called yesterday."

"Can't I be worried about my daughter?"

"I'm thinking it's the other way around and I should be worried about you."

"I'm fine."

"I'm fine," she said, repeating my line. "You sound like every other man I've ever met. They'll say, '*I'm fine*' in the midst of their final breaths."

"Well, I'm not on my final breath."

"How's the case coming against that psycho?"

"Captain Cook is trying to get a warrant. I'll keep you posted."

"Thanks. And sorry for jumping on you."

"It's alright. I'm just making sure my only child is safe."

"We're all good in San Diego."

"Say hi to that granddaughter of mine."

"Will do."

"Love you, Sherin."

"Love you, Dad."

CHAPTER 52

ROGER

In a matter of a few days, I'd received six offers on my apartment complexes.

I knew real estate in LA was desirable - that's why I'd gotten involved in the first place - but I didn't know rich people were like piranhas when a property opened.

I trusted my lawyer implicitly. I'd had him go to Knox and tell him Shane Doyle was the mark, after all. I asked him if I had to be in the United States when the deal went down.

"No, we can do e-signatures," Mason Croy III, attorney-at-law said.

He'd been with me since I'd bought my two properties. He'd been with me when a few tenants sued me for evicting them. He'd been with me when some women under twenty-one sued me for serving them booze at one of my parties.

And he'd stood by me when I was arrested for the murder of Billy Aybar. In fact, he was the one who suggested hiring Hilton Lund since Mason's specialty wasn't criminal law. He wasn't the judge-and-jury type. I'm not sure he'd ever done a full-fledged trial. He was more of a *'get shit done behind the scenes'* type of lawyer.

Per his suggestion, I hired Hilton Lund, even though it proved unnecessary in the end. Some shitty public defender would have won after we'd got Shane Doyle aboard.

Mason Croy III had made a lot of money off of me. And he was never going to turn his back on this cash cow. Plus, that whole attorney/client privilege thing. In other words, I could say anything to him.

"How about once the deal goes through?" I asked.

"What do you mean exactly?"

"Could you deposit the check into one of those accounts we recently set up?"

"Of course. For a small fee."

"There's no such thing as a small fee in your profession," I said.

Most people would have laughed at my comment, but Mason Croy III had the sense of humor of a salt shaker. It's a good thing he knew when to keep his mouth shut. I'd become proficient at eliminating people who stood in my way. Not that I was ready to off Mason. I needed him.

Speaking of becoming *proficient at eliminating people,* I hadn't forgotten about my dear friend, Noble Dunn. He was constantly on my mind. Flying out of the U.S. with millions of dollars secured in foreign bank accounts was sweet, but if I could find a way to kill Noble on my way out, that would make things all the sweeter.

As of now, there was only one thing that worried me about Noble. Him trying to get me on a no-fly list. That's why I wasn't publicizing the properties I was selling. My plan was to fly out of the country in a week or so and I just had to lay low until then. If I could last that long. Leaving a note about his daughter didn't exactly constitute *laying low.*

Even if Noble had convinced some of the dipshits at the LAPD that I might have been on a murdering spree, I hadn't been charged, so it's highly unlikely a no-fly list had been established in my honor.

And once I got to Europe? I'd continue monitoring the case from afar and if I heard from my lawyer that they were going to charge me with something in absentia, I'd go off the grid.

With all the money I had, things would be easy. I could just pay cash for a villa on the Mediterranean Sea. Mason Croy III had assured me that these Swiss and Grand Cayman-based accounts are basically untraceable so even if the LAPD decided to come after me, they'd have one hell of a time tracking me down. Banging a hot Greek girl in my Mediterranean villa wasn't exactly in their jurisdiction. And I'd probably have an assumed name at that point.

Maybe I'd even send Noble Dunn a postcard now and then, preferably with a gorgeous girl in the pic.

"Was Sherry this hot? Didn't think so. Maybe I'll invite Sherin out here to visit me. We could have a rollicking good time!"

That asshole would be seething. I loved thinking about it.

The man really loves his daughter. Even in the little time I observed them, that much was obvious. They had a warmhearted back-and-forth as they walked to the car. If that wasn't enough, he'd pulled a gun on me when I mentioned her at my house.

The man really loves his daughter, I repeated to myself.

A brutal thought sprang to mind.

As usual, I had no problem finding an address.

I'd have to thank Sherin for keeping her middle name along for the ride.

Sherin Dunn Silverton. 313 West Kalmia. San Diego, CA. 92101.

Do you know what would hurt Noble fifty times more than his own death?

His daughter's.

CHAPTER 53

NOBLE

On Monday night, I spent a solid twenty minutes debating whether any case had affected me quite this personally. Considering he'd threatened my daughter, I decided the answer was a resounding no. Roger Theus had gotten under my skin more than any other criminal I'd ever dealt with.

That's not to say he was the most reprehensible one. As horrible as he was, there'd been worse. A few necrophiliacs came to mind. Serial killers. School shooters.

But Roger Theus had - in record time - become the most personal.

Did I want to see him spend the rest of his life in prison?

To be honest, no. I'd much rather have shot him right through his big, shiny, sweaty forehead.

The guy had already avoided prison once.

I would have preferred not to take any chances.

I was still a detective, however. If I had to bring him in and let him rot in jail, then I would. I'd always prided myself on following the law. On being a good, honest detective.

I couldn't just toss my morals to the curb because this suspect had gotten underneath my skin.

As much as I wanted to.

～

I got to the office early on Tuesday morning.

Captain Cook wasn't in yet.

I talked to some of my fellow detectives and a few plainclothes officers. Not a single one asked how my case was going. They didn't mention Shane Doyle or Roger Theus. I don't know if it was intentional or not, but the Captain had seemingly kept this between us.

The obvious answer was - since he'd alluded to it several times - that after Roger Theus's acquittal, we had to tread more lightly than usual. And if he told a bunch of people around the office, it would get out. Cops are no better at keeping a secret than anybody else. In many ways, we are worse.

Now, if we secured a warrant, that would all change. There was no keeping that under wraps.

By 11:00, I still hadn't seen Captain Cook. I considered calling him but gave him the benefit of the doubt. For all I knew, he was trying to schmooze a judge into giving us our beloved warrant.

At 11:30, I received my answer.

A text came in.

"Come to my office."

It was the Captain.

~

"You owe me one, Noble," he said.

I looked up and noticed the same picture still hanging awkwardly.

"You were able to secure the search warrant?"

"After much ass-kissing and other things not usually in my repertoire."

"Thank you, Brendan," I said.

I'd accidentally called him by his first name. My subconscious must have told me he deserved it for what he'd been able to accomplish.

"Wasn't sure you remembered my first name."

I laughed.

"Sorry, Captain."

"Nothing to be sorry about."

"When are they going to execute the warrant?"

"In a few hours. Do you want to be there?"

"I'll assume that's rhetorical."

Brendan Glanville, a.ka. Captain Cook, a.k.a. my boss, started laughing.

"Yeah, that's what I thought. We are all meeting at two p.m. in Malibu. You can ride with me if you'd like."

"Sounds good."

"One thing though, Noble."

"What is it?"

"I wouldn't tell anyone else that you've been to Theus's house before. That might lead to a few awkward questions for you."

"Point taken. My lips are sealed."

"Come back around one. You know how it is getting to Malibu. The PCH could be a parking lot so let's leave early to be safe."

"I'll be here."

It's a good thing we left a few minutes after one because the Pacific Coast Highway was the exact parking lot that Captain Cook feared.

We got to our rendezvous at 1:45. It was a gas station parking lot off the PCH. As my fellow officers discussed how it was going to go down, I hovered in the background. I was a detective and higher on the ladder than the officers making this raid, but this was their area of expertise.

I gathered information in order to make it possible to get a warrant. I wasn't often part of the team executing said warrant.

After a brief five-minute meeting, the caravan set off for Roger Theus's house. There were five LAPD police cars and another three civilian cars.

We arrived a few minutes later, our car being the last to start up the hill to get to Roger's house.

He had an expansive driveway, but it couldn't fit all of us, so Captain Cook parked his car on the right side of the hill and we walked the remaining twenty-five feet.

The gathered police officers took a minute to get everyone into place. They had a small battering ram to break down the door if necessary. Two officers stood twenty or so yards back from the front door, guns locked and loaded.

It made sense. However Captain Cook was able to secure the warrant, he must have told the judge that he suspected the man of having killed several people. In a case such as this, the LAPD wouldn't be taking any chances.

The man closest to the front door started using his fingers to count down from five. He knocked forcefully on the door.

I saw there was a small piece of paper attached to the front door. It couldn't have been more than two inches by two inches, but it was unmistakable.

Not this again, I told myself.

I wanted to yell at the officer to read the letter first, but I wouldn't dare. This wasn't my shindig.

"Open the door, Mr. Theus," the man yelled. "It's the LAPD. We have a warrant to search the property."

Nothing happened for several seconds.

Captain Cook, who was right next to me, whispered in my ear.

"Do you see that piece of paper?"

"Yes. Why don't they grab it?"

"It's irrelevant to them. Their job is to get in that house."

"I know, but…"

My words just sat there in the air.

"Open the door, Mr. Theus!" the officer yelled, louder this time. "You are surrounded."

Still nothing.

Fifteen seconds later, the officer spoke again.

"This is your last chance, Mr. Theus. Come out or we're breaking the door down."

My heart was starting to beat way too fast. I was suddenly extremely anxious about what that piece of paper said.

"You had your chance. We're coming in."

The officer with the smallish battering ram approached the front door. Three officers got in line behind him. The man who'd been standing there and yelling once again started counting down from five on his fingers.

Once he ran out of fingers, we watched as the man sent the battering ram through the door. It splintered it in several places, but it didn't cave all the way in. He used it a second time and this time the whole door shot inward. A split second later, the three cops behind him were inside the house, guns drawn.

There was screaming and yelling, but no shots were fired.

A minute passed with more of the same.

By that point, I knew Roger Theus wasn't going to be there. What scared me - no, what terrified me - was contemplating where he could be.

Thirty seconds later, one of the officers came out and yelled, "There's no one here."

Two of the other cops walked into the house. They must have been there for collecting evidence and not part of the raid.

I looked to my right at Captain Cook.

He read my mind.

"Let's see what that note said," he said.

We briskly moved toward the front door.

One of the officers saw Captain Cook.

"What do you need, Captain?"

"There was a small piece of paper on the front door. May I see it please?"

"Are you sure? I didn't see anything."

"He's sure, " I said, as forcefully as I could.

"Alright, follow me."

I entered Roger Theus's house for a second time. We stepped over the splintered wood. Captain Cook looked at the main frame of the door but the piece of paper was no longer there.

"Told you there was no paper," the officer said.

I was livid.

"I'm detective Noble Dunn and there absolutely was a piece of fucking paper."

He was about to reprimand me - like I cared - when we saw someone approaching with the piece of paper.

His eyes looked towards mine. Not just in a glancing way. He was staring at me. I was frozen in terror.

"You're Noble Dunn, aren't you?"

"Yes," I said, barely able to get it out.

He uncurled the small piece of paper, just as I'd done at my house. He handed it to me. I took a brief glance over at Captain Cook who looked almost as petrified as me.

I started reading it and I'm not sure how I kept my balance.

My whole world started spinning.

The bottom of the piece of paper was in black ink and read: "Sherin Dunn Silverton. 313 West Kalmia. San Diego, CA. 92101."

The top of the paper was in red ink and somehow worse: "Hey, Noble! Your daughter was great fun. I'm sorry she had to expire so young."

I screamed at the top of my lungs - and a split second later - burst out in tears.

CHAPTER 54

ROGER

"Roger, I've got some bad news."

It was Mason Croy III. I'd been dealing with him a lot lately which wasn't a good thing.

"What now?"

"I've heard from one of my sources that the LAPD is trying to secure a search warrant against you."

"Fuck. Can't you stop it?"

"No. Warrants aren't something I can stop."

"Lawyers are good for fucking nothing."

"Do I need to reiterate all I've done for you lately?"

"Oh, fuck off, Mason. Let me vent."

"Alright, Roger."

I looked out of my window onto the Pacific below. The only thing I hadn't put on the market was this house in Malibu. Maybe I was hoping I'd be able to return here someday. That was getting less likely by the minute. The walls were closing in on me. I knew that.

Fucking Noble Dunn. He was to blame for this. I'd committed the perfect crimes and no one was the wiser. Until this freaking asshole came along. I couldn't wait to get my revenge on him.

"Are they trying to secure the warrant right now?"

"That's what my sources say."

"And when will they execute it?"

"If it's approved, likely within the next several hours."

"Fuck!" I screamed into my phone.

Mason kept quiet. Probably a good decision.

"And the warrant is for this house?"

"It may include the apartment complexes as well. Maybe your car or your cell phone. But it's a search warrant, not an arrest warrant."

"So I won't be arrested?"

"Depends on what they find."

The walls were getting ever closer.

"I'm not sure I want to take that chance," I said.

I thought long and hard.

"Do you still have that duplex in Hollywood that you rent out?"

Mason Croy III didn't answer for a few seconds. I knew he hated what I was asking. I also knew that he was scared of me and couldn't say no.

"It's available right now."

"Good. I'll be staying there. I'll swing by your work in about an hour. Come meet me outside and give me the key to the place."

"Alright, Roger."

"And one more thing, Mason. If you're thinking about growing a conscience and telling the cops that I forced you to give me a place to stay, just don't. I've got enough dirt on you to put your slimy ass in jail too."

"I'd never turn on you, Roger. Not just because of the attorney/client privilege, but because you're my friend."

"You're my sleazy attorney, nothing more. Be outside of your office at 12:30 p.m."

"Okay."

I started grabbing things from my house that I'd need in the coming days.

I hated the idea of hiding out at Mason's Hollywood duplex, but the possibility of getting arrested was worse. I'd been extremely careful at every crime scene, but it was possible I'd made a mistake. Now that the LAPD had a hard-on for me, I was walking a fine line.

I couldn't let them get ahold of my cell phone. They might be able to triangulate my whereabouts around the times that Alfonso Reyes and Bruce Palmer had been killed. I'd turned my phone off before entering Reyes's garage and Palmer's house, but I had been in the area and that would be tough to explain away.

I decided it would be best to turn off my phone immediately. I could hit up Mason for a burner.

As I started to pack, I thought about what I'd do once I got to the duplex. First off, I'd order a few hundred dollars of food that could last me a while. I certainly wouldn't want to be going in and out and drawing attention to myself. It's not like I was a guy who could just blend in. I was too big and inevitably stood out.

I realized my mistake. The search warrants might have included looking at my credit cards as well. I wouldn't be using them to order any food. I'd figure something out.

My mind was wandering. I didn't like it one bit.

I grabbed a bunch of my Tommy Bahama shirts and threw them in the car. I had some memorabilia of famous people that I'd like to have kept but now wasn't the time. The signed guitar I had from Eddie Van Halen was one of my favorite possessions. I'd find a way to get it back someday.

I quickly filled a duffle bag with some boxers, shorts, and my toiletries.

My phone told me it was 11:56. Mason had said the raid wouldn't happen for a few hours. That didn't set my mind at ease. I wanted to get the fuck out of here as soon as I could.

The final few things I packed were my laptop, desktop, and iPad. There was no way I was letting those pigs go through that shit. I'm sure I'd left something incriminating on them.

I was right about to lock the door behind me when I saw a certain piece of paper sitting on the table in the living room. I went and grabbed it.

Sherin Silverton. 313 West Kalmia. San Diego, CA. 92101.

I wasn't going to be meeting Sherin on this day, but I might be able to give Noble a heart attack in the meantime.

There was a red pen sitting on the table and I wrote the following: "Hey, Noble. Your daughter was great fun. Sorry, she had to expire so young."

I broke out in laughter. Even when I was the one being chased and attacked, I had a way of fighting back. I hoped Noble was at this raid. That would be fucking awesome. All the cops thinking I'd killed his daughter.

On the bright side, he'd be alerted to this letter either way.

I locked the door behind me and walked to my car, smiling the whole way, just imagining Noble's reaction to what I'd written.

Hahaha.

I cracked myself up.

CHAPTER 55

NOBLE

The crying only lasted a few seconds.

I quickly pulled myself together. If Sherin was still alive - please, God! - I had to contact her and alert her that she could be in grave danger.

Captain Cook proved the voice of reason.

"Roger Theus is a lying piece of shit, Noble. Call your daughter."

I reached for my phone, but my hands were shaking and it took me two tries to grasp it.

I called Sherin's number and held my breath the whole time.

There was no answer and my heart sunk further.

"Captain, can you call in a favor to San Diego and send some cop cars to this address?"

"I'm on it, Noble."

I handed him the paper with my daughter's address. The Captain took his phone and walked out to the driveway where there was less commotion.

I tried Sherin back a second time. Nothing.

I sent her a text: *"Call me as soon as you get this! It's extremely important!"*

As scared as I was, I couldn't let my mind wander. I'd become incapacitated if I went down that road.

Thirty seconds later, Captain Cook walked back in the house.

"Cops are headed to Sherin's house right now," he said.

I nodded. It was all I had the strength to do.

I saw many of my fellow cops staring in my direction. My scream had brought attention my way. Not that I cared one way or the other. All I was thinking about was my daughter.

And that's when I heard it. My phone was ringing.

I removed it from my pocket and looked down. It was Sherin calling.

If the voice on the other end belonged to Roger Theus, my life would never, ever, ever be the same. It would basically be over. I wouldn't want to continue living.

"Hello?" I stammered.

However long it took for someone to speak - and it was probably only a split second - was the longest moment of my life.

"What's going on, Dad? I saw your text."

I wanted to break out in tears of joy, but this wasn't the time.

"Are you at work?"

"Yes, I've got a child in my office waiting for me right now."

"Listen, Sherin. I'm going to send some police officers to your office right now. I want you to go with them, wherever they take you. Have them pick up Ava from daycare. And call Bobby and tell him to meet you."

"What the hell is going on?"

"Do you remember the guy Roger Theus I told you about?"

"Of course. How could I forget?"

"He threatened you directly and I can't take any chances."

"What do you mean he threatened me directly?"

"Sherin, I can't right now. I'll explain it all later. Just go with the cops when they get there."

"Are Ava and Bobby safe?"

"They should be, but let's not take any chances. Make sure the officers go and pick up Ava as well."

"You're really scaring me."

"You have no idea what I've been going through the last several minutes. Call me once you get settled with the police."

"Okay, Dad."

I hung up the phone.

There was no avoiding what came next.

I cried for the second time in a matter of minutes.

Captain Cook was on top of things.

He asked me what Sherin's work address was. I had to Google it.

A minute later, he told me the San Diego police were headed there.

I'd managed to get control of myself again.

"Thanks, Captain. Do you think Theus could be down there?"

I was done calling him Roger. The animal didn't deserve it.

"Better to be safe than sorry, obviously, but I doubt it. My guess is he was tipped off about the warrant and left the note to scare the fuck out of you."

"It worked," I said.

"I don't know what I would have done in your shoes."

"There's not much you can do. I felt defenseless."

"I'm just glad that Sherin is safe."

I noticed that there were no other officers standing within twenty feet of it. Word had now surely gotten out. They probably didn't want to approach me in case this was a worst-case scenario.

Mercifully, it wasn't.

My daughter Sherin was alive.

~

An hour later, Sherin, her husband Bobby, and their daughter Ava were all in the care of the San Diego Police Department.

We'd left Roger Theus's house and Captain Cook had dropped me off at our precinct. He said he was going to ask around and try to secure an arrest warrant for Theus. This was going to be tougher than getting the search warrant for his house, phone, etc. They'd found nothing at the house - at least, not yet - that proved he was involved in the murders of Shane, Lexi, Knox, Alfonso, or Bruce Palmer.

We could show them the letter he'd left, but with my daughter being safe, I'm not sure that would be grounds for an arrest warrant.

Where was Roger Theus?

The cell phone registered to him was powered down. A few officers had tried calling it.

I think Captain Cook was right. Theus had known about the warrant, grabbed what he could from the house, and powered his phone down so people wouldn't know where he was going.

And, oh yeah, found the time to leave the venomous note for me.

I'd told myself I'd behave as a man of the law if I was forced to bring him in. I no longer felt that way. I wanted him drawn and quartered. I wanted him to get the Breaking Wheel or the Iron Chair.

Roger Theus deserved a Medieval death.

CHAPTER 56

ROGER

Mason Croy III was indeed waiting for me when I arrived outside of his office.

Having people fear you had its perks. No one dared fuck with me.

I'd driven the blue Corvette. It was my favorite car and I wasn't going to give those pigs the satisfaction of impounding it.

"Here's the key to the duplex," he said. "You know where it's located, right?"

"You're not getting off that easy, Mason. Get in the fucking car."

He looked around as if some stranger on the street was going to save him.

"I don't have a choice, do I?"

"No."

He got in the car. I started heading towards West Hollywood.

"You're not going to kill me, are you Roger?"

He was genuinely scared. Good.

"Not today. You're here to hide this car somewhere. I can't have it sitting near your apartment in Hollywood. When I drop myself off, you're going to find a spot to hide this bad boy."

I stared at him.

"Understood?"

"Understood."

"There are a few other things. I need you to find out if they've put me on a no-fly list. If not, I'm out of here in the next few days. And you'll facilitate getting all of my money into my accounts once my apartment complexes are sold, which is going to come quickly."

It wasn't a question, but Mason answered as if it was one.

"Sure, I'll do that for you."

I'd already consolidated several million into my accounts with several more to come.

"Next order of business. I need you to get me a burner phone after you drop me off."

"Alright."

"You better make sure it's clean as a whistle because I'm going to be calling you on it. I'd say go to T-Mobile. Those crooks cater to burners."

"Consider it done."

I put my arm on Mason's shoulder.

"Why so nervous, counselor? I'm not going to kill someone who I need to help me get out of this country."

He looked white as a ghost.

"Yes, sir."

"I want you to drop the phone off at 10:00 p.m. tonight. Just set it on the front doorstep and keep walking. Make sure none of those Hollywood drug addicts see you. They'll grab that fucker before I have a chance to open the door."

"My condo is in a really nice part of Hollywood."

"That's the Mason I know. Arguing your point. Not this girly man who entered my car."

He just shook his head.

"Is there anything else you need, Roger?"

"I'd say ten hookers, but I probably don't want to cause a commotion at the condo."

Mason tried to smile, but it came off like he was constipated.

"Is that it?"

I remembered something.

"Actually, there is something else. In case they are monitoring me, I don't want to use my credit cards right now. No DoorDash or Uber Eats for me. So, I'd like you to bring me 2-3 days of the best food LA has to offer. Grab me some sushi, some pizza, and maybe something from Koreatown."

I was demanding as hell. Not that Mason was going to protest.

"Sure. I've got a question, Roger."

"Shoot."

"If you're not going to use your credit cards, how are you going to book your flight out?"

"You're going to do it."

"I was afraid you were going to say that. Aiding and abetting a criminal is a crime."

"Well, I'm not a criminal yet, so let's get this flight booked. Also, do whatever you can in your power to prevent them from getting an arrest warrant or charging me in absentia. Once I'm gone, I couldn't give a shit. I'm going to disappear."

Mason looked at me skeptically. He had a point. Disappearing and I wasn't often used in the same sentence.

"Is that it?' he asked.

"For now. Ditch the car and bring me a phone and a shit ton of food tonight."

"You going to make it without food until ten p.m.?"

"Is there any way they have an arrest warrant out for me yet?"

"No. Shit, they probably haven't even started with the search warrant."

I saw a Burger King fifty yards ahead and slammed on the brakes as Mason unnecessarily extended his hand to touch the dash. As if he was going to go through the windshield.

"You want anything?" I asked.

"I'm not hungry."

Fifteen minutes later, we'd arrived at his condo in West Hollywood. He was right, there were no homeless to be seen. This truly was the nice part of town.

"Where's the most inconspicuous place to park?"

"In the back," he said. "There's a rear entrance to the condo and you can take your clothes in through that door."

"Okay. Then leave the phone and the food in the back as well."

"Will do."

I tried to think if leaving my car in a separate part of town was advisable. Throw them off my scent. I decided it wasn't worth it. I needed to get Mason off the road and quickly. The worst outcome was him getting arrested and the police figuring out he was my lawyer. They'd have a few questions about when and where he'd been given the car.

"Where are you going to put the car?" I asked.

"I have a three-car garage at my house in the Palisades."

The Pacific Palisades was one of the more exclusive areas of Los Angeles, a city with plenty of beautiful locales.

"Alright, drive this directly home, park it in your garage, and leave it there until I tell you what to do. Under no circumstances are you to drive it again after today."

"Got it."

"And don't you dare speed on your way home. If you get pulled over, we might both be fucked."

"I won't get pulled over."

I parked in the back, took my clothes out of the car, and carried them to the back of the townhouse. By the time I came back, Mason was already in the driver's seat. I grabbed the remaining clothes and said goodbye.

"Goodbye, Roger."

"I'm looking forward to seeing your culinary choices."

"You're an asshole."

With that, he drove off. At a very reasonable speed, just as I'd told him.

Mason was going to do whatever I asked him in the coming days.

CHAPTER 57

NOBLE

There were times when I hated how sprawling the city of Los Angeles was.

Usually, it involved traffic and how it might take me an hour to drive ten miles.

On this day - the day after we executed the search warrant at Roger Theus's house - I was lamenting the size of Los Angeles for a different reason.

Theus had too many places to hide. I didn't even know where to start. He could be in Redondo Beach, Hollywood, the Valley, or outside of my house, peering in. Or a thousand other places.

My point is that if he was still in LA, he could be anywhere. It was basically pointless to canvas different parts of the city.

Then again, maybe he wasn't even in LA anymore. He could have driven to Las Vegas and booked a room under a fake name until this all blew over. We'd checked flights at all the airports around Los Angeles and he hadn't flown out. At least not under his own name.

There was one city that I feared above all others: San Diego.

Sherin's husband Bobby was a good man and a pretty tough one at that. He'd do anything to protect his wife and daughter. That being said, I don't think he was a match for the criminal mind of Roger Theus. And it worried me to no end.

I considered driving down to San Diego and staying with my daughter. Captain Cook talked me out of it. He said it was extremely unlikely that

Roger Theus would leave that note and then drive down there to try and harm Sherin. He'd have to assume that police were protecting her. And they were. We had a police car parked outside of Sherin's house twenty-four hours a day.

While Cook was probably right, *extremely unlikely* wasn't quite enough when referring to the safety of your daughter. After much thought, I decided to stay in LA. My gut feeling was he was still here.

But where?

"Noble, what are you doing in two hours?"

Captain Cook had knocked on my office door and then walked in before receiving my response.

"Probably what I've been doing all morning. Reaching out to any of Theus's acquaintances and seeing if they have any idea where he'd be hiding."

"I notice you aren't calling him Roger anymore."

"Fuck that name. And fuck him."

"Have you tried his attorney?"

"Of course. He was the first person I called. I got a no comment, just as I'd expected. We just executed a search warrant on his client, it's not like he was going to be very talkative."

"I know the guy. Mason Croy III. He's a jerk. But hey, aren't all people who have three I's at the end of their name?"

It wasn't exactly the time, but I couldn't help but laugh.

"Maybe not all, but the percentages certainly go up," I said.

"So, the reason I'm here is that I've got a meeting with a judge at 1:00. I'm hoping to secure an arrest warrant for Roger Theus. I'd love for you to tag along and make your pitch as to why he's likely committed these murders. You know the case better than anyone and could certainly sell it better than I can."

"Of course, I'll go. I'll charm the pants off of this judge."

Captain Cook laughed.

"Let's not go too far there, Noble."

"Which judge is it?"

"Judge Bryant."

"He's pretty liberal about giving out warrants, isn't he?"

"Why do you think I chose him?"

"That's why they pay you the big bucks," I said.

I was trying to make a joke out of everything. I was still extremely nervous about my daughter and I was defaulting to humor. It had long been my go-to when I was anxious.

"I'll swing by here at 12:30 and pick you up."

"We spent a day at my house, and now, two car rides with you. I can't wait for this case to end so we can get back at each other's throats."

I'd done it again.

"You can say that again."

With that, the Captain left my office.

~

Judge Jerry Bryant was getting up there in age. Generally, judges were already on the older side, but Judge Bryant was geriatric even for judges. He should have been the one hanging them up next year, not me.

He had a full head of gray, wavy hair, and the long hair might have made him look younger if the wrinkles hadn't given him away. I'd dealt with him a few times over the years, usually testifying for the prosecution in cases he was presiding over.

I'd gotten the impression that the ADAs liked Judge Bryant. He tended to look down on prospective criminals and not give them the benefit of the doubt, which made things easier for the prosecution. I'm sure defense attorneys despised him.

Cook and I parked outside of the Santa Monica Courthouse and made our way up to the fourth floor. We gave the clerk our affidavit, filed the prospective arrest warrant, and then asked to meet with Judge Bryant. He would read the affidavit that the Captain had put together and make his decision based on that. A little schmoozing never hurt and that's why he'd brought me along.

The clerk sent us to Department 37 where Judge Bryant was waiting for us in his chambers. He looked even older than I remembered. We all exchanged handshakes and he motioned toward the chairs opposite him. We sat.

"How are you Captain Glanville?" the judge asked.

The nickname Captain Cook was usually only used by his subordinates. Most judges would find it a tad hokey. They weren't wrong. Still, it was a bit odd to hear him called by his last name.

"Nice to see you, Judge Bryant. It's been a while."

"This must be an important arrest warrant. They sent you all the way here."

"Our precinct isn't that far from here."

"You know what I mean."

"I do. And yes, this is very important. Not only do we think Roger Theus has killed six people, but he's now threatened the daughter of Detective Dunn."

Captain Cook motioned in my direction.

"I know who Noble is," the judge said. "He's been in my courtroom over the years. Plus, he's been on the news a few times. I'm probably one of the few judges who pre-dates him being a detective."

I laughed.

"Thanks, Judge. I guess. We're not getting any younger. And I've always enjoyed my time in your courtroom."

"No one likes a kiss-ass, but thanks."

I smiled.

"He threatened your daughter?" he asked.

"He did."

I looked over at the Captain and he gave me a quick nod, telling me it was time to make my pitch to the judge.

I spent the next ten minutes going over everything I'd come to learn about Roger Theus. I'd made the same "speech" to Captain Cook a few days back so I had it down pat. Roger Theus hadn't left my mind since I'd started investigating him as a suspect in the Brady/Lexi/Knox murders. Detailing everything was easy.

Judge Bryant asked a few questions, but he didn't give away which way he was leaning. That's probably the sign of a good judge.

I closed with all that happened over the last several days.

The judge looked at me and asked his first question. It wasn't a good harbinger of things to come.

"Is it standard protocol for a detective to confront a potential felon at his home?"

"It's not standard protocol, but it's not unheard of either."

"What did you see as the advantages?"

"I wanted him to know we were on to him."

"We or you?"

"That's fair. It was mostly just me at that point. However, your honor, I was pretty darn sure that he'd killed the ADA Brady Doyle and the two other victims at that crime scene. I was also beginning to suspect he'd murdered Alfonso Reyes, but I'd yet to know about the murder of Bruce Palmer. I wanted Theus to know that someone - even if it was only me - was on to him. In my mind, he was eliminating potential witnesses and if nothing else, my visit would make him a little more cautious."

"That's well thought out Detective Dunn, but is that really what you were thinking when you confronted him?"

If there was ever a time for a white lie, it was now.

"Yes, your honor. It was."

"I have to say, it seems pretty coincidental that all of those people associated with the Roger Theus case are ending up dead."

Captain Cook jumped in.

"Our opinion is that it's anything but a coincidence, your honor."

"I know, Captain Glanville. I was being a bit facetious."

The judge had flip-flopped. I now believed him to be on our side.

"How exactly do you think the P.I. is involved?" the judge asked, looking at me the whole time.

"I think he was hired by Shane Doyle. There were some phone calls between the two during the potential timeframe and they'd worked with each other in the past. I'm not sure why exactly he was hired, but my guess is that once Theus was acquitted, he found out Palmer had been involved. By that point, he wasn't taking any chances. He was just killing anyone who could turn on him or stood in the way of his freedom."

The judge paused a few seconds.

"And you go along with all this, Captain?"

"I do, your honor."

"I'm sure you both realize that with Theus having already been acquitted of one murder, this is a touchy warrant."

"I understand," I said. "We wouldn't do this if we didn't think he was a big threat to the public."

"And your family specifically."

There was no use denying it.

"Yes, that is true. Although, I thought he was guilty of these murders well before he threatened my daughter."

"I'm sorry you had to go through that. I can't imagine the fear."

"Thanks," I said.

"I'm going to approve your warrant, gentlemen. I hope you're right about all this. There will be hell to pay if not."

This time, Captain Cook spoke first.

"Thank you for believing in us, Judge Bryant."

"Thank you, your honor," I said.

The judge looked at me.

"You keep that family of yours safe, Noble."

"Thank you. The San Diego police are taking care of it right now."

"Well, hopefully, this warrant helps you get Roger Theus off the street."

"Thanks for everything," Captain Cook said and I nodded in agreement.

With that, Judge Bryant made a motion signifying that we could leave his office.

~

The fact that we'd secured an arrest warrant was the good news. The bad news was that we still had to find Roger Theus. No easy feat.

His phone had been dormant since we'd raided his house. The search warrant had included the right to search his phone - or in case it wasn't discovered - to trace it. And it hadn't been turned back on since initially being turned off.

That would have been the easiest way to find him, but as I'd come to learn, nothing in this case was going to be easy. That's why Roger Theus was such a tough adversary. I had a feeling he was going to do anything to prevent going back to jail. That meant a violent ending was possible. Or probable.

There was some good news. The murders of Alfonso Reyes and Bruce Palmer had not involved a gun. Hopefully, the gun that Roger had left at the Shane/Lexi/Shane crime scene - the one he'd use to frame Shane for a murder/suicide - was the only gun he had.

If he'd managed to secure another one, I didn't see this resolving itself peacefully. Especially once he found out there was a warrant out for his arrest.

~

I left work at three p.m.

It was odd. At a time when I should have been up to my neck in theories on where Roger Theus might be, it was the opposite. I had no freaking idea where he was and couldn't even come up with any good prospects.

I told the Captain I could do just as much work at home and he agreed. There were now several other detectives working the case and it was not like I had to do it all on my own. Still, I'd brought it this far. I wanted to be the one to figure this puzzle out.

I called my daughter after walking in the door and plopping my butt down on the couch.

"Hey, Dad."

She sounded down. I couldn't blame her.

"I've got some good news."

"You caught Roger Theus?"

"Not exactly, but we did get a judge to sign an arrest warrant for him."

"That would be better news if you knew where he was."

Being raised with a detective father made Sherin very perceptive when it came to cops and the law.

"Yes, that's true," I admitted. "But when we do catch him, he's going straight to jail."

"Just to be acquitted again?"

"C'mon, Sherin. Have a little faith."

"I've got a cop car outside of my house and I haven't been to work in two days. Sorry if I don't have faith in the LAPD."

"Do you really want to go back to work?"

"Yes, I want to, but I'm trying to respect your wishes. Plus, I still worry about Ava."

"Why don't I come down there and watch her?"

"Thanks, Dad, but they need you in LA."

"It's killing me not being down there," I said.

"Theus is more likely to get caught if you're up there than down here bothering us."

I managed to laugh.

"That's probably true."

"Anything else, Dad?"

"I promise this will be over soon."

"You can't guarantee that. And listen, Dad, don't take this the wrong way, but if you haven't caught this animal by Monday, I'm going back to work. I'll take Ava with me if I have to. I have a life to live. I can't afford to be missing appointments day after day. If people start to think I'm an unreliable pediatrician, they'll gladly start going somewhere else."

It pained me to hear my daughter talking like this.

"I'm so sorry, Sherin. I'm only trying to do what's best for you."

"Best or safest?"

"To me, they are one and the same."

"Catch him by Sunday night, Dad."

It was time to be confident. Overconfident, you might say.

"He'll be in custody by then. Or dead."

"I guess we'll see. Be safe, Dad."

We usually tried to end our phone calls on a positive note. This was not one of those times.

~

I jumped up from the couch and grabbed a bottle of red wine.

I poured myself a large glass.

Amongst all the other unwanted things this case had brought, my drinking had increased.

I looked down at my phone, verifying what day it was. The days were all blending together. It was Thursday.

I had three days to catch the asshole.

CHAPTER 58

ROGER

"I've got some bad news, Roger."

The phone call was from Mason, but then again, it couldn't have been anyone else. He'd delivered the burner phone the previous night and was the only one who knew I had it.

"I feel like that's all you're giving me these days, Mason."

He didn't respond right away, probably because I'd used that very line a few times recently. He could have told me this was all because of my own actions and he would not have been wrong.

"Well, what is it?" I asked.

"They've secured an arrest warrant for you."

"With what evidence? They've got nothing tying me to those murders!"

"Who said it was for murder?"

"Oh, shut the fuck up, Mason. When I was incarcerated, I had you go to Knox and tell him that the ADA Shane Doyle would be the easiest to break. Then he gets Alfonso Reyes to flip his testimony. And then they all end up dead? Stop pretending you don't know what's going on."

"I know you're on a burner phone, Roger, but you really should be smarter about the things you say over the phone."

Mason was right. Not that I was going to admit it to him. He was starting to piss me off almost as much as Noble had. The problem was that I couldn't kill Mason. I needed his help with my properties and hopefully, getting out of the country. He'd remain alive. Still, I relished the thought of bashing his skull in.

As for killing Noble, it would purely be personal at this point. The LAPD had an arrest warrant out for me. Killing Noble wasn't going to stop a damn thing. And yet, like Mason, I was still delighting in the thought of Noble's demise.

My mind was wandering and I couldn't remember what the fuck we'd been talking about. I'd only been at his Hollywood condo for thirty hours and it was already driving me bonkers. I hated every second of it. It's like I was in jail again, albeit with a slightly nicer cell.

"What would happen if I tried to fly out of the country?" I asked, regaining my composure.

"You'd likely be arrested."

"Likely?"

"Well, you're not on the no-fly list since that's federal, so it's not a guarantee you've been flagged. But with an arrest warrant out for murder, you'd be taking a huge risk, so that's why I said likely. You just never know. Maybe a TSA agent isn't looking at his screen and you get through. I don't know."

"I'm not going to put all my stock in a distracted TSA agent."

"Nor would I."

"So, what are my options?"

"Turn yourself in."

"No thanks."

"You already beat the court system once."

"Have you got another DA we can bribe? How about another witness like Alfonso Reyes?"

"Those were likely one-time things."

"Exactly.

"What do you want me to say, Roger?"

"I want you to tell me you found me some boat captain and he's going to drive me to Cuba. Or to Catalina and from there I'll get on a plane that flies me to Europe."

"The Catalina airport is for small planes. There's nothing flying to Europe, Roger. Be realistic."

"No thanks. If I'm being realistic then I'm looking at a lifetime behind bars or killing myself."

"Hey, if you killed yourself, at least the cops wouldn't be on your tail anymore."

I didn't give him the satisfaction of laughing.

"I'm sorry, Roger. I didn't mean it like that."

"How did you mean it, Mason?"

He didn't answer and I let it go. Sadly, he was right. My death was going to be the only way the cops - especially Noble - would be off my back forever.

"I'll be honest, I'm not fond of these options," I said. "What else have you got?"

"I don't want to put myself in harm's way…"

I interrupted.

"You're already in harm's way, Mason. If I get caught, I've got enough to put you away for a long time. In fact, maybe I'll go to the police and trade my freedom for yours."

I was harkening back to my last meeting with Knox before being arrested. I'd threatened him in the same way, telling him I'd rat him out to save my own hide.

This was different and both Mason and I knew it. The police thought - correctly, I might add - that I'd killed several people. I wouldn't be able to trade my freedom for a pissant attorney who'd done all his crimes at my behest.

"Nice try, Roger. They don't want some small fish like me."

"Yeah, you're probably right, Mason, but I'll make sure to ask them just to make sure."

"I can't wait to have you out of my life."

"The feeling is mutual. Now get me a fucking way out of this country."

"I'll be in touch."

With that, I hung up.

～

I sat back down on an L-shaped couch and stared at the ceiling.

To most, a duplex in Hollywood was probably living in luxury. Not for me.

My house in Malibu had a view of the Pacific Ocean. Here, I watched a ceiling fan go round and round.

I needed to get the fuck out of this condo.

I ran through a few of my possibilities.

(1) Book a flight in my name and pray I wasn't arrested at the airport.

(2) Kill Mason and book a flight under his name.

(3) Stay at this apartment and pray that the police didn't knock on the door in the coming days.

(4) Go kill Captain Cook, Noble Dunn, his daughter, and just go out in a hail of bullets.

There had to be something I was missing.

I'd given myself the moniker of The Mastermind.

It was time to live up to it.

I thought long and hard for the next thirty minutes, my eyes never venturing far from the ceiling fan. Its rotating blades put me in some sort of trance.

Whatever it was, it must have worked.

A plan started to form.

It was risky, crazy, obscene, and almost impossible to pull off.

In other words, right up my alley.

CHAPTER 59

NOBLE

By 10:30 on Friday morning, two huge events had taken place. They both affected me; one directly and the other indirectly.

The direct hit was from a man named Sven Eriksson. He was Bruce Palmer's neighbor and had given an interview to a local news channel, KTLA, that morning. He claims that he saw Roger Theus in their neighborhood on the day that Palmer was killed. He'd assumed it was just some random neighbor until he saw an article yesterday in the *Los Angeles Times* about Roger Theus. It showed his picture and referenced the warrant for his arrest.

According to Captain Cook, he contacted KTLA, a well-known local news station, before notifying the LAPD. Mr. Eriksson's interview aired at eight in the morning and his call to the LAPD didn't come until 8:40.

I'm all for people getting their fifteen minutes but call the damn authorities first. You can do your unnecessary interview after we've had time to ask a few questions. His address was right next door to the deceased Bruce Palmer and despite me not liking the guy, he came across on T.V. as being quite credible. I was sure he was telling the truth.

The Captain sent someone else down to interview him, telling me my time was better spent elsewhere. I didn't think talking to Sven Eriksson would get me any closer to Theus, but it's not like I had much going on currently. I'd run out of angles when it came to locating Theus. I'd resorted to calling several AirBnBs to see if someone matching his description had checked in over the last few days. The most common response was that they leave the keys in a dropbox and rarely actually meet with the tenant. Just my luck.

～

The second piece of news - the one that indirectly affected me - was that Dax Everton had caught the person who'd murdered Parker Brody.

It was all over the news and dominated the talk around the office. I may not have liked it, but I understood why. Parker Brody was a prominent movie star and this was a national story. How often is a twenty-something celebrity killed in cold blood?

They'd arrested a twenty-two-year-old woman named Kimmy Wellington for Brody's murder. The news said she'd been a huge fan of his for years. Constantly writing letters and appearing at any public appearance that Parker Brody held. Two years ago, it turned ugly and she was caught roaming around the grounds of his Brentwood estate.

Brody filed a restraining order against her and since that time, there had been no police intervention until the murder. Who knows what made her snap two years later, but she ambushed him outside of the gate at his estate. Apparently, she was wearing a mask and had put duct tape over her license plate. There are lots of cameras in the rich part of Brentwood and it surely helped in prolonging her capture.

Still, Parker Brody had a restraining order against Kimmy Wellington. You'd think Dax Everton would have labeled her a suspect from the start.

I decided not to go there.

This was a tragedy and I shouldn't second guess one of my fellow detectives. I certainly wouldn't like it if they did the same to me.

What a shame.

A young man who had the world by the tail was killed by his stalker.

It was quite the world we lived in.

～

The news of Kimmy Wellington's arrest affected me because my case had now vaulted to the most publicized case in Los Angeles. Especially with the news that someone had seen Roger Theus in the vicinity of Bruce Palmer's house on the day he was killed.

The news was labeling him a serial killer. They were only a week behind yours truly.

All this should have made me happy. Roger Theus wasn't going anywhere. With his face plastered all over the television, his days were numbered.

And yet, part of it made me feel hollow. I was the only one who thought there was something suspicious about the Shane Doyle "murder/suicide." I was the first one to surmise that Roger Theus's prosecution had been a sham and Shane Doyle had intentionally thrown the case.

And now, with several detectives freed from investigating the Parker Brody murder, I was going to be just another detective.

It got worse.

Fifteen minutes later, Dax Everton walked into the precinct. I was in my office, but I could hear the commotion and all the ass-kissing he was receiving.

"Good for you, Dax!"

"Best detective in LA!"

Etc., etc.

I told myself to stop being a bitter old man and to be happy Dax had caught the movie star's killer.

And I probably would have until I heard Dax utter the following:

"Now that I'm free to help my fellow detectives, maybe I can help you all catch this Roger Theus guy. A serial killer is out there roaming free. That's not a good look for the LAPD. Maybe old man Noble should think about hanging up the gloves a little early."

I heard a few tempered laughs.

Part of me wanted to run out there and throw a haymaker toward the cocky little fuck. That wouldn't do anyone any good and it would probably just get me suspended. I decided to be the better man.

But boy did that comment hurt.

Maybe he was right. Maybe it was time to hang them up.

When I was younger, I'd have gone out and taught him a lesson. Maybe I was becoming too soft in my old age.

As for the Roger Theus case, I'd suspected him all along and hadn't been able to prove it. The only reason we got an arrest warrant was that Judge Bryant gave them away like he was Oprah giving away presents. And by that point, I'd lost Theus.

Fuck.

～

Captain Cook came by late that afternoon. I was cleaning up my desk and about to head home.

"I heard that asshole Dax Everton was here earlier," he said.

I didn't know if he'd heard what Dax said and I decided not to bring it up.

"He caught a stalker with a restraining order two weeks after the guy was murdered. What a detective," I said.

The Captain smiled.

"I'm not going to laugh, because an innocent person died, but your point is taken."

"I'm glad they caught her, obviously. I just can't stand that arrogant SOB."

"You're not the only one."

I didn't respond.

"I got more bad news," he said.

"Hit me with it."

"The SDPD said they are pulling the car off of Sherin's house come Sunday. They can't afford to just leave it there indefinitely."

"I understand. Sherin is going back to work on Monday regardless. See if you can get them to stay through Sunday night."

"Will do, Noble."

"Thanks, Captain."

"Alright, let's get back to Roger Theus himself. Is there something we are missing? Any connections of his that we haven't reached out to?"

"Call it a hunch, but I think that lawyer knows more than he's letting on. I've called him twice now and gotten the Heisman stiff arm both times. I'm sure that's what any lawyer would do, but something just felt off."

"Why don't you follow him around tomorrow for a few hours? It's Saturday and he won't be at work all day. See if he leads you to any unexpected places."

"Good idea, Captain. I might just do that."

~

When I arrived home thirty minutes later, I called my daughter and gave her the bad news. Nothing on Roger Theus's whereabouts. I now had Saturday or Sunday to catch him before my daughter headed back to work.

I decided that if Theus hadn't been killed or arrested by Monday, I was going down to San Diego. The thought of my daughter down there without police protection scared the hell out of me.

I consumed no wine on Friday night. I was going to follow around

Theus's lawyer early tomorrow and wanted to be on my A game. Not that a glass or two of wine made a huge difference, but I didn't want even the slightest hint of brain fog.

At eight p.m., I started getting ready for bed. I poured myself a glass of water and put it on my nightstand. As I did, I heard the sound representing a text message.

I walked back to the kitchen and retrieved my phone.

The text message read:

*"I've got information on the whereabouts of Roger Theus. If you meet me at Fisherman's Village in Marina Del Rey in thirty minutes, I'll tell you. But only if you come alone. If I see as much as one other cop, I'm out of there. That's the freaking trut*h. *Text me back right now if you want to meet."*

Sure, there was a chance that Roger Theus was leading me right into a trap. Shit, it might have even been likely. There was still no world in which I wasn't agreeing to meet this person.

"I'll be there by 8:45."

"Have your phone with you. Text me when you arrive. I'll tell you where we can meet. I'll make sure it's a public place just so you know this isn't Roger."

By the tone of the text, I really didn't think it was Theus. Maybe I'd be proven wrong - deadly wrong - but I was pretty confident I wasn't talking to him.

I guess time would tell. I quickly put my clothes back on and was out the door within five minutes, my gun by my side.

Fisherman's Village was a replica of an old New England fishing town. People would come for the views of the Pacific, the restaurants, and the chance to see boats entering and leaving the harbor every few minutes.

It was one of the more beautiful areas of LA and I'd usually try to take any visiting friends there. This was quite a bit different.

On my drive over, I considered calling Captain Cook, and yet, deep down, I knew I never would. Whoever the person texting me was had been adamant that he'd flee if he saw any other cops. I believed him.

And that would be my excuse when I was questioned. Deep down though, I knew the real reason. This case had become personal and I wanted Roger Theus for myself.

Was that the right point of view to take? No. A resounding no. I knew that, but it didn't matter. I was a stubborn old detective and was going to do what I wanted to do. For now, Theus was all mine. That could change, but I couldn't risk this whole thing falling to pieces because the person texting saw some other cops.

I parked my car and started walking towards Fisherman's Village.

Even though I knew it was there, I felt on my side to feel my gun. It was something I'd done since I'd joined the force oh so long ago.

And if I ever needed to confirm my gun was with me, this was the night.

It was almost nine p.m., but Fisherman's Village was still popping. It was late summer in Los Angeles and people were enjoying the warm nights with summer technically ending in a few days. Not that Los Angeles abided by that. The season may change, but Los Angeles remained "summer" weather for a few more months.

I grabbed my phone and texted: *"I am here. Where do you want to meet?"*

Thirty seconds later, I received a response: *"Whiskey Red's. And you better be alone because I'll be watching."*

"I'm alone."

My decision not to text Captain Cook may have been a selfish one, but it was probably the correct one as well. A bunch of cops converging on Whiskey Red's would have been obvious to anyone paying attention.

I started walking towards my destination. It was only a few minutes away.

Whiskey Red's was a bar and restaurant that sat feet from the Marina Del Rey harbor. You could throw a glass from the restaurant and hit the ocean. The food and drinks were solid, but everyone knew why people went to Whiskey Red's: Location. Location. Location.

It didn't hurt that the dinner cruises and booze cruises departed from mere yards away. It was a great spot to grab one last drink before you left on one of them.

I walked into the restaurant. My head was on a swivel the entire time, even though I thought it was less and less likely I was texting with Roger Theus. My gun was at my side and I was prepared if the opportunity presented itself. I was thankful I hadn't drunk any wine.

"I'm here," I texted.

"Walk outside of Whiskey Red's and take a right. There's a little kiosk about twenty yards down."

I'd have felt safer meeting in the restaurant itself, but there were still lots of people milling outside the restaurant. Unless Theus planned on committing a murder in front of scores of witnesses, this wasn't the place he'd set up an ambush.

I took a right and headed down to the kiosk.

"I'm here," I texted.

"Buy a ticket for the 9 p.m. Tiki Mermaid booze cruise. I'll meet you on the boat. One more thing. I can see you right now, Mr. Dunn. You're wearing a gray jacket. Now, once you buy the ticket, you are to set your cell phone down on the closest table. You are not to respond to this text and if I see you reach for your phone again - except to set it down - I'm out of here. I'll find you on the boat."

Fuck. I suddenly didn't like the way this was going.

It's not like I had a choice, though. I'd come this far.

I approached the kiosk.

"One for the 9 p.m. Tiki Mermaid booze cruise," I said.

"Lucky you. That's the last one of the night. And usually the most fun. Everyone is liquored up by that point."

"Can't wait," I said in a monotone.

"That will be $50."

I gave him a credit card and he gave me a ticket in return.

"It's already started boarding, so I'd hustle over."

"When does it leave the harbor?"

"Around 9:15."

I looked down at my watch. It was 9:06.

The clerk pointed in the direction of where people were loading.

I made a show of setting my phone down on the nearest table and started towards the boat.

My heart was beating a mile a minute.

As I got closer, I began to wonder if the vessel I was about to load was considered a boat or a ship. If I had to guess, it was about a hundred feet long. The front of the bow was probably twenty-five feet above the ocean. It was either a very big boat or a small ship. I couldn't decide. Maybe it was just an oversized yacht.

While part of my mind was debating this frivolous topic, the other half was taking in all of the people entering the vessel. I was assuming the guy who'd been texting me would be loading around the same time. If he'd really been watching me - and how else would he have known the color of my jacket? - then he'd been close to the kiosk. And you couldn't see the kiosk from the boat.

I looked around. There were lots of couples in their twenties and early thirties. Most of them appeared to have already had a drink or two. Or three. The insurance for these booze cruises must have cost an arm and a leg. Especially ones that left at night.

How the hell would you know if someone went overboard?

As I thought that, my heart started beating even quicker.

Could Roger Theus have picked a better place to try and kill me? A slight shove into the water would almost certainly be a death sentence, assuming we were far enough from shore.

I made it to the top of the loading zone.

"Ticket, please."

I handed him my ticket.

The couple who got on the boat in front of me couldn't have been more than twenty-five years old. It gave me an idea.

"Have you seen any other men about my age get on this boat?" I asked.

"No, I just take the tickets."

That's the fucking point! You get a look at these people.

I chose to approach it differently.

"Specifically, a white guy in his mid-fifties who is tall and heavy?"

"Sorry, man. I just take the tickets and tell them to get on the boat."

Another good idea that had amounted to nothing.

I walked the three-step plank and got on the boat. It was a lot windier than I realized and it was only going to get worse once we got out on the open sea.

Other people had taken notice as well. Just about everyone was inside at the bar.

There were three levels to the boat. The upper deck, which wound around the bow in the shape of a semicircle. There was a railing that surely gave a great view of the ocean below. If we were going to be allowed out there. The wind probably had other ideas.

The second level was where everyone was gathered. I could see at least two bartenders in the corner of the room. It had a roof over it and that was the reason everyone had gathered there. Well, that and the open bar.

The bottom level looked to be off-limits and I couldn't see much of it. I decided to roam around the upper level.

I figured the guy would be more likely to approach me if I was by myself.

A voice came over the loudspeaker:

"Welcome to Tiki Mermaid cruises. We are pushing off from the dock now. As most of you know by now, the bar is located inside on the second level. It's quite windy out tonight, so we'd prefer if you stayed inside if at all possible. We don't want a huge gust of wind taking you overboard."

And then the voice laughed. I guess there's nothing funnier than someone being thrown into the ice-cold water of the ocean.

I saw a few deckhands push us off the pier and we started making our way out on the ocean.

What the hell was I doing out here?

Why hadn't this guy approached me yet?

And why were we doing this on a boat?

I had way too many questions and no answers.

The voice from the loudspeaker spoke again:

"The name of the boat you're on is *The Singing Lady*. And we hope - after a few more drinks - that we get to hear a few of you ladies singing. Remember, the drinks come with your ticket fee so don't be shy with your bartenders. They do make their money off of tips, however, so make sure you throw a few bucks in their tip jar if you can. Thanks so much."

Out of the corner of my eye, I saw someone walking toward me. I put my hand on my gun, but then realized it was an employee.

"I think they want people inside," he said.

It was time for one of my infamous white lies.

"I got a little seasick, even just leaving the dock. I figured if I had to throw up, better out here than inside with all the partygoers."

"I guess that's fair. There are two bathrooms in the bar area if you need one."

"Great, thanks. Let me just get a few minutes of fresh air."

"Sure."

He was about to walk by me when I tapped his shoulder.

"Yes?"

"I have a friend who said he might be on this boat. He's a white guy in his fifties. Tall and heavy set. Have you seen anyone like that?"

"I'm sorry. I haven't. Why don't you try texting him?"

He wasn't trying to be a smart ass, but I couldn't help but laugh.

And with that, he walked away.

I peered in through the glass to look at the party people on the level below. I didn't see anyone resembling Roger Theus. Not that I expected it. If this was somehow a plan by Theus to throw me overboard, he'd be hiding somewhere and not visible to me.

Which got me thinking. I couldn't be thrown overboard from the inside. What the hell was I doing on the open air of the top deck? I decided to join the party people on the second level.

I doubled back toward the stern of the boat, where we'd entered. I took the little stairwell that took you to the second level. There was the real sense of a party going on. People were having fun.

There were a few older people than I'd realized. There were a decent amount of people in their forties and even a few who looked to be in their fifties. Maybe that's why they hadn't been able to ID Roger Theus. Or, maybe it's because he wasn't on this boat at all and my mind was just fucking with me.

The boat was now moving pretty quickly and we were getting further away by the second. I'm not sure if a fall - or a push - overboard would be a death sentence at this point, but it probably would be soon. Assuming no one was there to alert the crew.

I turned back to the party at hand. I wondered just how much I stood out. Not only was I the lone black guy, but I was one of only a handful of people who looked to be over fifty. Making matters worse, I was the only person hanging out by myself.

I hit the trifecta. Old, black, and alone. My daughter would probably say it was fitting and pretty much summed me up. Of course, she'd have a sly smile when she said it.

Nobody seemed to be paying me too much attention. They were too busy having fun. I looked out across the room but didn't see anybody looking in my direction.

The voice from the loudspeaker came on again:

"We're really sorry, ladies and gentlemen, but we've decided to restrict access to the open-aired upper deck. It's just too windy and we can't take the chance. To make up for it, we are going to uncork ten bottles of good champagne for everybody. On the house, obviously."

The room erupted in applause.

They didn't care about standing on the upper deck. They cared about getting drunk.

I saw a young couple in the corner making out feverishly. Oh, to be young again.

I thought back to Sherry's and my early days. We weren't opposed to some public displays of affection. That all changed when Sherin was born. Not that we were complaining. She had completed our life.

I wondered what Sherin would say about my current predicament. Probably something like, 'Call for backup and get off this freaking boat.'

Would she have been wrong? Probably not.

I was starting to feel safer, though. Roger Theus wasn't on this boat. I was sure of it.

If that were true, then why the text messages?

Was the plan to get me off land for ninety minutes? To get me away from my house? What was the possible motivation to get me out here on this boat?

I hadn't seen Roger Theus and there'd been no sighting of the mysterious guy who'd been texting me. Maybe this had all been a ruse to have me preoccupied for a few hours. But why?

Just then, I saw that someone was approaching me. It was a red-headed woman in her twenties. She looked to be pretty drunk. This couldn't be the person who'd been texting me. Could it?

"What's your name?" she said, slurring her words.

"I'm Noble."

She handed me a flute of champagne.

"You looked all lonely over here. I thought you could use some champagne."

"Thank you," I said, hoping she'd quickly go back to the bar.

She raised her glass to mine.

"You have to cheers," she said.

I clinked my glass to hers, still keeping my eyes roaming around the room.

"Cheers," I said.

"You didn't take a sip," she said.

"I'm not really a drinker," I said.

She started talking louder.

"Take a sip! Take a sip!"

She was trying to get people's attention and that's the last thing I needed. I decided to nip it in the bud and I took a big sip.

That didn't satisfy her.

"Chug it! Chug it!" she yelled.

She turned around, hoping others would join her. I heard someone else yell, "Chug it!"

A glass of champagne was the last thing I needed right now, but I also didn't want to become the center of attention.

I swigged the rest of my champagne.

"Thank you," I said. "Now, if you don't mind, can I get a little time to myself?"

"Okay, but I might be back in ten minutes with another drink," she said and stumbled back to the bar area.

The young woman undoubtedly had a good heart. She'd gone out of her way to include some old guy standing by himself. Under different circumstances, I'd have thanked her and maybe gone and joined her crew for a drink. Not today, though, and certainly not right now.

I glanced around the room for probably the twentieth time. If I had to guess, there were around eighty people in the room. No Roger Theus. And as of yet, the mysterious texter hadn't approached me. I was starting to think I was right. This had been a plan to get me off the land.

A few minutes passed. If I had to guess, we were at least a mile off shore by now. Maybe more.

Part of me wanted to go back up to the top level. Sure, they'd said they didn't want anyone going up there, but what were they going to do, put me in a straightjacket? There was also a lower level I hadn't examined yet. I was curious what - or who - was down there.

And yet, I remained where I was. That voice in the back of my head telling me that Theus couldn't get me if I stayed here had won out. There was only one thing that I wanted more than arresting/killing Roger Theus and that was seeing my granddaughter grow up. So I stayed put.

Another ten minutes passed and that now familiar voice came over the loudspeaker.

"I hope everyone is having a good time! The wind has only gotten worse, so I hate to inform you that we'll officially be staying inside for the remainder of the cruise. We will, however, be handing out more champagne soon! We'll get you so drunk you won't even remember you couldn't go outside."

Everyone cheered. This group was really putting the booze into booze cruise.

"We are now over two miles out to sea. In about fifteen minutes, we'll turn around and head back to shore. And I promise we'll drive slower on the way in. Give you some extra time to slam those drinks."

Another cheer from everyone.

"Over and out," the voice said, acting like he was the coolest guy in the world. Newsflash: He wasn't.

Fifteen more minutes passed.

I looked down at my watch: It was 10:00 on the nose.

The boat started making a wide turn and a few minutes later, we were headed back to shore. Sure, there were still forty minutes left in the trip, but the odds that someone was going to approach me were now slim and none.

A few more minutes passed. I'd taken to standing in the corner of the room. People probably thought I was a complete weirdo. I can't blame them. My actions were odd. Pay for a booze cruise and then stand in the corner by yourself while never approaching the bar. Even the kind-hearted drunk young lady hadn't approached me a second time.

I'm not sure exactly when I noticed there was someone standing on the upper deck. I was aware of a presence more than I was an actual human being. We'd been told to stay away so I figured it was just an employee.

Something made me take a second look and that's when I saw the impossible. It was Roger Theus. I couldn't see his face, but I could see the outline of his body and there was absolutely no doubt.

That little voice in the back of my head spoke again and told me I shouldn't go out there. I didn't listen to it.

Instead, I briskly walked towards the exit. There was someone monitoring it. I knew they couldn't lock us in. There'd been too many maritime disasters due to locked doors. Someone might have been watching the exit, but there's no doubt I'd be able to get upstairs.

I approached the guy, a tall, skinny guy with wire-rimmed glasses. He seemed out of place on this boat. He looked like he belonged in the library, not at sea.

"I'm sorry, sir, but the captain wants everyone to stay on this level. The wind is pretty brutal out there."

More than anything, I had to keep this info from getting back to the other passengers. The last thing I wanted was for them to find out and potentially walk up to the other deck. Roger Theus was an extremely dangerous man and I was assuming he had a gun with him.

I looked up onto the upper deck. The shadow of Roger Theus was still visible.

"What's your name?" I asked the employee.

"Gene."

"Listen, Gene. I'm going to tell you something, but you have to remain quiet. Okay?"

He had a curious look, which was to be expected.

"Okay."

I took my badge out but didn't show him my gun. That would have caused an unpredictable reaction.

"I'm an LAPD detective. And the guy up there on the upper level is a very dangerous criminal."

"You're joking, right?"

His words said he didn't believe me, but his face showed he was worried.

"No, I'm not. Now, here's what's going to happen. You're going to let me through that little gate and then you are going to shut it behind me. I'd prefer if you locked it, but if you really can't, then at least stand in front of it. This man might be armed and I can't risk any of your passengers storming the upper deck."

"Why don't you just announce that to everyone down here? The guy won't be able to hear you from up there. Not with this wind."

"People will start shrieking and moving around. I can't risk him knowing that I'm coming."

"There's no other way?"

"No. Now, I'm going to ask you to move. And if anyone sees me leave you can tell them that I was having a medical emergency."

He didn't respond.

"Open the gate, Gene."

He did just that and I took the little stairwell up to the deck above. I took the gun out of safety mode and proceeded very slowly along the deck. The captain wasn't lying. The wind had become a lot worse and would have been very unsafe. Especially for the drunk people below.

I inched forward a few more steps. I was about to move past the main part of the boat and I'd see whatever was out there on the bow once I did.

I pulled my gun out and set it by my side.

I subtly peeked around the corner. Roger Theus had his back to me. He was leaning up against the railing and peering out on the water below.

I had a weapon and he was in a non-threatening position. Which - contrary to logic - caused me to be more on edge. My heart rate was off the charts.

Taking a few steps closer, I put the gun in front of me and in a position to shoot.

"Roger Theus, I want you to put your hands over your head, and ever so slowly, turn around."

"Well, if that doesn't sound like my old pal, Noble Dunn."

"Raise your hands and slowly turn around."

"And if I don't?"

"I'll shoot you in the back. And don't think I won't."

I didn't hear anything from downstairs. I was hoping we weren't bringing attention to ourselves. Hopefully, it just looked like two people talking.

Theus raised his hands and slowly started turning around.

He was wearing a huge puffy jacket and not his standard Tommy Bahama shirt. In this weather, who could blame him?

"There's only one person who knows I'm out here. I can't believe my own lawyer ratted me out."

So that's who had been texting me. Mason Croy III. It was actually a pretty darn smart way to get your client arrested. Avoiding the tricky attorney/client privilege question that going straight to the cops would have brought.

"Maybe he was tired of you killing people."

"But I'm innocent, Noble. Or did you not hear the verdict rendered by the State of California."

"They acquitted O.J."

"I thought a black guy would have believed he was inno…"

"Shut the fuck up!" I said.

He laughed. But it wasn't the jovial, belly laugh I'd heard at his house in Malibu. This one was more of a nervous laugh.

"Plus, the State of California is going to have a second chance to try you know who. For Shane, for Lexi, for Knox, for Alfonso, and for Bruce Palmer."

"You're on a first-name basis with all of them. How cute."

"They deserve their day in court."

"I didn't know ghosts get their day in court."

"Fine, their families."

"Stop being a pussy, Noble. Just shoot me. That would please their families way more than a day in court."

I gripped the trigger tighter.

"I'm arresting you here and now," I said.

"Oh yeah, with what handcuffs?"

"I've got the gun."

He shook his waist as if to represent he had a gun in his pants. His arms were still raised. If he'd made that movement with his hands down by his side, I'd have shot him dead.

"Maybe I've got one too," he said.

"I don't think so. Unless it's the smallest pistol I've ever seen."

"Why don't you shoot me, Noble? You want to kill me and I don't want to go back to jail. It's a win-win."

"I'm an officer of the court. And because of that, I'm going to take you in."

"You're going to regret it."

"Oh, yeah? You got another DA like Shane to bribe or another witness like Alfonso to say 97%?"

"You do know a lot, don't you?"

"Not everything. Why don't you fill in the blanks?"

"Knox was my friend. He hired Lexi. She seduced Shane. The P.I. tried to bribe me. And Mr. Reyes could have exposed the DA. That about cover it?"

I'd have time to digest all of this later.

"Sounds like you just admitted to about five murders."

"Doesn't matter."

"Oh yeah, why not?"

"Because I'm not going to jail. You're going to kill me."

"Why would I do that?"

"Because you love your daughter."

"Excuse me?"

"Stop with that crap, Noble. You heard me."

The wind was loud, but I'd definitely heard him.

"What about my daughter?"

"Okay, here's how it's going to go. If you arrest me here tonight, I'll go to jail. And I'll make some friends out of my fellow inmates. They'll find out that I'm that rich landlord who paid off a DA to gain an acquittal. And they'll start asking me what it's like to be rich. And I'll tell them about all the money I have hidden on the outside and how - if they do me a favor - it can be theirs."

My hands were getting sweaty. I hated where this was going.

"I'd drop 100k and 200k as potential payoffs. They'll ask what they'd have to do for that much money. And I'd mention this young lady by the name of Sherin."

"Shut up!" I yelled.

"And they'll ask what exactly they have to do. And that's when I'll go into specifics about body parts and instruments that they could use."

"I said shut up!"

I could feel my emotions taking over. My grip on the trigger was tightening.

"I'll tell them that they get extra for each hour they keep Sherin alive. I want her to feel pain. No quick death for her."

"I'm taking you in," I said, but with no luster. I knew how close I was to shooting him.

"Do you want me to tell you some of the tools that I'll suggest to them?"

"Stop!" I yelled.

"This is your last chance, Noble. If you don't kill me right now, I'm going to have them terrorize your daughter. And you know me well enough by now. I will absolutely make that happen. It's me or your daughter. Who do you want to live?"

I did nothing.

"You just signed your daughter's death warrant. I'm going to make sure it's a two-day affair with every orifice getting its fair share of abuse."

I couldn't take any more.

I raised the gun and shot Roger Theus twice. Once on the left side of his chest and once on the right. He looked up at me, something resembling a smile appearing on his face. I hadn't killed him yet.

For the first time, I noticed the shrieking and hollering coming from down below. Even the wind couldn't drown out the sound of gunshots.

I raised my gun to fire one more shot. As much as I wanted to shoot him right between the eyes, I couldn't. I was committing murder - I knew that - and this was going to be investigated by Internal Affairs. I might as well make it look like I was doing everything by the book.

I took aim and fired straight at his heart.

The bullet pushed his body up slightly and he went somersaulting over the deck and into the freezing water below.

I went over to the edge and looked down, but it was too dark to see anything.

I spit toward the water. I wish I could have done something more dramatic, but it's all that I could come up with in the moment.

Roger Theus was an all-time scumbag murderer. His corpse deserved more than to be spat it.

It was going to take me a long time to try and unhear the things he'd just said.

And maybe I'd given him exactly what he wanted. A watery grave as opposed to a lifetime in jail.

It's a tradeoff I was willing to make. I'd gotten exactly what I wanted as well.

Roger Theus was dead.

As I stood looking off the railing of the boat, I heard a voice.

"Officer, do we need to call the police?"

It was Gene, the guy who had been watching the door. I looked down on the second level and all eyes were on me. I imagine it had been quite a shock for the people down there.

"Give me your phone, Gene."

I holstered my gun, not wanting Gene to think he was in danger.

I could call 9-1-1, but I needed to talk to Captain Cook first. I hoped he was still awake. Luckily, I knew his number by heart.

"Hello?"

"Captain, I just killed Roger Theus."

"Noble? Whose number is this? You did what?"

I told him all that had happened over the course of the last ninety minutes.

"And you're still a few miles from the shore?"

"Yeah. Listen, I don't think you want to bring the police out here to interview everyone. We're a floating, always moving crime scene anyway."

"You're right, Noble. Tell the Captain of the boat to drive back to the harbor and dock the boat. We'll be waiting at Fisherman's Village."

"Got it. And you may want to send the Coast Guard to recover Theus's body."

"I'll set that up as well."

"Sorry to call you so late, Captain."

"Stop with that. I'm just glad you got him. But on a boat? This is all very odd. I really hope this was on the up and up."

With that, he hung up the phone, his words floating in the air.

CHAPTER 60

NOBLE: A DAY LATER

I spent that night being interviewed by the LAPD. I knew it was protocol after an officer-involved shooting, but it still felt weird to be questioned by your fellow cops.

If you'd asked me to recollect most of the questions, I wouldn't have been able to say much. I was in a dreamlike state and it pretty much began the second Roger Theus went over the railing and into the Pacific below.

I still managed to answer every question I was asked. It just felt like someone else was doing it.

I didn't get home until after three in the morning.

By ten a.m., I was back at our precinct, this time being interviewed by IAD (Internal Affairs Division.) There were two sets of two and they took turns asking me questions.

They were trying to get a read on whether I'd handled everything correctly. I hadn't, but I wasn't going to admit that to them.

My story - which they had me repeat at least five or six times - was that Roger Theus was reaching for his pants when I shot him. At that point, it was almost irrelevant whether he had a gun or not. If an officer feels he might be shot, he can use deadly force.

Now, in my case, Theus wasn't reaching for his gun; if he even had one.

But I wasn't going to lose my badge or go to jail for a repulsive "human" like Roger Theus.

So I lied. And I lied. And I lied.

There were fierce winds so it would have been impossible for the people on the second level to hear us. That was a big benefit to me. If they'd heard the things that Theus had said about Sherin, IAD might have begun to suspect I'd become a little trigger-happy.

Furthermore, the people partying below us had a terrible vantage point to assess whether Theus had truly reached for his gun. One, you had to be in the back to even see us. And two, I was standing between them and Theus.

I thought IAD would have a tough time proving I hadn't told the truth.

I had been honest about everything else leading up to the shooting. How I'd ended up there. The young lady who made me drink a flute of champagne. Telling Gene not to let anyone on the top deck.

I got a quick dirty look when I described drinking the champagne, but I think they understood I was in a tough spot there.

They continually asked me why I didn't call for backup. I told them what the person texting me had said and that I believed it. If another cop was seen in the area, he'd vanish and I'd lose the chance to find Roger Theus once and for all. I told them where I'd left my phone and they confirmed they'd retrieved it last night and were searching through it as we spoke. Nothing on there would contradict my story.

I told them Roger Theus believed it was his lawyer who had ratted him out. I also reiterated what Theus had said about Knox recruiting Lexi to seduce Shane. It pretty much had gone down as I'd expected.

I explained that Theus also said Bruce Palmer had been trying to black-mail him. He must have discovered the plot along the way. And at that point, he stood no chance. Roger Theus had already decided he was going to kill everyone involved.

This wasn't my first time dealing with IAD. I'd had two other officer-involved shootings in my almost thirty years on the job. Not a bad record. They'd treated me fairly both times. Which might come as a surprise to some members of the LAPD.

IAD was genuinely looked down on by its fellow police officers. They viewed them as busting another cop's balls unnecessarily. I tended to give them the benefit of the doubt. I knew there were a lot of bad eggs on the force and if IAD could help get rid of them, I was all for it.

Then again, when you're the guy being interviewed for ten straight hours, it ain't that fun.

Finally, at eight p.m. that night, I was allowed to go home.

"Have they found Roger Theus's body yet?" I asked.

"No, not yet. He's probably been torn apart by sharks at this point."

With that, I drove home and proceeded to sleep for twelve straight hours.

~

I woke up on Sunday morning and realized I hadn't called my daughter yet.

In my defense, on Friday night, I was whisked into an interrogation room and answered questions until three a.m. And on Saturday, I was talking to IAD from ten in the morning until eight at night and passed out within minutes of getting home.

Still, I should have found the time.

For the first time in years, I actually had a valid reason to use the house phone I'd kept around. The police had confiscated my cell phone when they found it sitting on the table at Fisherman's Village on Friday night. I didn't know when I'd get it back.

Sherin answered on the third ring.

"Oh jeez. Finally Dad."

"I guess you've heard the news?"

"I sure have. Captain Cook called me on Friday night. I've been trying to call your cell phone ever since."

"The police took it and haven't given it back yet. Plus, I've been getting interviewed every second of every day."

"You could have found a way."

"You're right. I'm sorry, honey."

"It doesn't matter. I'm just glad you're okay and that monster is gone."

"Thanks. It's been a long few days, I can assure you that."

"Are you being interviewed by IAD?"

As always, Sherin knew the ins and outs of being a cop.

"Yeah. They do this for every officer-involved shooting and as you know, this is a big one."

"They believe your story, right?"

It's almost like my daughter knew. I'd never be able to tell her the full truth, however. I could tell her I'd shot Theus, but I couldn't regurgitate the words he'd said about her.

"Yeah, I think they know I'm telling the truth."

I hated lying to my daughter, but it had to be done.

"You've got a pretty good track record," Sherin said.

That was very true. I still wanted to change the subject.

"I'm assuming they removed the SDPD cars from outside your house?"

"Yeah. Thanks."

"That wasn't me. Probably Captain Cook."

"He's a good man, Dad."

"I know."

"But you guys butt heads a lot."

"He's been my boss for twenty-plus years. It's going to happen."

"I think you should buy him a nice bottle of wine."

"Hey, I'm the one who had to face off with Theus. What the hell did he do?"

I heard my daughter laugh. It was about the sweetest sound in the world.

"Well, you'll always be my hero, Dad."

I stand corrected. Those words were the sweetest sound in the world.

"I'm going to come down and see you soon. Say hi to Ava for me and tell Bobby I'm sorry for all you guys had to go through."

"Don't worry about that. Just glad you're safe."

"Talk soon, honey."

"Bye, Dad."

I felt naked without a phone so I went down to my local Verizon store and bought the cheapest phone they had. It's not like I knew many numbers by heart - my daughter and Captain Cook were the only two I could think of - but I just felt better having one.

They asked if I wanted my old phone number and I told them for the time being just to give me a new number. I didn't know if activating it would screw up IAD's investigation so I just went with a new number.

As I drove home with my new phone, I thought about the person who'd been texting me. Was it Mason Croy III? Certainly seemed likely and that's who Theus said it was. Not that he was, in any sense of the word, reliable.

And why would Croy alert me to the fact that Theus was on the boat? The obvious answer was that he knew Theus was a menace to society and wanted him out of circulation.

Hopefully, I'd get a chance to interview Croy myself.

Assuming IAD bought my bullshit story and reinstated me.

~

I laid low the rest of Sunday.

I called Captain Cook and thanked him for all he'd done. I told him my daughter relayed the same.

He thought that IAD would likely come down with their decision on Monday and he saw no reason why I wouldn't be fully reinstated as an LAPD detective.

"Sometimes these things can take weeks. That won't be the case with you, Noble. Roger Theus was a wanted criminal and you have an impeccable track record. This will be over soon."

I thanked him again.

"One last thing," I said. "Have they found Theus's body yet?"

"Not yet. The sharks probably got him."

The fact that he'd given the same answer as IAD made me a bit uneasy.

~

Tuesday proved a great day for me and a not-so-good one for Mason Croy III.

I was reinstated, just as Captain Cook had anticipated, although it was a day later than he'd guessed. Not that I was complaining. They even returned my phone to me.

As for Croy, he'd made a huge mistake. The police followed the GPS of the phone that had been texting me. It had been at Fisherman's Village at the same time as me, just as I'd suspected. He knew the color of my jacket, after all.

Croy's mistake was that he didn't turn that phone off until he returned home. By then, the GPS had already recorded the address. And it was the home of Mason Croy III. He'd been smart enough to get a burner phone, but too dumb to remember to turn it off.

The timing of these two things couldn't have worked out better, because I was going to be allowed to sit in on the questioning of Croy. I wouldn't be the lead, probably because of what happened on the boat, but I was just happy to be in the room.

The meeting was set up for nine a.m. on Wednesday.

~

"Detectives, it's nice to meet you. I'm Mason Croy III."

I'd never met him in person. He was even seedier than I'd expected. He had dark, oily hair and an expression that said he knew more than anyone else in the room.

He was wearing an expensive pin-striped navy blue suit with the requisite yellow tie. He was also a little shorter and skinnier than I'd expected. He was the polar opposite of Roger Theus. Except for the "I'm smarter than you" look. They shared that.

The three detectives assigned to this interview all shook his hand. Benny Yarborough, Cliff Claxton, and myself. Benny and Cliff were in their late forties and almost as geriatric as I. They were good cops and I was happy they were leading this. If it had been Dax Everton, I might have just retired on the spot.

We took Mr. Croy to an interrogation room and led him through the requisite jargon. We told him he wasn't under arrest and he agreed that he was here on his own accord.

Investigation rooms were usually only meant for one to two detectives as well as the individual being interviewed, so we had to make some inventive chair rearrangements to fit me at the table. In fact, I was just off the edge of the table between us and Mr. Croy, so it was obvious I wasn't the lead.

I was alright with that.

Only a few short days ago, I was being investigated by IAD. Now I was back on the case.

Benny Yarborough asked the first question.

"Mr. Croy, is it true that you texted Detective Dunn on Friday night?"

He looked in my direction.

"Yes."

"And you were trying to alert him to the fact that Roger Theus was on that boat?"

"Yes."

"Why?"

"This is where it gets tricky for me. As you guys know, being a lawyer I have to abide by the attorney/client privilege. And I don't want to lose my law license. The problem is that Roger was starting to make allusions to having killed all those people."

"Which people exactly?"

"The DA and the two people killed with him. The witness, Alfonso Reyes. And the private investigator, Bruce Palmer."

"He admitted to killing them?"

"No. He made subtle references to killing them. He was too smart to come right out and say it."

Cliff Claxton jumped in.

"And you were tired of him getting away with murder?"

"Yes, but also he'd become totally unhinged. I was afraid he might kill again. And attorney/client privilege doesn't extend to that. I also thought he might be trying to flee."

"We'll get back to that in a minute. First off, who do you think he wanted to kill?"

Mr. Croy pointed at me.

"Detective Dunn here."

"He told you that?"

"As I said, he only alluded to things. He said his whole life had been wrecked by Detective Dunn - although he called him Noble - and that he would seek revenge, but he didn't actually come out and say he was going to kill him."

The only thing that surprised me thus far was that Theus would tell his attorney all this. I had no doubt he wanted me dead. That part was obvious.

Benny Yarborough jumped back in.

"Why would Mr. Theus go on this cruise? His face was all over the news. Why take the chance?"

It's a question I'd been wondering and was glad Benny asked it.

"He was taking a dry run."

"A dry run for what?"

"He wanted to see exactly where that booze cruise went. He was considering having someone pick him up from the boat sometime in the future."

"And then what?"

"Take the boat to an island or something I guess. Maybe get a plane from there. I don't know. Like I keep saying, he wasn't very specific."

"Why not just take a boat from the harbor? Why go through all the trouble of going out a few miles on a booze cruise?"

My fellow detectives were asking all the right questions.

"He worried that there would be cameras all around Fisherman's Village and they'd see what boat he got on. That wouldn't be the case if he was picked up at sea."

The rationale seemed a bit convoluted to me, but it was possible. The camera thing was true.

"Who was he going to have pick him up from the booze cruise?"

"I have no idea. I don't think he was that far along yet."

"You do know aiding and abetting a criminal is against the law, right? Even if you are the man's attorney."

"I know. I said earlier I was afraid he might be trying to flee. That was the other reason I wanted him arrested."

The interview went on for another thirty minutes. I hadn't asked a single question yet. I thought he might be a little less receptive to me, considering I'd killed his client. Then again, he'd led me down this path with his texts.

We were about to wrap up when Cliff Claxton turned to me.

"Is there anything you want to ask, Noble?"

There was one question I felt hadn't been asked.

"If you felt so strongly that Roger should be arrested, why did you only contact me?"

I stared at Mason Croy III, trying to read his body language. He was a slick speaker and might be able to talk himself out of this question, so I tried to read the man, not the words. It was my own little game of poker.

"Roger is a really smart guy. If I'd told you to bring ten cops, he'd have sensed it and never got on the boat. He has a second sense for pigs. Sorry, his words, not mine."

His jab at my profession aside, I tried to decide if I believed him. The part about Roger having a second sense about cops was likely true. It still rang hollow, however.

"What do they call lawyers?" Cliff Claxton asked rhetorically.

He hadn't taken the 'pig' comment so well.

"I was just using Roger's words."

"Nice clients you pick there, Mr. Croy."

"They all deserve a defense."

"Could you have picked a less generic line?"

Mason Croy III stood up a little higher in his seat.

"I helped deliver a dangerous criminal to you guys. I should be getting championed, but instead I'm being insulted and given the third degree."

Was he right? To be fair to him, we'd still be looking for Roger Theus if it weren't for Croy. But he was such a conceited jerk that he made it next to impossible to shower praise on him.

"We're just trying to get the full story, Mr. Croy," Benny Yarborough said.

"I'm giving it to you."

I wasn't so sure.

Something stunk. I'd had that feeling when I was being interviewed by

IAD the day after shooting Roger Theus. It all seemed to tidy up too easily. I felt like I was missing something.

And Mason Croy's interrogation had done nothing to quell that fear.

$\sim$

I had a nightmare that evening.

After I fired the third shot - the one to the heart - into Roger Theus, he just started laughing. I shot him a fourth and fifth time and still, all he did was laugh. That same deep, bellowing laugh I'd heard at his Malibu home.

I shot him five more times, but nothing could kill the guy. His laughter grew more intense with each shot I fired into his chest.

Then I shot him in the leg and he fell to the ground and cried out in pain.

And that's when I woke up.

$\sim$

This wasn't just a random nightmare.

I'd had a feeling since the beginning that something was off. I hadn't been able to place it, but the nightmare kickstarted my brain.

I thought back to the night in question.

Especially the moments where I shot Theus.

His body didn't look like most people I'd seen shot. He took two to the chest and remained standing. While it is true that he was leaning against the boat's railing, I'd still have expected him to slump to the ground. But no, he remained upright. And then, with the third shot, it raised him up on the railing and sent him tumbling over.

Was that possible? Of course. Your body reacts in strange ways when a bullet tears through it.

I was also dubious of Theus's expression right before he went over. It's almost like he was smiling at me. Who does that after being shot three times?

And then there was the matter of his large, puffy jacket. During the course of my investigation, everybody I talked to said that Theus wore one of his silly Tommy Bahama shirts at all times. It didn't matter if it was fifty degrees out or a hundred. Sure, there was quite a bit of wind on the night in question, but did he really need a huge jacket? It had been a warm day.

I didn't envision Roger Theus putting on a big thick jacket before getting on the boat. It just didn't seem to fit his personality. Nor his style.

Theus would equate covering up to taking a loss. It's hard to explain, but that's how he'd feel.

Unless he was hiding something under the jacket and had to wear it.

I thought back to when I fired the first two bullets.

Did it make the usual sound that a bullet makes when it pierces the skin?

Maybe I was going crazy, but I don't remember hearing that signature sound.

Usually, it makes a bit of a high-pitched sound as it ricochets through.

This sound was more like a thud.

Almost as if something had caught the bullets.

In the moment, it hadn't registered. There was so much going on and it was definitely windy up there.

But looking back, the sound was off. I was almost positive.

The third shot was the same. No high-pitched sound.

I was starting to comprehend why Roger Theus might have needed to wear an oversized jacket.

Holy fuck.

~

I woke up the next morning and my anxiety had only gotten worse.

I wanted to tell Captain Cook my crazy idea but thought better of it. Since being cleared by IAD, I'd just spent the last few days being lavished with praise for killing Roger Theus. If I came out now and said there was a small part of me that worried he was still alive, I'd be laughed out of the precinct.

I made myself two fried eggs and some toast and sat down at the kitchen table.

After I ate and washed my dishes, I sat down on the couch.

As I was prone to do, I started going over everything in my head.

Being a detective was almost like solving a math problem. A long, complicated problem that sometimes took several repeat viewings.

If my asinine theory were true, a few things had to be true.

One, Roger Theus had someone with a boat following the booze cruise. I don't care how indestructible Theus appeared to be, he wasn't lasting more than ten minutes at sea. We weren't in the shallows, but a good three miles from the shore.

Two, he would have had on a bulletproof jacket. If not, he was surely dead. No man survives three shots to the chest, especially if the last one is straight to the heart.

Three, if Roger Theus pulled this off, he surely had Mason Croy's help. The guy was texting me and was already down at Fisherman's Village. Plus, the guy came off as shady as fuck. I left our interview thinking he was hiding something.

The problem was that we had checked the GPS and that phone was back at Croy's house in the Pacific Palisades by 9:45 that night. That meant there's no way that Croy had been the one who'd rescued Theus at sea.

That part didn't make any sense.

Theus already had Croy hanging around Fisherman's Village, texting me. He was likely Theus's closest friend - and possibly only friend - left. Everyone else knew he had a warrant out on him for murder and wouldn't touch him with a ten-foot pole.

So why would Theus have Croy in the perfect location to follow behind the booze cruise and then not use him for that? It made no sense.

But GPS didn't lie.

I spent the next two days away from the office.

People were already starting to forget about Roger Theus. The allure had worn off. There was a new shiny little object amongst the LAPD. And this case was a doozy.

Someone was leaving body parts in mailboxes around Los Angeles. A wrist there. An ankle there. Yesterday, somebody walked out to their mailbox and found a nose waiting for them.

The LAPD was currently doing tests, but the assumption was it had been more than just one body being left around town. That meant we may have another serial killer on our hands. And we all know how the American public can't get enough of serial killers. Just look at all the Netflix shows that dominate the ratings. The Night Stalker, Jeffrey Dahmer, John Wayne Gacy, and Ted Bundy. There are multiple documentaries/movies about all of them.

We can't get enough.

So this became the case that had the LAPD talking.

And while everyone else was forgetting about Roger Theus, I certainly wasn't.

He was also a serial killer and I believed he might still be alive.

So I stayed home. It gave me more time to think. And that's what I needed to do.

~

My working premise was that Mason Croy III was a very intelligent guy. And once he'd seen me get on the boat, he would have powered down the burner cell phone he'd been texting me with. He would have known better.

So the fact that we were able to trace the phone to Croy's home made me think that's exactly what he wanted. Or, maybe, it was what Theus wanted. His "fingerprints" were all over this.

If my premise was correct, then the question was why. Why did Mason Croy want us to think he was at home? And if he'd actually helped Roger Theus, how did his phone end up at his house?

~

After two full days of thinking everything through - starting with the moment I received that first text from Mason Croy - I'd finalized another one of my crazy theories.

I'd gone through twenty different plots/plans/schemes that Theus could have thought up, but I kept coming back to the one that made the most sense.

I'd done a little research and Croy had been married for eighteen years to a woman named Geraldine Bohanan. She appeared to still go by her maiden name.

My theory was this: Croy's wife had been with him at Fisherman's Village and she drove home with the phone while he remained behind and picked up Roger Theus when he went overboard.

They only had one child and she was sixteen years old. Even a scumbag like Mason Croy wouldn't have his teenage daughter doing his dirty work for him.

If I was indeed correct, the plan was actually quite genius.

If some crazy cop came along - namely, me - and thought something was fishy about what happened at sea, Croy could deny any involvement.

The GPS of the phone would absolve him. Croy could say he was nowhere near the boat.

Now, Theus and Croy would never have expected it to get that far, but they'd cover their bases just to be safe. They'd assume the LAPD believed that Roger Theus had died at sea.

And all of them had. Except for me.

I knew I was fighting an uphill battle. If I was right, there was no way that Geraldine Bohanan would turn on her husband. The wife of a lawyer knew to always keep her mouth shut.

Still, I had to find out.

～

The following morning, I drove up to Mason Croy's home address and parked about thirty yards down from his home.

It was 6:30 a.m. I had to see him leave before I approached their door. If I walked up and he was still there, he'd shut the door in my face and warn his wife never to answer a question from me.

The home itself was beautiful. Not that was any surprise considering I was in the Pacific Palisades. I wondered how much money Roger Theus had paid Croy over the years. A million? Three million?

He'd been Theus's lawyer for a long time. Did he know about the drug dealing? The murders?

Croy was nowhere near as evil as Theus, but I was pretty sure he was a criminal nonetheless.

At 7:44, my wish was granted. I saw Croy walk from the front door to the adjoining garage. A few minutes later he sped off in his silver European sports car. I couldn't even make out if it was a BMW, a Mercedes, or an even more expensive manufacturer. I just knew it was something I couldn't afford.

I waited a few minutes.

When I knew he wasn't doubling back, I approached Croy's front door. Or, should I say, Geraldine Bohanan's? She was the one I was here to see.

I hit the big brass knocker twice against their front door. It was the face of a lion with the knocker itself coming out of the lion's mouth. It was as conceited as it sounds.

A few seconds later, a woman came to the door.

Geraldine Bohanan had on white shoes, a ruffled white skirt, and a white Polo shirt. As if there wasn't enough white, she was wearing a white headband as well.

Now, I was no tennis aficionado, but if she was on her way to doing anything else, I would have been shocked.

Her tanned legs and arms were probably the result of a lot of these tennis mornings over the years. She was a beautiful woman, probably somewhere in her mid-forties.

"How can I help you?" she asked.

As always, I was in civilian clothes. I didn't want her to know that I was a cop. She'd know that soon enough, but I wanted to read her reactions first.

The first reaction seemed to say, 'What is this black guy doing up in the Palisades?'

"It's nice to meet you."

"Thanks. Now how can I help you?"

I'd thought long and hard about how to broach the subject. If I got too cute and asked too many questions, she'd know something was up. So I just decided to go straight for the jugular.

"How long after your husband was done texting me did you drive back up here with that burner phone?"

I stared directly at her, not breaking eye contact for even a split second.

She brushed her hair aside before she answered.

"Excuse me. I have no idea what you're talking about. Who are you, exactly?"

She was lying. I knew it and there was zero doubt in my mind. It would have been less than zero if there were such a thing.

"I don't believe you, Mrs. Bohanan."

"What don't you believe?"

"Honestly, not a single thing you say. Let's start with you asking who I am. I think you know exactly who I am. If you watched any T.V. over the last several days, you saw split screen pictures of myself and Roger Theus."

"I'm sorry, I don't watch much T.V."

"You're husband is Theus's lawyer. I'm not buying that crap. Try harder," I said.

She stared at me, daggers in her eyes.

"I'd like you to leave."

"I gotta say, it was a pretty ingenious plan. You drove up here while your husband stayed down there and helped Roger Theus. You know he's still alive, right?"

She did a brief double-take and the slightest of smirks appeared. It was almost imperceivable, but not to me. My God. She knew everything.

"Holy shit. You know."

"I'm calling the cops," she said.

"Oh don't worry about that. They are already here, and by that, I mean me."

"Screw you," she said and slammed the door in my face.

I tried the lion head's knocker one more time, but I knew she wasn't coming back. She was likely on the phone to her husband at that very moment.

I went back to my car with renewed vigor for this never-ending case.

It wouldn't last.

∿

A week passed.

I'd gone to Captain Cook and explained everything I'd learned.

"I'll never doubt you again, Noble," he said. "But literally everyone in the LAPD with the exception of yourself thinks Roger Theus is dead. A suspicious reaction by Croy's wife is not enough to get you a warrant in this case. In fact, you may not like hearing this, but the LAPD and people like Judge Bryant would prefer if this thing just went away. As I said, I'm not discounting your theory. I'm just telling you it's not going to go anywhere."

I hated to admit it, but he had a point.

I had my theory, but not much else. I couldn't exactly ask for a warrant based on the fact that Geraldine Bohanan had a dubious reaction when I confronted her. I'd be laughed out of the judge's chambers. And I knew there was no way that either Mason Croy or his wife would ever talk to me again.

So what did I have?

Not a whole lot.

But I hadn't given up just yet.

I spent the next several days calling businesses that rented out boats. I called from Santa Barbara all the way down to San Diego. I asked if they'd had any rentals paid for by the last names Theus, Croy, or Bohanan.

No such luck. That would have been a game-changer.

I did the same in trying to find places that sold bulletproof vests.

I struck out there as well.

I had a few other strikeouts along the way and my investigation slowly started to peter out.

I still thought there was a good chance that Roger Theus was alive, but I was running out of ways to prove it.

~

I confronted Mason Croy one day. He was outside of his office and I asked him three or four rapid-fire questions.

He didn't answer any of them, but it somehow got back to Captain Cook, who called me to his office.

"I say this as your friend, Noble. People are starting to talk. They say you're holding on to this case too tight. I heard someone refer to you as *'The boy who cried Roger Theus.'* You've only got a few months left on the force. Don't let this be the lasting impression you leave."

I left his office that day knowing my time on this case had just unofficially ended.

~

I went home that night and called my daughter.

"Hey, Dad."

"I'm coming down to San Diego tomorrow."

"About time. Is there nothing new on the Theus case?"

"The Roger Theus case is over, honey."

I heard her exhale.

"I'm glad to hear that, Dad."

It was time to spend my time on people that matter: My daughter and my granddaughter.

I'd spent enough of the last few months dealing with - and thinking about - Roger Theus. Maybe everyone else was right and he really had been shark bait. I'm not sure I totally believed that, but regardless, it was time to move on. Captain Cook had made that clear.

A few days with Sherin and her family sounded like heaven.

"You know what, I guess I'm glad it's over too," I said.

"I can't wait to see you tomorrow."

"I can't wait either. I love you, Sherin."

"Love you too, Dad."

CHAPTER 61

ROGER

I died on September 29th, 2022.

At least, according to *The Los Angeles Times.*

In reality, it had only been five days since the day I'd planned and executed the best fake death in the history of mankind. Unless Jim Morrison or Tupac were still alive somewhere. Doubtful.

But I had - against all odds - achieved the impossible. Faked my death and fooled the LAPD. The *LA Times* as well. For all intents and purposes, I was now considered deceased.

That meant no more warrants. No more manhunts. And most importantly, no more worrying when I used the airport. Which, ironically, I was at right now.

I am flying to Europe in minutes. I'm currently waiting at the gate.

Rome is my first destination and then we'll see where the wind takes me. I am going to be a ghost never to be captured.

At least not by the LAPD.

And certainly not by Noble Dunn.

∾

THREE WEEKS EARLIER

My ludicrous plan had been met with much resistance by the guy whose help I dearly needed: Mason Croy III.

"There are easier ways, Roger. Why not just go missing?"

I'd given him the thumbnail version over the phone and he came over to his Hollywood apartment where I was staying. I'd garnered some sort of karmic energy looking at that ceiling fan and my plan materialized in a matter of hours.

What had really launched the idea was when Mason said the LAPD would only truly be done with me was if I were dead. That got the old pistons churning.

We sat on the table in the kitchen. I reheated some of the pizza he'd brought that first night, but neither of us touched it. This conversation was too important and food didn't interest either of us.

"If I just stay missing, this will never end. They'll continue searching for me forever. And unless they think I'm dead, the airport is a no-go for me. I have plenty of money in my offshore accounts. I can live a long, debaucherous life in Europe or South America. I can't do that here. It's worth the risk."

"How about just jumping off the boat once Noble sees you?"

"He'll assume I lived. I know the fucker well enough at this point. I need to have him shoot me. And you think I'm taking some big risk by doing this. I'm really not. Everyday detectives are taught to shoot for the chest."

"What about long-distance marksmen?"

"You answered your own question. That's a different thing altogether and they have to shoot for the head from that distance. There's more surface area in your chest than in your face. That's why cops aim for it."

"You're insane."

"Possibly."

"And you're not going to drown or freeze to death before I pull up in the boat?"

"I'm putting some little arm floaties in the thick jacket that will be covering the bulletproof vest."

"Arm floaties? Are you fucking serious?"

"I only have to stay afloat for a minute or so. Piece of cake. And remember, don't have the fucking lights on in the boat. Once the booze cruise takes the U-turn, you're to tail behind the boat by fifty yards or so. It will be dark out and your lights will be off. No one will see you. And once you see me go overboard - that you will see! - wait a good thirty seconds before you come to me. Just to be safe."

"Yeah, because this plan is all about safety."

I managed to laugh.

"This has like a 25% chance of succeeding," he said.

"Want to bet your share?"

Mason didn't respond.

"That's what I thought."

He stayed mum once again.

"You're having your wife pay for the boat in cash, correct?"

Mason's wife Geraldine had kept her maiden name so he had floated the idea of having her pay for the boat with her credit card. I told him that just to be safe, better to have her pay in cash. She might have to overpay with a cash deposit, but they'd fall for Geraldine. She was a sexy woman with awesome legs. She'd get by with paying in cash.

We were going to rent the boat out of San Pedro and drive it up and dock it at Fisherman's Village, so I didn't think we had to worry. I was being meticulous. More so than I'd ever been. And that included the murders.

"Yes, she'll pay in cash. We're going down there tomorrow morning and she'll do all the work. Don't worry, they won't see my face."

"Good. You're being smart."

"So, what's else? I want to make sure we have this down pat."

"Once you see Noble step on the booze cruise, go get on the speedboat and start tailing us. You can be far back for the first forty minutes. It's not like you'll lose a boat that size."

"Got it."

"And then when it does the U-turn, you start getting closer. Look for a handsome, fearless, charismatic, indestructible, cop-hating property owner going over the railing of the ship. And then come and get me. Easy."

Mason, the man with no sense of humor, managed to laugh when I used all the adjectives to describe myself.

"And then, once the night in question is over," I continued. "you'll tell the cops that you called Noble in order to get me arrested. I'd started to fess up to my crimes and you were going to be a good samaritan and get me off the street."

He asked me a few more questions and I guided him down the path I'd set up. He was to say that I was doing a dry run on the booze cruise. For a later getaway.

He was to tell the pigs that he didn't call 9-1-1 because I would be able to sense they were coming.

"Noble will buy that," I added. "He thinks I've got a God complex."

By not denying it, Mason had confirmed he felt the same way.

"Alright, I'm in," he said.

Like he had a choice.

"Of course, you are," I said. "And the house in Malibu is yours. With an asterisk."

Mason also handled my will so we could do a few alterations in the coming days. Obviously, he'd make it look like I'd done this months or years ago. No reason for the LAPD to be privy to some late-inning shenanigans.

"I figured."

"Once it sells, you'll deposit 100k per month in my oversea accounts for the next two years. That's 2.4 million and I think we both know the place in Malibu is probably worth four million or so. That's a cool 1.6 for you."

"What do you want me to say, Roger? I've already agreed to do this."

"Stop making this out like you're taking one for the team. I'm the one getting shot and you're making 1.6 million for driving a boat around. You're not some hero."

"What night are we doing this?"

"Likely tomorrow night. I called the booze cruise company and learned a few interesting details. One nugget was that tomorrow was going to be very windy and they expected everyone would be forced to stay on the second level where the bar is."

"Why is that a nugget?"

"Because I'd prefer it just be Noble and I on the roof."

"Why?"

"If it's just me and him, I'll be able to convince him to shoot me. If other people are on the top deck, it adds a variable I don't need."

"How will you convince him to shoot you?"

"Enough fucking questions, Mason. You sound like a crooked fucking lawyer. Oh, that's right..."

He didn't respond.

"Also, the boat doesn't usually disembark until around 9:15," I said. "Then at 10:00 or so, when they are about three miles offshore, they'll make that U-turn. And I'll go overboard a few minutes later."

"How can you be sure this doesn't happen earlier?"

"Because I'm going to hide downstairs or in a bathroom or somewhere else until we've made that u-turn. No need to do this earlier."

"Because they'd be more suspicious if you went over closer to the shore?"

"See, you're learning. No one can survive three gunshots and then going overboard three miles out at sea. The LAPD will consider me as dead as a doornail."

"I hope you're right, Roger."

I didn't bother responding.

I stared down at the old, stale pizza. The next time I had pizza I wanted to be in Naples, eating it with some hot Italian girl. While the pieces of shit at the LAPD were trying to catch the latest LA dirtbag, I was going to be living it up. My life was going to be so much better than theirs.

Assuming Noble didn't just shoot me in the face.

And if I said the things about his daughter that I'd planned, I almost couldn't blame him.

On the bright side, even that was preferable to returning to jail.

The night in question went by without a major hitch.

There were a few minor hiccups, but with something so grandiose, that was inevitable. I was standing on the top level of the boat for a few minutes longer than I wanted. I started to worry. Why hadn't Noble come up here yet? Maybe he was calling the cops.

I'd had Mason make Noble leave his phone on the dock, but he could have been using someone else's. I didn't think that was likely. This had become personal to us. Noble would confront me first.

Maybe he just couldn't see me. I walked closer to the window and looked down at the floor below. With my imposing figure, he'd know it was me.

A few minutes later he was on the upper deck and from there, it went about as I expected. Early on he told me he was going to shoot me in the back so I quickly turned around. My fear remained that he'd shoot me in the face after some of my comments about his daughter. Luckily for me, that's not how it transpired.

The shots to my bulletproof vest hurt more than I'd expected. It really does knock the air out of you. I'm sure there would be massive welts. It felt like being shot by a paintball. Not very fun, but not the end of the world either.

I still managed the slightest of smirks as I went tumbling over the railing. I pushed myself up against it and flew over after the third gunshot. I imagine that looked very believable.

I was still out of breath when I hit the water below. I didn't have the time nor the oxygen to inflate the floaties I'd hid in my jacket. Instead, I just doggy paddled as well as I could. The water was somewhat docile for such a windy night and the waves were manageable. As long as Mason was out there, I knew I'd make it.

I heard the light noise of the engine a few minutes later. The boat was now a few hundred yards ahead of us and there was no way they could see us in the dark, especially with the boat's lights pointed towards Fisherman's Village and away from us.

It took a few yells back and forth between Mason and I before he located me. From there, it was easy. He threw me one of those circular inner tubes attached to a rope. I grabbed it and pulled my way onto the boat.

"You're a psychotic genius," Mason said.

I thought about hitting him with an oar then and there and going all *The Talented Mr. Ripley* on him. I could leave him dead in the middle of the Pacific. But then they might find his body and this whole scheme would have been for naught.

Plus, he was managing my will and my money. I knew I couldn't kill Mason. Oh well, it was at least fun to think about it.

Instead, I just said, "And don't you forget it."

He shook his head in amazement at what I'd pulled off.

"Truly amazing."

"Ye of little faith," I said. "Now, drive in the opposite direction of the big boat and go fast, just in case they already called the Coast Guard. When we get far enough away from this location, we'll head due south and take this thing back down to San Pedro."

"Yes, sir. I still can't believe you pulled this off."

He'd said basically the same thing three times now. Maybe I deserved it. This was an all-timer.

I sat in the back of the speedboat and took in the heavy breeze, the ocean, and even the sight of the moon.

Yes, even a psychotic genius like me can enjoy those types of things.

We arrived back in San Pedro and docked the boat. It was late enough that no one saw us. I kept my head down just in case.

We walked to one of the Croy's two family cars. His wife had driven the other one from Fisherman's Village to their house with the burner phone on the whole time. It supplied Mason with his alibi if they ever got suspicious about my death.

"You remember the rest of the plan, right?" I asked.

"Yes."

"I will see you one more time. And that's when you give me the passport and the airline ticket on October 12th."

"You sure that's enough time for this to die down?"

"Should you be doubting me right now?" I asked.

"Fair point."

I decided to answer anyway.

"They'll search for my body for 2-3 days. It will be a big story during that time. Then they will probably declare me dead on day five or six. It will continue to be in the news for a week or so, but then it will die down. Americans have a short attention span these days, Mason. Even that Parker Brody murder is starting to lose steam and my story can't compete with that. Unless they knew I was still alive. Then I'd be the toast of the town."

I laughed quite loudly at that. Mason looked at me like I was a maniac.

Hey, if the shoe fits…

I was going to be spending the next three weeks squatting at a house in San Pedro that Mason had found. They were clients of his who traveled half the year and never had anyone staying there when they were gone. It was a nice house off the beaten path and no neighbors were within a quarter mile.

Part of me had wanted to put an oar in Mason's head, but truth be told, I couldn't have done all of this without him. I just hoped he held it together when the police came to interrogate him. Which they inevitably would.

He dropped me off at the house. He'd already supplied it with five days of groceries.

"Five days? You're going to be there for three weeks, Roger," he had said at the time.

"I'm going to be losing a lot of weight over the next three weeks. I'm also going to shave my head and ditch the oversized Tommy Bahama shirts. No one is going to recognize me. I might even shave my eyebrows and start wearing a fanny pack."

"You're crazy."

"As a fox."

Back in the present, we said our goodbyes.

"I'll see you on the 12th," Mason said.

"And if something happens to you, your wife knows to drop the passport and ticket off?"

"She knows, but I'm not going to be in jail."

"That's right. You're going to be a hero. The man who turned in the serial killer Roger Theus."

"I hope they buy my story."

"They will. Just stick to what I told you. They'll likely just think that you'd grown sick of me and wanted me behind bars. That's our hope. If Noble comes digging about what happened on the boat, you needn't worry. They will GPS that phone and realize you couldn't have been helping me out at sea. Your wife drove directly home, right?"

"Yes. I handed her the phone right before I walked to the boat. I told her to drive home and turn the phone off once she arrived."

"Perfect. Geraldine is a gamer."

"She is."

"We're going to get through this, Mason."

"I'm starting to believe you."

"That's a wise decision. If the LAPD hasn't gotten me yet, they ain't never getting me."

"Promise me one thing, Roger."

"What?"

"You'll be an upstanding citizen once you get to Europe."

I laughed.

"Sorry, I can't promise that. I am who I am."

"Try to stop murdering people, at least."

"We'll see. I've grown to enjoy it."

~

PRESENT DAY

They just started boarding my plane.

I gotta run.

Looks like I've accomplished the impossible.

The Mastermind is alive and well and on the move again.

Arrivederci, Los Angeles.

Ciao, Rome!

CHAPTER 62

NOBLE: 5 MONTHS LATER

I retired from the police force two weeks ago.

It was a huge affair. Not at my request, but Captain Cook made sure that I got the send-off that he thought I deserved. Maybe he was right. I'd put thirty years into the LAPD and had been highly reputable for 29.5 of them. What happened with Roger Theus on that boat would probably be described using a different adjective.

But I'll always defend what I did. You don't talk about someone's daughter like that. Especially someone with a gun.

There were times when I wondered if he was still out there.

No one had believed my crazy theory back then and now, five months later, hardly anyone even talked about Roger Theus anymore. Life moves quickly. There is always a new criminal-du-jour for the LAPD.

So I didn't bring him up.

But he was still on my mind.

⁓

I'd made a big life change.

I decided to start dating again. Sherin had nagged me long enough. Her quote that finally got me was this:

"Dad, you're freaking in your early fifties. You've got thirty good years left. Now go spend it with a nice woman. Mom would be disappointed if you didn't. And to be honest, so will I."

She was right. I'd waited too long.

It's early on, but I think the woman I'm currently dating is a keeper. Her name is Denise and she's forty-four years old. Sherin gave her age a thumbs-up, saying it would be weird if I was dating a girl around her age.

~

It was a cold night in February - yes, LA has cold days - when I went out to my mailbox to retrieve the day's mail.

Denise was at her house but coming over in an hour. There was already talk of us moving in with each other. I wasn't against it. It was time. I'd have to put away all the pictures of Sherry and me. Out of sight, but never to be forgotten. It was time for that as well.

I looked through the mail and saw the usual crap. Bills, clothing magazines, and other stalwarts.

At the bottom was a postcard. That was something new.

I walked back into the house and threw all of the mail on the counter. Except for the postcard. I was intrigued.

On the front, it said, *"Howdy, my fellow American! Greetings from Europe."* It was playing up the whole 'All Americans are Cowboys' angle.

The city said Antwerp, Belgium.

I turned the card over. It was handwritten. I hadn't even read a word, but I had an idea what was coming. I told myself I should just throw it away. But I couldn't. Against my better judgment, I started reading:

"Hey, old friend. I've been keeping tabs on you. I saw that you retired. Congrats. That doesn't mean our little game is over. I don't know if it's going to be in six days, six weeks, six months, or six years, but we'll be meeting face-to-face sometime in the future. I've become bored in Europe and will be returning home soon. We'll resolve this once and for all. And we both know who is going to win. I can't fucking wait!

P.S.: I haven't decided whether to include that sweet piece-of-ass Sherin in our little game. I'm leaning towards yes. Time will tell, my friend. Keep your head on a swivel. I'll be seeing you soon."

ALSO BY BRIAN O'SULLIVAN

A huge thanks for finishing *The Mastermind!*

I really hope you enjoyed it and would be honored if you left a review. Cheers!

If you're not done with me yet, I'd recommend *Revenge at Sea,* which is Book 1 of my Quint Adler series. It's a wild one!

And if you haven't read my first multi-narrative thriller, The Bartender, what are you waiting for?

It's not always easy being a self-published author, I can assure you that. But you, my readers, make it all worthwhile.

Thanks for your support.

And if you want to tell a friend or five about me, I'll be forever grateful.

Have a great day!

Sincerely,

Brian O'Sullivan

Printed in Great Britain
by Amazon

24608929R00172